Unspeakable

Unspeakable

Dilys Rose

Dilys Rose

FREIGHT BOOKS

First published 2017

Freight Books
49–53 Virginia Street
Glasgow, G1 1TS
www.freightbooks.co.uk

A CIP catalogue reference for this book is available from the British
Library.

ISBN 978-1-911332-15-2
eISBN 978-1-911332-16-9

Typeset by Freight in Plantin
Printed and bound by Bell and Bain, Glasgow

the publisher acknowledges investment from
Creative Scotland toward the publication of this book

Dilys Rose is a novelist, short story writer, poet and librettist. She has published eleven books and received various awards for her work, including the Macallan/Scotland on Sunday Short Story Award, the McCash prize, two Scottish Arts Council Book Awards, a Society of Authors' Travel Award and a Canongate Prize. She lives in Edinburgh.

Other books by Dilys Rose

Fiction
Our Lady of the Pickpockets
Red Tides
War Dolls
Pest Maiden
Selected Stories
Lord of Illusions
Pelmanism

Poetry
Madame Doubtfire's Dilemma
Lure
Bodywork

Poetry for children
When I Wear My Leopard Hat

For Geraldine

It is a principle innate and co-natural to every man to have an insatiable inclination to the truth, and to seek for it as for hid treasure.

Thomas Aikenhead, January 8th, 1697

Part One

Elephant

When he is taken from the Tolbooth in chains and escorted by armed guard down Leith Wynd to the Gallowlee, Thomas Aikenhead will recall standing amongst close-packed adult legs, straining to see the elephant.

The creature, from India, is the first of its species to which the city has ever opened its gates. For the whole morning a gangly, outlandishly garbed showman and his tow-headed drummer boy tramp up and down the High Street, announcing that a marvellous creature from the Eastern Indies will be on view, for a price, at dinner-time.

On a platform assembled at the Mercat Cross in readiness for the arrival of the main attraction, two tumbling girls entertain spectators with supple coilings and writhings, leapfrogs and somersaults, crab walks and headspins. The girls are slight and lithe, cinnamon-skinned, with lips as purple and juicy as damsons, flashing eyes and crow-black braids worked into topknots. Their arms are ringed with bracelets, their ankles with jingling bells.

They twist into such an array of fankles and launch into such leaps that they might have springs for bones or wings attached to their sharp little shoulders. Thomas, not yet five years old, thinks them beautiful but possibly malevolent, like the faerie folk, sprites that pinch and pull your hair and might steal you away to a land beyond the hills where you must live in silence for seven years. He can't imagine how it might be to stay quiet for such an eternity; he loves to talk.

In the cold winter light it is evident that the tumbling girls are only human: bruises on their legs and arms stand out like archipelagos inked on the maps of their skin. When the crowd cheers at some marvellous contortion, the girls bow so low that their topknots graze their knees. They never smile.

Throughout the morning a raw wind blows up from the Firth of Forth, a pale streamer below the hills of Fife, which, on this November day, are hazy. The sky is thick as broth. Snow begins to fall, light smatters at first, drifting around then pouring down from the heavens, settling on bare heads, on hats and hoods as the elephant, with the drummer boy astride its shoulders and his bare legs kicking about the animal's great lugs, plods up the street.

The showman is garbed in a raspberry cloak and matching breeks. His head, on the end of a scrawny neck, nestles amid layers of yellow satin.

The mannie's got a tulip for a heid! says Thomas.

And a seedpod for brains! says a fat man beside them. A bunch of shoelaces dangle like rats' tails from the pocket of his cobbler's apron.

A great cratur like yon must cost a king's ransom tae stable.

Whit's a king's ransom? says Thomas.

Weel now, says the man, it's a sum few can pit thir haunds on.

The showman struts by the elephant's side, affecting an air of pomp and ceremony. He carries a stout, sharpened stick and grips the end of a heavy chain attached to one of its forelegs.

Is the elephant a prisoner? says Thomas.

Efter a fashion, the cobbler replies.

But whit's he done wrang?

Stole a bannock? They'd be for packin him off tae the New World wi aw the sinners they dinna hae space for in the Tolbooth, but he'd mair than likely sink the boat!

Where's the New World? says Thomas. How d'ye get there? Efter ye cross the ocean, d'ye haveta fly?

Stap yir pesterin, says his big sister, Katharine.

Nae hairm, says the cobbler. If he disna ask, he willna ken.

He niver stops. Even when naebody wants tae hear, he prattles on and on. There's a time tae talk and a time to haud yir tongue.

You tell him, lass, says the cobbler, ruffling Katharine's hair, which she doesn't like one bit.

When the elephant approaches the ramp leading to the platform it halts, shakes its head, extends its monstrous trunk and blares a great trumpeting across all the assembled snow-dusted pates. The crowd's initial wariness gives way to amusement. The showman jabs the elephant. When it doesn't respond, he jabs it again and thrashes the loose end of the chain against its leg.

He's hurtin it, says Thomas. Why is he hurtin it?

Because he'll no mak money frae a beast that disna dae his biddin, says Katharine.

The elephant gives another trumpet, is jabbed and beaten again until it lumbers forwards, head rising and dipping, trunk coiling and uncoiling; it raises one huge foot after another then heaves its great bulk onto the creaking, swaying platform.

From the adjacent gibbet where, like the hanged man on a tarot card, they have been demonstrating the art of dangling upside down from a single slender foot, the tumbling girls right themselves, leap off the gibbet and land neatly on the elephant's back. They stand on tiptoe and snake their arms about, causing their bracelets to rustle like wind shaking the barley. At a nod from the showman, they sweep the drummer boy off the elephant's head and fling him out onto the street, where he lands with a flourish.

The girls tumble onto the street then flit around, collecting payment. Though slight, they are fierce and tenacious, with a way of catching and holding a person's gaze. Again Thomas thinks of faeries and magic spells, of the evil eye and how it might snare a person, drag him into its orbit and not let go.

The drummer boy unhooks the panniers which hang either side of the elephant's head and brings out three loaves and six jugs of ale. As for the elephant, grey as the day itself, it turns in obedient circles, giving onlookers who have flocked from all over an opportunity to observe its novel anatomy. They marvel at the big blunt feet – which, at some point in the future, will become velvet-topped stools in the house of a wealthy merchant with a predilection for curiosities – the spindle tail; the restless, freakish trunk; the curved tusks; the hide ridged and wrinkled as bark; the great, flapping, skatefish lugs; the eyes which glint like nails driven deep into its skull.

So, my Guidmen and Guidwives, the showman roars, it's a cauld wind blaws up frae the Forth the day but I'll warrant the cockles o yir herts are warmed by the spectacle afore ye! This beast, niver afore tae grace the shores o this island and purchased for the princely sum o *Two Thousand Pounds*, has come here by way o a lang slow tramp frae the soothern extremity o the land. And afore that, aw the way frae the far side o the kent world! Aw weel and guid but whit, ye might wonder, can such a curious cratur dae? Whit special accomplishments hae been bestowed by the Almighty and why, ye might ask, have I, at great personal expense, fetched it here for yir inspection?

That's whit we're here tae find oot! comes a cry.

Cut the craik! comes another.

But thir's ane thing ye need tae ken, says the showman, and ye'd be wise tae pay heed. It's in an elephant's nature tae attend tae aw aboot him. His een may be sma but they're sharp as tacks.

The showman knows this is a lie but it is a convenient lie and not a soul challenges him on it. So, he continues, if onybody hasna yet made it his business tae haund ower tae my lovely dusky lasses the requisite fee, act now or regret it at yir leisure. Oor auld mannie here – ye can see for yirsels by inspectin the undercarriage that this is undeniably a *bull* elephant – has spent elevin year on God's earth. At hame he'd hae control – and let's be honest, the *sweet freedom* o a haill herd o coos. But, in the absence o the carnal pleasures in which beasts indulge thirsels at nae cost tae thir immortal souls – because, as ye ken, they dinna hae sauls! – oor auld mannie here has become a veritable miser. Whit's mair, he's been kent tae play an ill trick on cheapskates and – doot me at yir peril – ye widna wish it played on yir guid sel. And by the bye, as he and I'll no be gaen onywhere hastie-like, here's anither scruple o information ye'd be wise tae mind: the elephant possesses a prodigious memory.

Amid some mutterings of disbelief, a fair few seek out the

tumbling girls and make a show of parting with their money.

That's mair like the thing! Now then, as ye havena cheated an honest man o his livelihood, ye can enjoy yir entertainment wi a clear conscience.

Honest is as honest does!

Show us whit the beast can dae.

Aw in guid time.

We havena got aw day, man.

Some o us hae proper work!

Thomas ignores the banter but uses the showman's stalling tactics to edge forward.

Richt ye be. First things first! This cratur hails frae a heathen land and believe you me, if some o ye Presbyterians find it ill tae stomach the ways o the Episcopalians, and some o the Episcopalians find it vexatious tae thole the idolatry o Papists, and the Papists amang ye tae abide the preposterous habits o the Quakers, and the Quakers—

Get on wi it, man, for pity's sake. We dinna need yir balderdash.

I ken, I ken. But aw ye guid, God-fearin sauls should tak a moment and try and picture the kinna abominations tae be foond in his hameland. I'll no lee, snakes are venerated. Monkeys, rats! Tae tap it aw, they worship a God that's hauf laddie, hauf elephant and credited wi ridin on the back o a moosie! As a corrective, the first thing I kent it needful tae teach the beast wis due reverence. So, can I hae yir attention please!

Ye've already got it, man. But ye'll lose it if ye dinna get a move on.

When the showman is satisfied that his girls have extracted as much coin as possible, the lad hitches his ragged breeks and sets his sticks against the drumskin in a long, dramatic roll. The showman prods the elephant until it slowly folds its cumbersome forelegs into a kneeling position and lowers its heavy head.

The elephant remains awkwardly in an attitude of reverence, ears undulating, trunk slithering over the straw-strewn platform.

In response to another prod it drags itself back into a standing position. Snow continues to fall. It settles on its head, turns into sleet and drips into the wrinkled fissures around its eyes.

Is it greetin? says Thomas.

Naw, says Katharine.

How d'ye ken? Perhaps the dribbles are tears as weel as sleet. Or the sleet's makkin it greet. Or the mannie pokin him.

Wha kens? says Katharine.

Can dogs greet? Can cats?

I dinna ken, Thomas, and I dinna care.

But if dogs can greet, they must be sad. And if they're sad, they must hae sauls.

Ask the minister the next time ye're in church.

I dinna like the minister, says Thomas. He's aye cross.

If he's cross it's on accoont o haein tae thole nincompoops like you, says Katharine.

Whit's a nincompoop?

Lord have mercy! says Katharine.

Where Thomas is, right at the front, with his sister's skirt pressed against the back of his head, his eyes are level with the elephant's feet. The pads are covered with cuts and sores from walking on mud and stones and standing for hours on end, on damp straw.

D'ye think the elephant's cauld? D'ye think he's dule?

How dae I ken, Thomas? How could onybody ken?

When Mither drooned the kittens in the Nor' Loch, the cat wis dule. I sweer she wis. She wis aye searchin for her kittens. She stappit huntin rats. She didna greet wi her een but made a greetin soond in her thrapple.

Cats are no the same as elephants, says Katharine.

Thomas tries to picture a land where elephants roam free, where tumbling girls sit on sun-baked rocks, braiding each other's hair and stringing bracelets onto their arms, and everything is bright and colourful but has little to compare it to. The buildings, the sky, even the few trees standing on the High Street are grey or black. There's brightness from the snow but it's a harsh brightness, the kind that pains the eyes. Apart from a few extravagantly becloaked gentry and a couple of young women – that Katharine calls jades – in showy robes, the tradespeople wear subdued colours and the labourers, hodden grey.

What, Thomas wonders, could be wrong with colour? How might the wearing of coloured cloth offend God? Didn't God make flowers in every possible hue? Doesn't his own father, who knows so much about how things are put together, say dyes are made from roots and leaves, petals and stamens, from powdered rocks and tinted clay? Why, if God made Heaven and Earth, wouldn't He wish His people to make use of all the cheerful colour He provided?

The showman jabs the elephant. With deep groans and choked squeals, it rears up and props its forelegs against the gibbet. The showman produces a musket and makes a great palaver of loading it with gunpowder. He fixes a metal cage over the elephant's head, chains it to the gibbet so its head juts upwards, then slides the musket into the cage. In some unfathomable manner the elephant manoeuvres the gun between its grey lips and fires a shot at the sky. Again there is much cheering. Its head is freed from the cage and the elephant is permitted to stand once more on all four feet.

But now tae my final demonstration, for which I offer ye a unique opportunity! Buy the beast a hunk o breid and a pint o ale and ye'll hae the privilege o feedin it yirsel! Believe me, nocht in the world is as curious as an elephant's way wi bit and sup.

A tall, broad-shouldered man in a claret cloak holds up his purse.

Guid sir, a baker's apprentice calls out, if ye pay me thirteen and sax I'll eat the breid and drink the ale. And piss it oot again – gratis!

Where's the novelty in that? his neighbour replies. Ye piss yir ale agin the wa a dizzen times a day as it is.

The man in the claret cloak ignores the jests and moves through the throng with his entourage: two flame-cheeked bairns bundled up against the elements, two sturdy manservants and a pair of panting, piebald hounds.

Thomas nudges Katharine.

Is yon Maister Hepburn feedin the elephant?

The same, says Katharine. Tossin awa coin oor faither pays him in rent!

Why?

Because he can.

Think on the miracle o the loaves and the fishes! comes a cry from another quarter.

Could ye no mak yon breid and ale fill the bellies and slake the drouth o guid, workin men?

Now that wid be a sight worth seein.

Isna an honest man mair deservin o bit and sup than a dumb beast?

Aye, and a heathen beast at that!

The showman allows the banter to run its course. He knows how it goes. People need a chance to jape and jibe, to argue the toss.

Watching the elephant snuffle up a hunk of bread is entertaining but nothing to seeing it take in a whole jug of ale, twirl its trunk this way and that, as if intending to spray onlookers, and then, after more furling and unfurling of the monstrous appendage, direct a jet of ale into its own mouth.

Children laugh, grown-ups laugh, even the elephant with its curled grey lips seems to laugh. Once the first jar of ale is consumed, Hepburn and his entourage have seen enough. Master and his brood in the lead, servants and dogs following close behind, they cut a swathe through the crowd and proceed down the High Street towards the Palace. Almost immediately, another snugly clad member of the gentry approaches the stage, eager to pay for a repeat performance.

Whit's its limit? the fat cobbler calls out. Whit quantity o ale can the cratur consume afore it fa's doon mortall?

I couldna richtly say, says the showman. But time will tell.

The elephant's limit becomes the question of the moment.

Some reckon ten jugs, some twenty. Wagers are made, more ale is purchased and laid at its feet. When the supply runs out, the drummer boy is dispatched to the nearest tavern for replenishments.

In the interim, the elephant pisses a steaming yellow arc over the snow-covered straw. After another half-dozen jars it emits several gargantuan belches. Men toss their hats in the air. At sixteen jars the elephant's coordination deteriorates: it begins to miss its mouth with its ale-loaded trunk. People hoot and roar as if they too have consumed vast quantities of drink. It occurs to the showman that persuading the elephant to walk back to the stables at Restalrig – which offer the most reasonable rates – might be far from straightforward. Then again, his audience is riding on a wave of its own extravagance and it's always best to let such things run their course.

The truth is, he now has little control over the situation. People are betting wildly. Flashing dark eyes and daring folk to ignore them at their peril, the tumbling girls continue to collect payment for further victuals. Cadies run wagers hither and thither.

Just as weel Faither's no here, says Katharine.

Does he no like elephants? says Thomas.

He'd like this ane. He could pit a wager on it.

Wid he wager the rent for Maister Hepburn on it?

He might. Mair's the pity.

At eighteen jars, squirting ale from its trunk and splattering ordure from its backside, the elephant flumps into a sitting position.

Come awa, says Katharine. A mortall elephant is no a laughing maitter.

But awbody else is laughing.

They're aw ignoramuses.

Whit's an ignoramus?

A body wha kens nocht. Come awa. Come awa hame for yir dinner.

Thomas does not protest as Katharine guides him through

the braying crowd. When they reach their door, the shop sign hanging above it creaks in the breeze: blue letters on black, the painted mortar and pestle, and the set of yellow scales proclaim his father's name and his trade: James Aikenhead: Chirurgeon Apothecary.

The snow has stopped falling. The street is furred with white. At the cross, the tumbling girls are once more dangling by dainty feet from the gibbet. The elephant sways on its great haunches and waves its stubby legs in the air, for the moment a jolly Ganesh against the dark backdrop of tenement buildings. And then, trumpeting feebly, foolishly, pitifully, it topples over in a drunken stupor. A full-throated roar rises and once again money changes hands.

A Receipt for Happiness

Did ye no hear the rousin bell? snaps Helen Ramsey. Whit did I dae tae deserve such layabeds as bairns?

She pulls open the shutters. Thin winter light glances in and the world begins to reassert its solidity, its proper shapes, dull lustres and sharp shadows. Morning brings the glint of glass bottles lined up on shelves back into being, the soft gleam of earth-toned glazes on ceramic jars, the brassy shimmer of the scales. It picks out the twitching tail of a rat as it slips behind the sacks, and the cat's tawny gaze as it considers whether or not to give chase.

Thomas wiggles his toes but stays put. Anna's arm is thrown out across the blanket. Her yellow hair is a dandelion clock about her round, creamy face. Her eyelids flip open, shut. Her brow furrows. She snuffles and burrows her face into the crook of Thomas's arm. His little sister, who is only a year younger than he, is not fond of mornings, especially cold ones. Nor is his mother, especially when others are slow to rise, and lets everybody know it, clattering at the grate and grumbling as she rakes out the ashes.

If I wis meant tae muck oot alane, why did the Lord gie me a family? Thomas, Anna, shift yirsels.

Katharine is already up and doing. She combs her hair – which she makes a point of doing before she'll attend to any chore – pulls on her boots and wraps a plaid about her shoulders.

Dinna be daunerin by the well, says Helen.

As if I wid, Katharine replies. I've better things tae dae.

No whit I've heard, says Helen.

And whit, then, Mither, have ye heard?

I've heard that if Jeremiah Skaill's within a stone's thraw o the pump ye'll gie yir place tae ony auld wife.

Ye shouldna believe aw ye hear, says Katharine.

Anna shifts, snuffles, blows plumes of misty breath across Thomas's chest.

Why no? says Thomas, keeping the covers drawn up to his chin as the bigger members of the family clack about.

Because, says Katharine, folk are ower fond o stretchin the truth.

Ah but a scruple o truth can gang a lang way! says his father.

And you'd be the best judge o that, says his mother, and nae mistake.

If my guidwife didna waste her braith on scoldin and argy-bargy, life would hae a sweeter taste.

Unlike yir ain vices, James Aikenhead, talk is free.

Tell that tae the Kirk Session, says his father.

If ye stretch the truth, says Thomas, can ye no mak mair truth than ye had tae start wi?

Lord help us, says his mother. We've no got aw day tae debate whys and wherefores.

At least the lad's got a keen heid on him, says his father.

Onybody think ye'd faithered a prodigy, says Katharine, the way ye big Thomas up.

It may be I hae, says James. It may be I've faithered three prodigies! Or three dunces!

There's the rub, says Helen.

Katharine hefts the pail onto her hip and makes for the door.

Mind and no tak aw day, Helen calls out, as Katharine steps onto the street.

His father, who has less quarrel with mornings than his mother, lights his Dutch pipe. The plug of tobacco crackles and glows red. He blows a string of smoke rings which drift, wobble, break up and disperse, then sits at the counter and opens his beloved Culpeper, which he reads from every morning the way others read the bible. He is a chirurgeon in name only, trusting more in the healing powers of herbs and potions than in the virtues of the knife. He enjoys taking risks on the gaming tables but would rather leave the risks of surgery to those who've studied anatomy longer than he.

Thomas is transfixed by motes speckling in pale sunbeams. He welcomes the arrival of morning and would rather see the dust in all its dancing brilliance than conjure it gathering in places where the sunlight can't reach. In the night the contents of his father's jars – the sticks and stones, the dried animal skins, the bones and hair and teeth – unsettle him in a way they never do by day. In the night, nothing, to his mind, needs to keep to its proper place or shape; the dried frogs and vipers might somehow come back to life and leap out of their jars, the bones and hair and teeth reassemble into living breathing creatures.

His sisters both sleep sound but Thomas wakes at the slightest disturbance. In the cold black dead of the previous night, he was snatched from dreams by his mother talking in her sleep: *Balance the books,* she was saying, not loud but distinct and clear, cutting through the sooty darkness. And chiding, chiding. *Balance the books, for pity's sake balance the books*! His father's snores were small burbles of pleasure, as if he were in the midst of some distracting entertainment. A rat scrabbled. The cat padded over the bedcovers, its meaty breath hanging in the blackness. He listened for his mother to say more but all she did was toss and turn and sigh in a vexed way before she too began to snore in short, impatient snorts. Lulled eventually by the body heat of his sisters, he sank back into sleep.

His mother sets the match to the fire. She hunkers down and blows on the coal until it flings up a shower of red sparks and unfurls an eye-smarting coil of smoke. It will be a while before there's any heat to speak of. Thomas rolls onto his back.

Faither, he says, staring up at the dark ceiling, how d'ye balance books?

His father puffs on his pipe, coughs, mutters.

D'ye pit them on the scales?

Ask yir mither.

No the now, James, says Helen. Ye ken as weel as I that this is no the time for cogitation.

James whistles softly and turns over the page of his Culpeper.

Outside a cart clatters by. From the floor above the sound of neighbours raising their voices to the Lord filters down to them; the rumbling bass of the man of the house (a kirk elder), the unwavering line of the devout mistress of the house, the quavery warble of her invalid mother who has lived with the family as long as anybody can remember, the reedy, tuneless voices of the children. It is not the most uplifting chorus.

When Katharine returns from the well with a near full pail of water, her eyes are bright and her grin broad.

Somebody's in fine fettle, says James.

I'll hazard a guess, says Helen, that a kenspeckle body wis settin up his faither's luckenbooth at the verra moment when oor Katharine had taen hersel doon the brae.

Could it no be I'm but feelin the love o God in my saul?

It could that, says Helen. Then again—

Then again, Mither, piety's no yir strang suit.

Kathie, says Anna. Will ye kaim my hair?

Aye, says Katharine. If ye say yir prayers douce-like.

The canary groomed by the craw, says Helen.

Yir mither's a fool, says James. Yir treacle locks are braw. They'd mak a grand periwig.

My hair, Faither, was destined tae set on my heid and that's where it'll stay.

I'll wager it wid fetch a guinea or twa.

You'll wager nae such thing! says Katharine.

Whit the eye disna see, the hert disna grieve ower, says James.

Kathie, kaim Anna's hair!

I will, says Katharine. And no the way Mither wid dae it. No aw rough and tuggy but gentle, like ye're a princess and I'm yir lady in waitin. Wid ye like that?

Anna nods seriously.

If ye were a princess, Anna, says Thomas, ye'd be waited on haund an fit. Is that whit ye wish?

Anna continues to nod.

For why? Thomas continues. Is it no better tae dress yirsel

and kaim yir ain hair?

No! says Anna, shaking her fluffy head vehemently.

Katharine, who has more appetite for worship than the rest of the family put together, leads them in prayer. James is loath to leave his Culpeper – but once they are all on their knees, Katharine thanks the Lord for their blessings, the food they are about to eat, the roof over their heads, their livelihood. She beseeches the Almighty to deliver her family from sin. Today, in addition, she urges Him to look kindly on those He took from the living in their infancy, in particular their own lost sisters, Jonet and Margaret.

Amen, say the Aikenheads, and rise to their feet.

Why the day, Katharine? Helen asks bitterly. Why stir up the pain o the past the day?

Why no? The Lord needs us to be mindful o oor sins.

Bairns die, whether ye're a sinner or no.

We're aw sinners, Mither.

After the womenfolk leave for the market, with the bickering between Helen and Katharine fading into the distance, James's mood lightens. He whistles and shuffles around the shelves, pulling down this and that and preparing for business. Thomas is glad to be alone with his father. Without the bustle, he is free to think. Today he is thinking about Jonet and Margaret, the lost sisters he never knew. The Lord takes bairns for Himself but why does he need so many?

Katharine saw Jonet and Margaret but says she can't remember what they looked like. Thomas wishes he could picture them. Names are not enough to fix his lost sisters in his mind and he wants to fix them, not to let them drift away like shadows in fog. Would Jonet's hair have grown in treacle brown like Katharine's or his mother's, or chestnut like his own, or yellow like Anna's? Would Margaret have become lean and freckled or plump and pale? If the Lord hadn't taken them, would there have been room in the bed for all of the children? Would there have been enough food to go round?

There's a rap on the hatch and a large face, puce as a glazed ham, leans in.

Are ye open for business, man?

Aye, and guid day to ye, Doctor, his father replies in a hearty voice. Whit ails ye?

Doucely, man, doucely! I've a heid like a rattlebox and a fearsome drouth.

So a grand time wis had at the tavern?

Ower grand. No that I'll regret or repent o it. Whit's life withoot a splurge once in a while?

Wid that we aw had yir constitution, sir. And yir brazenness.

I'm no brazen the day. There's no a whit o brazenness left in me.

Archibald Pitcairne is a sturdily built young man, full of chin, eager of eye and with a gluttonous sheen to his cheeks. His chestnut periwig is long and luxuriant. The buttons of his plush coat strain across an incipient paunch. He is a regular customer and as he pays on the moment for what he purchases, a welcome sight.

Wis ye mortall, Doctor? asks Thomas.

No, no, lad. No, no. Fou certainly. Perhaps a mite mair than fou. But no fou mortall!

Did ye spy the mortall elephant? says Thomas. It drank twenty jugs o ale then fell ower. It wis greetin.

Wis it now? I expect the poor thing's heid hurt as bad as my ain!

I've some first-rate Brazilian coffee, says James. Fresh up frae the port o Leith. Just the thing for slakin a drouth, sharpenin the wits and purgin the vitals.

Pitcairne groans and massages his temples with the tips of his gloves.

The question is, dae I wish my wits sharpened? Perhaps I should gie mysel ower tae saftheidedness, partake o a scruple o bhang? Dear me, if a man canna decide how best tae treat a trivial affliction whit hope o success when greater pains present thirsels?

I widna ken, says James. I keep my mind on sma aches and agues.

And richt ye be. Leave the rest tae Providence. Divine or itherwise.

Maister Hepburn paid thirteen and sax tae feed the elephant, says Thomas. And Kathie says that if Faither had been there he'd've pit a wager on how much ale it could drink.

Does she now? says James.

Heh, heh, says Pitcairne. Ye'll hae nae secrets wi yon laddie.

I've nae need for secrets, Doctor.

Then you must be ane fortunate chiel and no mistake. Now look here. I've a mind tae investigate a new medicament for The King's Evil. I'm in little doot that His Royal Majesty means weel by availin his royal palm tae the pates o the afflicted. Aw the same, as a man o science, I fear in this instance, scant benefit is tae be had frae a royal pat on the pate.

Faith in the efficacy o a remedy, says James, can work a power o its ain.

A king might effect mony changes in this world – though the changes this pairticular monarch wid effect are o the dubious kind – but scrofula is scrofula. And requires a medicament.

And where would an apothecary be if aw that wis required tae cure a body o its ailments wis faith?

Weel said, man. And where wid physicks be forby?

Pitcairne reels off a list of ingredients as long and broad as the sleeve of his plush coat. The doctor is not one to stand on ceremony: he will hold a clinic in the tavern as soon as in the college, allowing a line of patients to form while he delivers a diagnosis to the first in line. While his father attends to Dr Pitcairne, Thomas sets out scales, mortar and pestle, and the sectioned box which contains his own miniature pharmacopoeia. His father's enthusiasm for new remedies and elixirs – combined with a profligate nature – means that he often orders surplus to requirements. As for scraping the last grains from a sack or a sea-chest, a twist of paper or pouch of muslin, or draining a bottle of every drop, this is often left to Thomas.

Needless to say, James keeps the precious and the poisonous clearly marked and out of harm's way. Needless to say, like any curious child, Thomas is drawn to what he is denied. Quicksilver holds a powerful fascination. Its brilliance draws him, the way it races and slithers, how it splits off into rebellious beads which roll away on individual trajectories then reunites as a gleaming puddle in the palm of his hand. And the way the shiny slippery stuff expands when heated and contracts when cooled. This, his father says, is a clear demonstration of the goodness of warmth and the badness of cold.

James is a man who seeks the heat. He will muffle himself up in all seasons and talk eagerly of warmer climes, of plants which thrive beneath the rays of a burning sun but could not survive the rigours of a Scottish winter, of snakes and lizards which bask on sun-warmed rocks, so still you'd think they'd already been stuffed and then, with a sudden flick of the tongue, trap their dinner.

Thomas delights in watching the brass pans see-saw as he adjusts quantities of this or that until they settle into equilibrium. It never ceases to amaze him how a single knuckle of bone will balance fistfuls of tobacco or lavender. There is even more enjoyment to be had crushing seeds and pods, roots and leaves, grinding them together until they are no longer recognisable as themselves, until they have become something altogether new.

People come to Thomas's father for all kinds of remedies and treatments. Some have knowledge of simples and purchase what they require to make up their own plaisters and topicals, purges and vomits. Others, and this irks his father, will ask what receipt he recommends for this or that and then, after he has consulted Culpeper and his own prodigious memory, ignore all recommendations and make their own choice. Some, who have little faith in physicks or lack the wherewithal to pay for treatment, describe their symptoms and trust him to supply a cure.

Of some afflictions folk speak loud and bold and shameless: warts and boils, dyspepsia and the lasque, agues and chills, toothache and sleeplessness. Thomas himself could already suggest a remedy or two: clove oil to be rubbed on the gums for toothache; for sleeplessness, the leaves of belladonna placed on the eyelids – easy! For other more difficult things – the curse of barrenness, the bringing out of a dead child, or worse, the putting away of a living one before it comes to term, a woman – always a woman – will cover her face and drop her voice to a whisper.

Thomas wonders why anybody might wish to put away a child before it had seen the light of day. As it is, so many die at birth or soon after, too soon even to be baptised and take their name to heaven. Katharine says it is wrong to question God's will, that Jonet and Margaret have been saved from sin and are in heaven with the angels, but Thomas knows that the dead lie in the ground, with the worms. Unless, as his father is fond of saying, someone has a mind to dig them up.

People come to his father not only for aches and pains of the body. They also seek cures for bad dreams and choler, for potions to banish melancholy and dark humours. And what of happiness? Would it not be grand to have a potion that would make a body happy? If you could put happiness itself on the scales, it would be airy as a spray of camomile. As for sadness, it would be dark and heavy as a lump of pitch.

That's whit I like tae see, says the Doctor, stowing his purchases in a leather satchel. A lad taen efter his faither, learnin the trade.

The lad craves activity, says James, and whit better way tae occupy hissel?

Indeed, says Pitcairne. Let him learn tae weigh and grind his simples, try his haund at makkin pastes and plaisters, potions and tinctures. And whit, laddie, wid ye maist wish tae concoct wi yir simples?

A receipt for happiness, says Thomas.

Ah weel, we'd aw wish for the same. But yon elixir, I fear, will continue tae elude us, mountebanks and honest apothecaries alike.

HEAVEN'S
ALARM
to the
WORLD
Or
A SERMON, wherein is shewed,

That Fearful

Sights

and Signs in Heaven are the *PRESAGES*

of great *CALAMITIES* at hand.

By Mr. *INCREASE MATHER*

And the third Angel sounded, and there fell a great Star from heaven, burning as it were a Lamp &c.
Revelations 8.10

Everyone sees the Great Comet. How could they not? It appears faint and hazy in the sky one night then clarifies into a nub of brightness trailing a flaming tail. By the estimation of William Whiston, astronomer, the world has not seen this magnificently plumed phenomenon since it brushed against the earth after the fall of Eden and, so many in Christendom believe, set in motion the cataclysm which goes by the name of Noah's Flood.

Everyone sees the comet unless they are sightless. Some of the visually afflicted claim that they too can see it, that something special about its light acts upon their eyes in an unprecedented and astonishing manner; others that they can sense its presence, as well as its fundamental and ominous significance. Some claim they can hear it whirring through the firmament like a celestial spinning top.

Spectacular in size and luminosity, the Great Comet can even be detected at midday, when the weak winter sun is often little more than a spectre. All over Europe and North America, drawn by morbid curiosity, people of all callings venture out of doors to crane their necks and gaze in awe. In Edinburgh, in the belief that permitting the comet's retributional light to penetrate the retina will further encourage God's wrath and prompt Him to direct His dire judgements on those who dare to look the comet in the eye, a number of the faithful no longer leave their homes after dark.

The skies are hard and bright. Frost blooms on windowpanes and in the crannies of drystane dykes. A skin of ice glazes the hard ground and masks the foul waters of the Nor' Loch. Extra care is required to pick one's way up and down the slippery High Street and the wynds sloping off it. Horses skitter and shy, carters struggle up the long Leith Wynd with whatever fish and provisions from overseas the boats bring in.

The ice thickens and the comet grows brighter. As a rainbow is interpreted as a token of divine favour, the *fiery besom* is a token of divine wrath, foretelling plague and pestilence to be visited upon the land by an Almighty who has been sore provoked by His creations. All over the country, the continent, over much of the western world, admonitory sermons are preached from pulpits: repent of your sins before it is too late; cease your fornicating, drunkenness and gluttony, your laziness, greed, your cheating and gambling but, above all, abandon any doubt regarding the omnipotent and vengeful nature of the Lord. See how the fingertip of the Almighty lights up the sky and think on what else He might choose to effect should His subjects on earth lack sufficient piety, obedience and fearfulness.

Not everyone, however, is in thrall to the theistical interpretation of such a sign, such a wonder. Astronomers track the comet's progress and note its changing aspect. For the first time ever a fiery besom has been observed by telescope and Gottfried Kirch of Guben, while cocking his eye at the moon and the planet Mars, is the first to make sense of what he sees.

Thanks to earlier efforts by Robert Hooke, Antonie van Leeuwenhoek and Baruch Spinoza, that atheistical Jew, lens-making has become increasingly sophisticated. The quality of blown glass is now more pure and true in what it reveals, and fine grinding enables greater distinctions of calibration. Not only is it possible to look more closely at celestial bodies but miniature life, invisible to the naked eye and hitherto unknown, can also be observed, by means of a miscroscope, in all its wriggling glory.

Magnification has opened up whole new areas of knowledge and raised new and dangerous questions. Those most directly engaged with such questions – Flamsteed, Halley, Brattle, Newton – currently working on his *Principia*, and employing it to test his theory of gravitation – spend many a clear night hour with an eye pressed to the glass. The astronomers differ in how they interpret their findings. Some differences are superficial – a discrepancy in the calibration of an instrument, for instance, a mathematical error, variable visibility – but other, fundamental differences of interpretation arise. Which have sent men to the stake. The vocation of astronomy is not short of martyrs. Perhaps the elevated ambition of these men – and women – eclipses fear of reprisal. Perhaps. For some more than others.

In Edinburgh, stargazing is little more than an amateur passion. In the taverns, amongst the wits and the wags, the sceptics and the freethinkers, informed debate and idle speculation turn to angles of incidence, the temperature of the nucleus, the length of the aphelion and perihelion. The fiery besom continues in its hairpin orbit, first in one direction, then in the other. Opinions on the comet's significance, other than those which conform to the ecclesiastical explanation – that it is part of the Almighty's grand design – are kept, where possible, from the ears of the Kirk.

With all the pulpit-thumping and warnings of hellfire it can muster, the Kirk urges its preachers to urge their congregations to prepare for punishment and doom. A day of fasting and humiliation is instigated. The pious press chilblained palms together and set knees on freezing flagstones until their joints lock and their shins bleed. The only fire they feel is the flare of hunger in their bellies.

Nevertheless, with one eye on the fiery besom, townsfolk tap the ice on the Nor' Loch, press an ear to the cracked notes of its creaking or drive poles through the surface to determine its thickness. They step out gingerly, primed to leap back to the safety of the bank should the surface shift and craze. As it remains intact, they sharpen the bone blades of their skates.

As the Nor' Loch takes the place of a city wall, the Town Guard also pays heed to the thickness of the ice. A frozen pond is easier for vagabonds and destitute beggars to negotiate than putrid water and there's no telling what kind of trouble might, with the assistance of the fiery besom's nocturnal show, infiltrate the city. The comet has upset the normal order of things. If the worst is imminent, what is the point of piety? Why not live for the moment, take pleasure where one finds it?

And so, as the freeze continues, on the next clear Saturday folk flock to the frozen Nor' Loch. Braziers are set up on clumps of stiff reeds and the aroma of roasting chestnuts sweetens the air. Hot pasties and mulled wine are on sale. By a clump of bushes, a makeshift bog house is constructed. Cherry-cheeked children tumble and shriek. Ballad sellers launch songs of bonny earls and wayward gypsies across the ice, of calamity and derring-do, of tragic love. Skaters glide, curlers slip-slide, golfers pitch and putt, fishermen bide their time beside holes in the ice, in the hope that some sluggish perch or eel might nose into their nets.

A horse-drawn sledge jingles along. Clumps of burgesses and merchants, resplendent in fur-lined cloaks and rabbit-skin hats, exchange news from the coffee houses: unrest in the English court, atrocities in far-flung colonies, scandal on their doorstep. Temporarily relieved of their chores, domestic servants gossip, snipe and flirt. Chittering in frills and flounces, a pair of African slaves trot behind their muffed and masked mistress, raising the hem of her gown free from the churned-up ice as she skates, a goblet of mulled wine in her hand. Wrapped in the blankets they slept in, beggars work the crowd for alms. Even one or two men of the cloth are out on the ice, skating in a leisurely and dignified manner, skimming the fringes of the throngs like narrow black boats, keeping an eye out, as ever, for sin.

The Aikenhead family are all at the Nor' Loch, except Katharine, who is at home, determinedly reading a sermon on the fearful signs and wonders which has found its way from Boston, New England, where it was delivered at the beginning of the year. All the same, if her mother is to be believed, Katharine is also hoping that Jeremiah Skaill might happen by and find her at the window, alone, the cold sunlight falling on her cheeks.

James skates out towards the middle of the loch, heedless, it would appear, of everything but the sting of chill air on his cheeks and the strength in his legs.

Thomas tugs at his mother's arm.

Can we gang hame?

Did we come aw the way doon the brae only tae climb back up again? Awa and play wi yir sister.

Anna has joined a group of lads of an age with her brother. They have made a slide and take turns hurling themselves along it, as often as not plumping down on their arses before they reach the end. Undaunted by the boisterousness of the boys, she revels in the rough and tumble and the endless repetition of the same action; before the day is done her fervent wish is to master the art of staying upright while moving at speed.

Some of her playmates are familiar to Thomas: the lad who helps his father to sell horn spoons and calf skins. With meaty haunches and the stolid gaze of a young bullock, he makes a great thump when he takes a tumble. A pair of brothers in matching blue bonnets scrap and scuffle when it's not their turn on the slide. Thomas has seen them in church, and their father cuffing them for fidgeting. Smaller than the others and poorly protected from the elements, a copper-headed lad, whom

Thomas can't place has, by virtue of speed, daring and some sly kicks, established himself as the leader. His sharp features and fixed frown give the impression that he's older than his years. When it's his turn on the slide, what an ado he makes of it, ensuring he has the others gawping before spreading his arms wide and hurling himself forward.

Come on, Thomas! Anna calls out.

Thomas is taken aback that Anna is so bold today, so needless of him. He is used to her trailing behind, pressing her fluffy yellow head into the small of his back, digging her fingers into his palm. But here she is, shrilling and carrying on.

Naw, he says.

Why no?

It's cauld!

Aw! Aw! It's cauld! mimics the copper-headed lad.

It's easy, Thomas, says Anna. Dinna be feart.

I'm no feart! Thomas shouts. I'm no feart!

Whit's the matter wi ye? says his mother. Aw the ither bairns are fair enjoying thirsels.

The matter is that Thomas is suspicious of the ice, and anxious about what lies beneath it: tangled weeds and rubbish, the jagged jaws of perch and eels, the decaying remains of boats and bodies. Witch drowning is a thing of the past but the previous summer, when flies hung over the water in a dense black swarm, his mother drowned a litter of kittens. She put them in a sack with a rock, knotted the sack and flung it as far out into the water as she could. He remembers the yowling, the hollow plop, the ripples. He tugs on his mother's arm:

Dae cats hate water because they ken folk droun kittens?

I couldna say. Awa and play for pity's sake. Dinna mak a laughin stock o yirsel wi yon lads or ye'll niver hear the end o it.

Dae cats hae sauls? If cats hae sauls can they gang tae hell?

That's a question for the minister.

A strolling fiddler approaches, sawing out a bright air and his mother, who can never resist a bonny tune, hands him a coin. As the sun goes down, Thomas can pick out the smokers by the glowing bowls of their pipes and thin columns of smoke rising into the purple dusk. There is not a breath of wind. The air is hard as glass. The comet skinkles. Such a lovely sight it is; like a bird of paradise with a long, golden tail. How could something so lovely be a sign of God's wrath? If Thomas were God and wanted to show the world he was irked, he'd offer up a dark and ugly sign, a sign which made a terrible clanging and gave off a terrible stink.

Helen would be enjoying the outing more were Thomas not so clingy and James so oblivious to the children. She regrets that she does not own skates: the women who skate look so graceful and assured, as if at any moment they might take to the air. Helen often wishes she could fly away to some warm, gentle, far-off place. As James embarks on yet another turn around the frozen loch, she ponders her choice of husband. He had been *her* choice. Her brother Thomas, the Minister of Duddingston, uneasy that an apothecary might have ideas which didn't sit well with his parishioners, had done his damnedest to prevent the match. James has made her bed warm and can still, on occasion, make her blood jump but his devil-may-care nature, that once she'd have walked over thistles to defend, now keeps her awake at night.

Beyond the far side of the loch is a wilderness of frost-coated stubble and limp, blackened stalks. A group of ragged men roast small birds over a meagre fire. From their pitiful, insufficient garb they are Highlanders, starving Highlanders from their sunken cheeks and wild eyes, risking the perils of proximity to the town, like deer, or wolves, coming down off the hills. The frigid air magnifies each sound: bird bones snapping, spit hissing as it hits the flames, the Gaelic. And then there's a sudden commotion and the men are up on their rag-wrapped feet, jabbering and clacking their weapons against the hard ground.

Several of the Town Guard, in greatcoats and cocked hats, tramp doggedly over the lumpy ground at the edge of the ice, clutching muskets and antiquated Lochaber axes. There's more pomp about the Town Guard than circumstance, and more complaints about taxes levied to finance it than praise for its attempts to keep the peace. Like the old dogs that they are, however, once they've got their teeth into a piece of meat, they don't give it up without a fight. James is relieved that they have not come for him but knows his relief can only be short-lived.

His father moves across the frozen loch, small as a waterboatman. How can he seem so small when he's on the far side of the loch and so big when he's up close? Thomas is wondering how big and hot and bright the comet would be if he found himself up close to it when there's a crack in his ear like a gunshot, and another, and then he's eye to eye with two slavering hounds.

Curb yir dugs! shrills his mother, as Thomas shrieks and tugs at her skirts.

Guid day tae yirsel, *Mistress* Ramsey.

Keep yon beasts awa frae the bairn.

They're only barkin, Mistress. It's in a dug's nature tae bark, tae alert its maister tae unforeseen perils.

Where's the peril tae yir hounds in a young laddie?

A lad becomes a man. If it pleases the Lord.

It's in a dug's nature tae bite! says Thomas.

Hepburn of Blackcastle is tall, hammer-jawed, with eyes so hooded it's hard to be sure there's anything behind the heavy lids. He tightens the leashes on his panting hounds and claps their milk-and-liver haunches.

I see yir man, as aye, is shirkin his responsibilities.

Wid ye prevent a man stretchin his legs?

He'll no find the rent money on the Nor' Loch.

A man's life is mair than work.

Aye, Mistress Ramsey. There's prayer forby. I widna wish ony tenant o mine tae short-change the Lord. Or mysel. This kind o idle amusement—

Is ane o the few pleasures left tae workin folk! And whit brings *you* here, Maister Hepburn, if it's no tae amuse yirsel?

A man needs tae educate hissel in the foolish, sinful ways o the vulgar. I trust ye'll remind him o his dues.

Why no remind him yirsel?

No the day, Mistress Ramsey. The sun's dipped beneath the Calton Hill and I've better sport tae consider than chasin efter a guid-for-nocht.

Hepburn drags his hounds into the deepening dusk. Lanterns are lit and orange beams of light spray across the ice. Anna's playmates, who paused in their game to observe the arrival of Hepburn and his hounds, resume their sliding. Once again Helen encourages Thomas to join the other children but the copper-headed lad is mimicking a barking dog and Thomas will not shift.

The Sweet Singers of Borrowstounness

A city set upon a hill cannot be hid.
Matthew v.14

The city has vanished. Nothing of it remains but dense, damp haar, ringing with hollow wails. The tall lands have melted away, the church spires become spectral fingers pointing at nothing. The ghostly wailing dips and soars.

It is deils come tae steal oor sauls?

Dinna be daft, says Katharine. Deils stink o burnin sulphur. D'ye smell rotten eggs?

Thomas can smell fresh-baked bread, which he and Katharine are on their way to buy. He can smell ale and coppery blood, the thick stink of fish guts and the soursweet tang of mule dung but not, this morning, rotten eggs.

Whit is it then?

I dinna ken. But if the Lord's hid whit He's sent us behind a cloak o haar, it'll no be a penny weddin.

Is a penny weddin braw?

Once the menfolk hae a drink in them there's as much argy-bargy as on ony ither occasion.

Why wid God wish tae hide whit he sends us?

It's no for us tae question the ways o the Lord.

But why does He mak a mystery if He wants us tae understand?

I dinna ken, Thomas, and I dinna care.

The wailing swells. Faces appear out of the haar then fade away: woeful, tormented, fearsome apparitions. Thomas and Katharine are close enough to feel the body heat of the distracted, raggle-taggle psalm singers and smell the rot of the peatbogs on them. They are flanked by an equally unkempt troop of dragoons who jab at them with muskets and sprang them about the head if they attempt to stray from the convoy.

Oh God, why hast thou cast us off? Is it for evermore?
Against thy pasture-sheep why doth thine anger smoke so sure?

Whit did they dae? Thomas whispers.

Katharine tells him what she has heard: that the psalm-singers find sin in everything; that they feel themselves so immured in guilt they abandon the comforts of the hearth to live on the high heath like rebel Hill Folk; that they are wilder even in the convictions they profess than fanatical field preachers.

They disown the government. Disown an unconvenanted king, refuse tae work or pay taxes. Call for vengeance for the execution o two martyrs. They were sure that frae their vantage point on the hills they'd witness the sinful city burn tae the ground and that they, as servants o the true God, wid be spared. When the troops arrived they set up their psalm singing and havena ceased since.

How d'ye ken? says Thomas.

I heard tell.

Aye but how d'ye ken whit ye heard is true?

How long, Lord, shall thine anger last? Wilt thou still keep the same?
And shall thy fervent jealousy burn like unto a flame?

Keep yir distance, says a brawny dragoon. Yon folk are sair afflicted wi some unkent devilment. I widna wish a bonny jade tae catch the Borrowstounness epidemy.

I'm nae jade, sir! Katharine replies.

He lurches towards them. His front teeth are missing and his lips are all but hidden by a heavy beard.

Keep yir distance, sir! Keep yir distance—

Or whit? Whit'll ye dae, jade?

Dinna cry me jade, sir!

Thou makest us a strife unto our neighbours round about:
Our enemies amongst themselves do laugh at us—

Shift yirsels, ye sorry lot! commands the dragoon, cuffing any who pass within striking distance. And gie the blessed psalms a rest.

Why are ye hittin them? Thomas pipes up.

A loose tongue is a dangerous thing, says the dragoon, catching Thomas by the ear and twisting it. And a bonny jade is a sair temptation.

With his own tongue snaking over his whiskers, he's about to advance on Katharine when a bare-headed lass with a shock of white hair looms out of the haar and screams in his face:

My God, them like a wheel, as chaff before the wind, them make!
As fire consumes the wood, as flames do mountains set on fire!
Chase and affright them with the storm and tempest of thine ire!

Fare ye weel, jade.

The dragoon grabs the lass by the hair and kicks her back into line. On bare, torn feet she hirples forward and is consumed once more by the haar. With much roughness and cursing, the ghostly psalm singers are escorted to their place of confinement. The men are led towards the Tolbooth; the women to the House of Correction.

Whit will happen tae them? says Thomas.

They'll be punished, says Katharine. That's whit the House o Correction is *for*. Tae punish folk. Mak them see the error o thir ways.

But whit did they dae?

I've already telt ye. They made a song and dance o thir beliefs when they should've kept thir faith safe and quiet in thir herts.

The haar lifts and the city, once again hard and clear in the February light, goes about its business: the measuring and cutting of cloth, the printing of sermons and other edifying pamplets, the slaughtering and butchering of beasts, the gutting of fish, the plucking of fowl, the schooling of children, the preparation of medicines and the passing-on of tavern gossip. Outside the bakery with his sister, breathing in the aroma of fresh bread, Thomas hears the crack of the lash and the howls of pain. In the Tolbooth and the House of Correction, in the wardens' belief that their charges are receiving an effective treatment for driving out the devil, the Sweet Singers of Borrowstounness are being soundly thrashed, for the good of their eternal souls.

A-Maying

His mother is singing. She has a strong clear voice when her spirits are up and today, as they skirt the mills clustered on the banks of the fast-running Water of Leith, her eyes shine and her step is sure.

The trees they do grow high and the leaves they do go green,
And many's the cold winter's night my love and I have seen.

The path is dry and crisp underfoot, the air warm and scented with yolk-yellow broom. Blossom drapes the hawthorn like veils of creamy lace. In a loose line on the water, fuzzy ducklings putter behind their mother. A swan rises from her nest, wings spreading, neck curling into a dangerous question mark.

Growing, Growing, oh my bonny boy is young but he's growing.

Being a Sunday, Thomas has the feeling that his mother shouldn't really be singing a song about love for anyone but God but it is a pretty, slow air and chimes with the lilt of the river. Being a Sunday, they should be in church – as Katharine has already reminded them more than once – but Mayday only comes once a year and his mother says the Lord can surely do without them for once. Thomas is content to take his mother's word for this: it's much nicer to stravaig in the sunshine than to sit in church and listen to a long sermon.

Now at the age of sixteen he was a married man,
And at the age of seventeen the father to a son,

Anna skips ahead. Thomas chases after her, brandishing a branch of hawthorn.

If I tap ye wi my wand, ye'll turn intae the queen o the faeries!

Anna squeals in delight at the prospect, slows to let Thomas gain on her, then speeds off again to prolong the thrill of the chase. Katharine considers herself too old for such games but though she walks sedately by her mother's side, she holds a seductive image of Jeremiah Skaill in her mind's eye: his malt-brown eyes, peat-brown hair and milky skin, freckled like a mavis. It's no secret that she will invent excuses to visit his father's fine house in the Canongate.

Merchant Skaill has a walled garden with a choice array of fruits and legumes. He also has a keen interest in the cultivation of exotic herbs, as good a reason as any for an apothecary's daughter to visit, though Katharine cares little for herbs unless they might promote the object of her affection to fall at her feet. Piety might bring its own rewards but if it doesn't, Katharine does not entirely rule out other possibilities, though she would not admit such sinful thoughts to a living soul. One way or another, she hopes at some point soon to be done with living amid bottles and jars, with people expounding on their ailments and displaying wounds and eruptions as if they were trophies won in a tug-of-war with life.

Growing, growing, cruel death soon put an end to his growing.

More than a score of men, women and children have already arrived. The sun beats down like a blessing, rekindling the bodily pleasures of being alive. At this moment ministers might glare down from the pulpit, count vacant seats and fulminate to the devout and fearful about respecting the Lord's Day but the weather is so fine, days like this are so rare and the old ways have a hold on the imagination which admonishments from the Kirk can't always break.

Helen finds a spot for herself and the children on the river bank, a little apart from the others: she is not one for idle chatter. Thomas stretches out face down on the grass, the sun warming the back of his neck, his ears filled with the clicks and chirrs of insects, the twittering of tits and finches, the babbling water. Katharine has an expectant air about her, glancing this way and that, noting who is already there and hazarding a guess as to who might yet arrive. Anna wanders hither and thither, entranced by a dragonfly which hovers, wings aglint, in mid-air, then vanishes, only to materialise somewhere else.

Everyone present knows that, in the eyes of the clergy, being at the healing well constitutes a transgression. But Mayday offers something other than what the Kirk can provide; or take away. They do what has to be done: they pin clouts on the tree; throw trinkets in the well; raise palmfuls of spring water to their lips and make silent requests to the old spirits.

In some, the reason to have broken the Sabbath is evident: a lame child, another with a fist-sized struma on its neck, a lass with the green sickness languishing in the shade of a rustling beech, a woman black and blue at her guidman's hand, another twitching from worry and sleeplessness. But this is always how it is. Folk come to the well with their aches and pains, their sorrows. They quit the filth of the city, the crush of towering, close-packed buildings which block out the sun and the narrow, stinking wynds where there is no option but to live in each other's pockets and eat out of each other's mouths, and take themselves off for a day in the open air...

Growing, growing, I'll watch all o'er his child while he's growing.

Helen has not come A-Maying to rid herself or her children of physical afflictions. She's not even sure that the powers of the well concern themselves with the kind of problems she needs to solve. To all appearances, James's business is thriving: doesn't he always buy more than his fellow apothecaries, doesn't he fill the shelves with stock which has travelled the oceans from Batavia, Barbados, Barbary? He won't rest until he finds a way to satisfy a request but some requests entail a long wait, so long a wait that by the time the root or branch, the seed pod or skin arrives, it may no longer be required.

The trouble is that James buys plenty but does not sell enough, nor soon enough. And even when he does sell, the payment he receives is never enough, nor soon enough. They owe and owe, and though Hepburn had once been prepared to let one year's debt slide into the next, he has lost all patience and generosity. If he ever had it. What Hepburn gives, he gives with conditions. To hand out freely to those who cannot help themselves is not, in his estimation, a virtue; encouraging profligacy is only asking for trouble.

Overhead, a heron surveying its feeding ground flaps by, its broad slow wings creaking. Ale, cheese and fresh bread from the great ovens in the village of Dene are shared out, as are songs of love, to the sad pleasure of the women, the puzzlement of the children, the tolerant, knowing nods of family men and the faint scorn of the young blades who are here only for sport – and where else might they find sport on the Sabbath? They do not seek cures or answers to prayers – or if they do it's the kind of healing offered by female flesh and blood rather than well water.

Helen's voice cuts into Thomas's dwam.

Weel now, Katharine. It wid appear that somebody's wish has already been answered!

Hush, Mither.

Pretending to be a fox, Thomas peers through the long grass at the riverside path.

Jeremiah's comin doon the brae, he says.

Hush, says Katharine, directing her gaze to the treetops, as if some exotic creature has caught her attention.

Katharine refrains from acknowledging Jeremiah. When he begins to hum *Kathie by the Burn* she pretends not to hear him. When he waves at her, she pretends not to see him. Though gratified by the attention, she sets great store by propriety and dreads being made a laughing stock.

The young men Jeremiah joins on a flat rock are keener on horseplay than on ridicule and before long they are stripping off shirts and breeks and splashing into the river. When the little ones see what fun the big lads are having in the water, of course they want to join in.

At first Katharine resists Anna's pleas to paddle with her but the water sparkles so prettily and the mood is so festive, she too tucks up her skirt and steps in, gasping at the coldness of the water. Jeremiah splashes towards them.

Anna, lass, if ye gie me yir ither haund, he says, ye'll be able tae walk on water!

Katharine wants to disapprove – walking on water is the prerogative of the Lord Jesus – but Anna is too delighted by the notion to refuse her. While she and Jeremiah swing Anna between them, unseen beneath the fast-flowing water, Jeremiah strokes Katharine's ankle with his toes.

Thomas wants to do more than paddle and some of the young men have found a pool deep enough for swimming. The feel of the cool smooth stones underfoot, their slipperiness and the drag of the current, makes every step an adventure.

Look at me! he shouts.

With arms outstretched, he steps from one smooth stone to another. The young men pay Thomas little attention; they are too taken up with douking each other and splashing a stroke or two.

Look at me! he shouts again, as he loses his footing and falls smack on his arse.

Now the young men do look at him, and laugh loudly as he gets back on his feet, the Water of Leith pouring out of his breeks.

He'll hae tae gang bare-arsed for the rest o the day!

Or don ane o his sister's petticoats!

★★★

If they were frank with each other, the two black-coated elders lurking behind the broad tree trunk on the far bank would admit to thoroughly enjoying their time in the open air, free from coccyx-numbing pews and the asphyxiating odours of humanity which accumulate between kirk walls during a Sunday sermon. Elders Mathieson and Morrison might even be experiencing more enjoyment than those gathered at the well; *their* absence from kirk, after all, is fully sanctioned.

They have been sent by the Kirk Session to seek out those who have gone A-Maying, to identify, both with the naked eye and the application of a spyglass, each and every Sabbath breaker. So as to be thorough in their task, all observations are noted down in a small black book, with names where possible, descriptions where not. Mathieson holds an inkwell and Morrison writes; they have already listed a fair few sinners but the sun has not yet reached its zenith and the more names they add, the better. They agree to tarry a while.

In the meantime, as it would be a waste to leave the spyglass idle, Mathieson and Morrison take turns to observe the bird life on the river, to familiarise themselves with the ways of God's own creatures. Upstream, a heron stands on a rock, hunched and motionless, to all appearances doing nothing at all then, quick as a blink, it stabs the water and pulls out a fish, wriggling in the clamp of its beak.

The heron resembles us, says Mathieson to Morrison. It kens how tae bide its time, tae be vigilant. And when the moment is richt, tae mak its move.

Vigilance is aw, says Morrison to Mathieson. I believe yon's a kingfisher upon the brig. Might I tak a turn o the gless?

And so the pair pass a pleasant while, noting plumage, behaviour and song, admiring the banks of curly bluebells and starry globes of wild garlic. Alerted by the whooping and splashing further down river, the elders turn the spyglass, with its admirable magnification, in the direction of the bathers.

It is Anna who first notices the dark shapes of the elders moving between the trees and with a pointing finger shows Katharine where to look. Katharine in turn shows Jeremiah. When he spies the peeping elders, he alerts his fellow bathers and they act swiftly. When a stone the size of an egg lands with a dull thud just short of their feet and is followed by many more, Mathieson and Morrison realise their mistake too late. Stones continue to be thrown. Mathieson is struck on the temple, Morrison on the knee. Slurs and jibes continue to fly across the water.

Thomas picks up a stone but it's too big and heavy and his aim is awry. It hits the far bank then clunks back into the river.

Try a sma stane, says Jeremiah. Ye'll have mair success wi a sma stane.

Ye'll try nae stane at aw! says Katharine. Maister Skaill, ye should be ashamed o yirsel, encouragin a bairn tae insurrection and disrespect tae men o the claith.

Nocht but dugs in the manger, says Jeremiah.

Whit's a dug in the manger? says Thomas.

Niver mind, says Katharine. Pit doon that stane!

Whit dae the elders want? says Thomas.

Tae meddle in awbody's lives, says his mother.

But why?

Because they can. Because the Kirk gies them licence tae meddle.

Dodging the volley of stones, Morrison and Mathieson can no longer note down who says or does what. Increasingly fearful that some young strong men might ford the river and do them a serious mischief, they scuttle off, stumbling in their haste, tearing the knees of their breeks, regretting their lapse of vigilance, yet reassuring each other as they flee that, come what may, the following week, they would see a goodly number of Sabbath breakers on the stool of repentance.

Lozenges for Love

It is a hazy summer morning. Thomas sits by the open hatch, writing labels for his father: Agrimony, Amaranthus, Asarabacca, Belladonna, Briony, Epithymum, Feverfew, Pennyroyal. He knows that all the substances must be treated with care but repeats their lovely lilting names under his breath. The High Street jangles with the squeals and bellows of beasts being slaughtered, the squawking of caged birds and the hoarse barks of vendors offering wine and wool, plums and panniers, cabbages and rat-traps.

Buttery light spreads across the flagstones. His mother is at the stove, preparing the mid-day meal. Katharine is letting out the cuffs of the jacket he has almost outgrown. Anna dangles a length of string above the cat's head and laughs as it leaps up in pursuit of the tail end. His father is resting a tobacco-stained finger on a page of Culpeper on which the words 'Venice Treacle' appear several times.

Whit's Venice Treacle? asks Thomas, standing on tiptoe at his father's side.

Anither name for Mathiolus's *great antidote against Poison and Pestilence*, says his father. Some say it can cure maist ills. Some say it's poison but by dint o being poison itsel draws ither poisons frae the body. And some say it can mak a man reject the poisonous sin which has entered his saul. Now that wid be a fine thing indeed.

Could ye mak it, faither?

I'd fair like tae try. But there's ower mony rare and costly ingredients. I'd be taen a great financial risk...

While James ponders the possibility of concocting Venice Treacle, a woman darts up to the hatch and leans in.

Apart from her wide green eyes and smooth brow, her face is obscured by a heather-coloured plaid. She glances down the busy street as if someone were hot on her heels, then leans in close to James's ear, uncovers her mouth and begins to whisper. Thomas, in his best hand, writes *Bella*. He listens hard but cannot hear her request... *donna*. She is serious and businesslike but when she's done his father lets out a laugh and declares loudly enough for any passerby to catch it:

So it's lozenges for love ye're efter!

Shush! They're no for me.

I didna say they were. I widna have thocht a comely lass wid be needful o such a remedy. But wha, I wonder, has a mind tae chairge up thir pleasure?

It's no for ye tae ask, and no for me tae tell. Can ye gie me whit I'm efter or can ye no? I'll gang elsewhere, if need be.

James tamps some tobacco in his pipe, lights up and takes a deep, leisurely draw.

Patience! he says, eyes sparkling with mischief. A virtue aye required in matters o love.

James watches the smoke from his pipe blue the air. He appears to have forgotten all about the young woman drumming her little fist on the counter and keeping an anxious eye on the street.

Faither, says Thomas. Is belladonna no the same as deadly nightshade?

Aye.

Why does a plant hae twa names?

Now ye're askin. But this is no the time for me tae be tellin. Awa and see how the dinner's comin alang, there's a lad.

Sensing a ruse to be rid of him, Thomas stops at the door. His father spreads his elbows on the counter and looks the lass straight in the eye:

Meddlin in a body's affections, tamperin wi Divine Providence – the Kirk widna be likin that, now, wid it?

I dae whit my mistress bids.

So it's a woman wants tae disrupt the natural course o things? That disna bode weel... James's voice is sonorous with mock solemnity.

Haud yir tongue, I beg ye!

For *you* lass, and mair sae if ye're *beggin* me, I'd haud my tongue till Kingdom Come. But whit ye seek disna come cheap.

I can pay the price, she says, and lays coins on the table.

Thomas! says his father, sharpish this time. Awa through tae yir mither.

But it's no dinner-time yet. The gill-bells havena even rang.

Dae as ye're telt.

Reluctantly Thomas does as he's bid.

In the kitchen, his mother is grating an onion into the pot. Her eyes are red and streaming from the pungent juices.

Whit're ye efter, Thomas?

Faither asked me tae see how the dinner fares.

Could he no come and see for hissel?

He's got a customer. A lady's maid's efter lozenges for love.

His mother wipes her eyes.

Is she now?

Faither shouldna stock such things, says Katharine, biting the end off her thread. It's agin the Lord's wishes.

Whit isna agin the Lord's wishes?

Meddlin in affairs o the hert is the deil's business.

Ay, Katharine, the auld mischanter's a busy man.

His mother drops the remaining chunk of onion into the pot.

Whit dae I tell Faither?

Tell him dinner will be ready in its ain guid time.

How lang is that?

As lang as I wish it tae be!

When he returns to the shop, his father is making a show of searching the shelves – though he knows the precise location of all his stock – peering at the rows of jars and bottles and making light of the lass's flounces of impatience. At length he plucks a narrow bottle from between a jar of powdered earthworms and one containing the papery skins of vipers. He pops the cork and tips a handful of deep pink tablets onto the table.

Pink tae mak the laddies wink, he grins.

Whit's in them?

A bit lovage, stalks o royal fern as a base. Cochineal for colour. But the receipt in its entirety is a secret o the trade. Where wid a humble apothecary be if he gied awa ilka receipt in his possession? He'd be on the street, that's where, beggin a crust. But I believe these'll dae the trick. He slips the tablets into a muslin pouch, scoops up the coins and commences to whistle a merry tune. The young woman draws her plaid across her face and hurries away.

So how's the dinner?

Mither says it'll be ready in its ain guid time.

Mercy, that's how she is the day? We'd best mind oor manners.

Whit's lozenges for love?

Weel now, says his father, glancing out at the street, that wid be tellin.

The Stool of Repentance

If there's anything worse than a cold empty church it's a hot, overcrowded one. The sun has been pouring through the windows since early morning, warming the benches, dappling bare walls and scant furnishings. The church stinks to the rafters. The better-off worshippers inhale scent from the phial hanging at their throats but all the perfumes of the Orient can't counter the stench of a gathering of their fellow men and women. Spruced up in a manner befitting the Sabbath, the congregation has settled on a motley assemblage of stools and benches, or secured a patch of wall to support them for the duration of the sermon.

For the Aikenhead family and others the shame of public humiliation taints their day of worship. Is it worse for Helen Ramsey, standing for the sixth week on a raised wooden form situated directly beneath the pulpit, from which she and her fellow sinners may be scrutinised by the congregation? Or is it worse for James to see his wife squirm, and feel the hot hands of his children press their sharp little worries into his palms?

Does Katharine revel in her mother's public humiliation? Does she search her mother's expression or bearing for signs that she has been cured of her irreverence? If so, she sees more defiance than repentance. Does she wish her mother to suffer for longer in the hope that it might curb her pride? Would she rather help her mother down from the bench and usher her back into the body of the kirk or does she, having herself escaped public censure, feel little more than relief that she too is not standing there, on the stool of repentance?

What goes through the young minds of Thomas and Anna when they see their mother standing there week after week, gawped at from the first prayer to the final Amen, unable to hide her face? At home she has been her usual self, if anything a deal more irascible, quicker to fly into a rage at their tardiness in the mornings, quicker to curse the cat for getting under her feet or berate their father for his spending. From one Sabbath to the next they've seen her slighted by friends and neighbours, heard tongues start to wag even before she was out of earshot. Were some of the scolds who malign her not also at the Maying? Just because the elders failed to note down their names does not change the fact that they too enjoyed their time in the sunshine.

That others who'd been at the Maying have not also been punished for Sabbath breaking irks Helen almost as much as the punishment itself. Not a single stone-thrower stands beside her and surely stone-throwing is a more serious offence than name-calling? Jeremiah Skaill, whose family attend a church in the Canongate, has been excused penance and it's likely his father's generosity was a consideration: over the past year the man has donated three pairs of Dutch chairs and a carved font from Germany. Whatever list the elders might have gathered from their investigations, only some individuals have been picked out for punishment.

It must be some comfort to Helen that she is not alone on the stool of repentance, though her fellow penitents are a motley crew. There are the card players: one plum-nosed and bandy-legged, the other with a wandering eye and a pot belly. Together these men fritter away the hours of worship in a dank tavern in Fleshmarket Close, oblivious to everything but the breathless bond of the bluff. James has lost money to both. There is the scrawny widow, reported to the Kirk Session by prying neighbours for lying in the arms of her amour. Her husband, a stone mason, died young, in an accident at work, and the long winter nights hit her hard. Has James not provided her with valerian for sleeplessness? Perhaps lying next to a warm body made it possible for her to sleep sound. Some folk just can't leave well alone.

Amongst the drinkers and gamblers, the fornicators and Sabbath breakers, James might also have found himself upon the stool: he has become over-fond of the tavern as well as the gaming tables. There's no telling which way the lackeys of the Kirk Session will turn: one week they'll be sniffing out the lemon sellers at their unofficial business, the next, skulking outside the taverns at the ten o'clock bell to note whoever is unsteady on their feet. With so many zealous informants and so many punishable misdemeanours, it's hard to know who might be next.

Thomas is oddly proud of the fact that his mother stands with her head held high, her eyes dark with rage. When she is angry with *him*, he'd rather cower with the cat, but when she's blazing at the entire congregation, that's another thing altogether. Others hang their heads, simper, twitch and blink, or cast their eyes to the rafters where the sparrows are chattering. Chattering in church! Sparrows committing a sin! Perhaps the minister will see fit to punish them for interrupting his sermon.

Brazen besom, a voice mutters behind him. Scowlin at the God-fearin sauls in the body o the kirk when she should be hingin her heid in shame.

The Chief End of Man

One: *What is the chief end of Man?* – Farquar.

Man's chief end is to glorify God, and to enjoy Him for ever.

Six: *How many persons are in the Godhead?* – Ogilvy.

There are three persons in the Godhead: the Father, the Son, and the Holy Ghost; and these three are one God, the same in substance, equal... in power and glory.

No excuse for hesitation, Ogilvy. The words of the catechism should come oot yir mooth as easy and natural as breathing. Number Twelve: *What special act of providence did God exercise toward man in the estate wherein he was created?* – Aikenhead.

When God had created man he entered into a covenant of life with him upon condition of perfect obedience forbidding him to eat of the tree of the knowledge of good and evil upon the pain of death.

Are ye on a runaway steed? Tak yir time and gie the response the due attention it deserves.

Yes, Maister Armour, sir.

Nineteen – Lennox. *Wherein consists the sinfulness of that estate whereinto man fell?*

The sinfulness of that estate... whereinto man fell, consists in the guilt of Adam's first sin, the want of... the want of...

Of original righteousness, Lennox. Something you are surely in want of.

Original righteousness and the corruption of his whole nature, which is commonly called Original Sin; together with all... actual transgressions... which proceed from it.

Bernard Armour raises a skinny arm, opens his mouth wider and wider, then trumpets a dust-raising sneeze. A ripple of hilarity runs around the benches. While the dominie is occupied with his capacious handkerchief, his charges get up to the kind of mischief schoolboys have always favoured: a lad in the back corner sets a frog on another's shoulder. The frog leaps from one shoulder to the next, then onto a lap, a knee and finally the floor where it hops around the room, prompting further hilarity.

De… de… desist! sneezes Armour, simultaneously whacking his cane against the desk. Armour is a stickler for proper procedure and prepared to persist for however long it takes to extract the required responses from his pupils.

Twenty One – Grieve. *Who is the Redeemer of God's Elect?*

Andrew Grieve, a dazed, fearful boy, quakes.

The only Redeemer o o o o o o o of Go o o o od's elect is the Lo o o o o rd Jesus Christ, who, being the eternal Son o o o o of Go o o o d—

Spit it oot, son, for pity's sake.

…God God God God became man, and so waswaswaswas and co co co co continueth to be, Go o o o d and man in two distinct natures, and one perso o o o n, fo o o o o r for for for EVER!

Well, thank the Lord that's done wi. Number Twenty Two – Craig. And tak that smirk off yir face. Did ye hear me, Craig?

Aye, Maister Armour.

Yes, Maister Armour, *sir.*

Yes, Maister Armour, *sir.*

Well then, Craig. If ye please, supply me wi the answer tae Number Twenty Two: *How did Christ, being the son of God, become Man?*

Christ, the Son of God, became man, by taking to himself a… a…

A whit, boy? By taen tae hissel a whit?

I canna mind, sir.

Please, sir, says Thomas, I mind. I mind, sir!

It's no yir turn, Aikenhead. Ye've already had yir turn. It's no my job tae teach ane pupil but tae teach the haill class.

But I ken it, Maister Armour, and can gie it due attention. Please, sir!

Verra weel… Craig. Craig! Prick up yir ears or I'll prick

them up for ye.

Christ, the Son of God, became a man, by taking to himself a true body, and a reasonable soul, being conceived by the power of the Holy Ghost, in the womb of the Virgin Mary, and born of her, yet without sin… but sir, if we're aw sinners how can the Virgin Mary be—

Keep yir queries for Judgement Day, Aikenhead, as I've telt ye mony a time… Number Thirty Nine – Craig. Let's see whether ye can redeem yirsel – for the time being, at least. *What is the duty that God desireth of Man?*

The duty which God requireth of man is obedience to His revealed will.

Correct. And the duty I requireth o this class is obedience tae *my* will. And dinna forget it.

The dominie does not, however, have eyes in the back of his head however useful such a facility might be in his profession, and when his back is turned the boys once more get up to their tricks: pulling faces, launching paper birds across the heads of classmates, tossing chuckie stanes across the flagstones, nudging and shoving, whispering and sniggering. Since the beginning of the daily recitation of the catechism, Mungo Craig, who is new and older than the others, has been plaguing Thomas with kicks and pinches and repeating a tiresome joke about his name: Have ye got an achin heid, then? Thomas recognises him; he's the same copper-headed lad who commandeered the ice slide in the winter of the Great Comet. His kicks are vicious but Thomas hasn't cried out: no-one likes a pickthank. Besides, the dominie has promised them a story at the end of the day but only if they're well enough behaved. And if Thomas is the one to cause extra Latin instead of a story, he knows he'll pay for it.

Thomas has been at school for nearly a year. Armour has praised his application and his reading and writing skills but has taken the stick to his back for his chattering. As Maister Armour insists on doing almost all the talking almost all of the time, the hours of sitting in school, especially on a dark winter day, can be long and wearisome, if it were not for the prospect of a story.

In spite of a few minor transgressions which the dominie, in the scheme of things, is prepared to overlook, the boys have behaved well enough. The light from the windows is fading and despite Armour adding a few lumps of coal to the fire, a chill creeps through the classroom. To gain some warmth, the boys pack themselves as tight as a bed of mussels then settle, with arms folded and eyes closed. Even those who have been at loggerheads earlier in the day are prepared to put their differences behind them and listen, with held breath, to a story.

Bernard Armour sets his bony arse on the bench and tugs at his blue nose. He trims the candle wick, hoots into his handkerchief then begins:

Weel now, my young pups. Ye may spy an auld dug afore ye but this dug has had its day. This auld dug has consorted wi princesses, and djinns! A lang way frae here, there's a land abune the clouds. Ye haveta tramp through the clouds thirsels and feel thir wet mist on yir shanks and airms, and climb and climb. Ye think ye're gaen aw the way tae heaven. Once ye're through the cloud the light's that bricht it pains yir een and the mid-day sun can burn a man's skin until first he's reid, then broon, then dark as treacle. In the forests, the foliage is dense and the trees tall, and once ye're deep in their midst, ye've need o a shairp blade tae hack yir way oot again. There's craturs ye widna believe unless ye'd seen them wi yir ain een.

Maister Armour, sir. Maister Armour!

Whit is it, Aikenhead?

I saw the elephant, Maister Armour. At the Mercat Cross. It was greetin and pissin. It wis mortall.

That's as may be but this isna a tale aboot an elephant.

Wheesht Aikenhead! says Mungo Craig, and dunts Thomas in the ribs.

Now whit wis I sayin? says the dominie. Queer craturs, wi muckle horns and tusks, and jaws that can snap a man's airm in twa. Birds which staund higher than a man and big cats that creep up on ye withoot a soond then claw oot yir vitals. Bats that suck the blood frae a man's thrapple. Snakes that can crush the life oot o a man, and coontless ither beasts.

But even mair streenge is the spirit world. Folk say the spirit world bides side by side wi the material world – just beyond yir glimpse, just oot o earshot but there are times when the twa worlds mingle and then ye truly hae tae mind yir step.

Today I'll tell ye aboot the time I crossed swords wi a djinn. Now, the first thing ye hae tae ken aboot djinns is that they're free tae dae as they will. They're maistly invisible but can tak the form o beast or bird, or a mannie forby. Djinns live in the taps o the trees wi the monkeys and can leap frae branch tae branch and rin like the wind. There are times when, for spite, they cairry off a human lass tae thir spirit world.

If a djinn gets ye, d'ye hae tae bide wi them for aye? says Thomas.

Why d'ye care if they're only efter lasses? says Mungo Craig.

Enough, says Armour. Ony mair interruptions and ye'll hear nae mair.

A shushing spreads through the classroom before silence reigns once more.

Weel, now, says Armour, once I wis the guest o a prince wha had a dochter he loved ower dearly. A horde o suitors came askin for her haund but the prince aye found faut wi them: ane wis ower lazy, anither ower vain, ower auld, ower crabbit, ower niggardly, and so on. The lass accepted her faither's decision but didna wish tae bide in her faither's hoose for aye.

Ane nicht she wished tae walk in the rose gairden, alane, and her faither, nae wishin tae rouse the housemaid, asked if I'd escort her and staund gaird. I agreed, thinkin I might be fendin off fierce craturs o the forest. It wis a balmy scented nicht, the monks were chantin for poya and the moon wis fou; a heavenly nicht and tae tell the truth I wis slippin intae a wee dwam when I heard her cry oot:

He wants me for his bride! The djinn wants me for his bride!

I hastened through the rose gairden tae find the princess

wailin piteously and tearin at her hair. I could see naebody but the princess hersel but she insisted the djinn had taen the form o a lang mannie in white robes.

Save me! she said. Save me!

I believed she wis prey tae her ain imagination but I wis chairged tae protect her. Feelin a mite sheepish, I drew my sword and cried:

Show yirsel, whitiver ye be! in God's name show yirsel and fight like a man.

There wis a rush o air and a white flame flared then skirled aboot my sword. I could feel heat, smell burnin. I could hear heavy pantin, like a dog that's chased a fox, but couldna see ocht but the skirlin flame. I thrust my sword this way and that, then lunged at the hert o the flame. Wi an eldritch howl it curled and twisted, and wis sucked up intae the firmament. The princess fell on my chest and wept. Once I'd ascertained that she wisna hairmed, I escorted her back tae the palace – carefully mind! Efter daein battle wi a djinn, a lass disna wish her dainty feet torn by thorns!

When I related whit had transpired, the prince vowed tae find his dochter a mate, and did by the next fou moon, which goes tae show whit can be done when a man maks up his mind tae act. I stayed for the weddin, a maist lavish and lovely affair, wi days on end o feastin and dancin.

The dominie falls silent and gazes over the bowed heads of his charges.

But Maister Armour, sir, says Thomas, sitting up straight. How could the princess see the djinn but you couldna?

Ah weel. The princess believed in the djinns but I didna. And if ye dinna believe in them, ye canna see them. That's how I understand it. But I tell ye, o a balmy nicht, the kind we rarely hae in oor land, when oot o naewhere comes sudden rush o air, or a streenge glimmer in some lightless place, my een aye search for a lang mannie in snowy robes.

At Lucky Lorimer's

A change has come over the house, a sour mood crept in like some malignant spirit and taken up residence, draining the life from everything. James no longer whistles while he works nor takes time to instruct Thomas in the proper names of compounds or the properties of roots and leaves. He no longer rhapsodises about new cures nor seeks out marvels imported by merchant ships. He rarely jokes with customers, such few as there are. Instead, he leans too hard on them to purchase more than they came for; they make their excuses and leave.

James paces like a bear on a chain, a sick bear, coughing and spitting and grinding his teeth. Helen has run out of sympathy. Heal thysel! she chides, shrewish. If he's sick, surely he can find a cure on his own shelves and if he can't, what sort of apothecary is he? James accuses Helen of household extravagance, of buying from costlier merchants; Helen declares that only the costliest will grant them credit. It is James and James alone, she insists, who has loosened the purse strings, neglecting debts which grow in the dark, like mould on old bread.

She harries him to inspect the ledgers, and balancing the books sets off bitter wrangles and long, vicious rows. For his part, James sees little point in thinking about debts he can't repay all the livelong day, and so they remain at loggerheads. Thomas and Anna are cowed but Katharine burns with shame; their parents' broiling will bring disgrace upon the family and who will pay the price of such disgrace?

James has become niggardly with his ingredients, tipping every last grain from a sack, forbidding Thomas the least gleanings. Rather than discard leftover material from a volatile compound, he stores dregs and scrapings long past the duration of their efficacy. Once he would have had qualms about passing off a paste as freshly-prepared but now he cares more about eking out his dwindling stock.

Though now he does not dare dispense aphrodisiacs, when it comes to the unwanted *results* of ardour, he no longer has any qualms about supplying pennyroyal or tansy to a lass who, feigning she seeks to rid her bed from infestation, is in fact after an abortifacient. In the past he might have outlined the danger in tampering with the course of nature but now he keeps his own counsel: if *he* won't provide what a customer demands, somebody else will.

Not all of James's customers have deserted him, the Lord be praised. Archibald Pitcairne, hot on the trail of some new medicament, still drops by. Absorbed by his own investigations, oblivious to the Aikenheads' troubles, Pitcairne brings with him a breath of boozy cheer. And some sorely needed coin. But the moment he draws on his gloves and sets off down the street on his bowed and buckled shoon, the malignance in the house reasserts itself.

When business is too slack and his wife's remonstrations too shrill, James calls upon Katharine to mind the shop and makes for Lucky Lorimer's, one of the few taverns which still offers him something of a welcome. And credit, albeit limited. Over the years he has done Peg Lorimer some favours. He has provided her with purges which, dropped in a tankard of ale, will send most miscreants packing. Peg Lorimer is a woman with a long memory.

Amid the fug of pipe smoke and the comforting aromas of ale and mutton broth, the mishap caused by the aphrodisiacs is not treated with the solemnity with which it was dissected in court. Though it can't be denied that Jonet Stewart, servant to advocate William Dundas, was taken exceedingly ill and is likely to remain poorly for the rest of her days, the tavern sages take a more sanguine view. Life has dealt these men some cruel blows. To make bearable what remains of their own sorry existence they chew on the tribulations of others with the same relish as they suck meat from the bones in Peg Lorimer's broth.

So they say the Mistress Edmonstoun gied the tablets tae the servant lass—

In front o several witnesses—

Wi the lass's knowledge?

Naw, sumph. The Mistress Edmonstoun feigned they were sweetmeats.

Weel, there ye hae it. Gie a lass a poke o sweeties and a lass wi a sweet tooth, is it likely she'd only tak a cautious quantity?

She likes the taste, she wants anither.

And on until the poke is empty.

Gluttony's yir culprit, then.

Naw, it wis duplicity. The cause o the hairm wis her that gied yon tablets tae the lass.

And why, ye wonder?

Aye. Why trick a lassie intae taen such a thing?

Tae mak her sin then see her chastised for it?

That's low, man, verra low.

Next yon Mistress Edmonstoun'll be requestin a potion tae mak a body birl roond the room!

Wha wis the intended object o the lass's wantonness?

Wis it her ain maister, Dundas, or Maister Edmonstoun?

Now ye're askin.

Did Mistress Edmonstoun wish tae mak the maid amenable tae advances frae her ain guidman and thereby keep him frae her marriage bed?

Man, yon's a sin tae be sure, tae keep yir guidman frae his conjugal richts, his just deserts!

And hae a maid snuggle up tae yir guidman in yir stead?

That's low, ower low.

Ken whit I'd dae wi a woman like yon? I'd whip her roond the toun like a common whore. Drag her through the mire tied tae the back o a cart then see how fine she thocht hersel.

But whit if the maid wis meant tae be wanton wi her *ain* maister, Advocate Dundas? And whit in that case wis the Mistress Edmonstoun's intent?

It's ill luck the lass's maister's an advocate.

At least the cratur didna dee.

Near as dammit, mind.

Wis she comely, James?

The Mistress Edmonstoun?

Naw, naw, the lass. Jonet Stewart.

No when I saw her, she wisna. Nor's the Mistress Edmonstoun. Mind, the maid Edmonstoun sent in her stead wis a sonsie wee hinny, says James.

And d'ye think she had a fancy for Dundas, the advocate?

Wha, the maid?

Naw, the Mistress Edmonstoun.

And wis the lass, Jonet Stewart, in fact enamoured o Dundas or Maister Edmonstoun?

Did the tablets dae thir proper work afore they made her seik?

Ah now, we havena thocht on that…

It is not facts that fire the imagination of the drinkers but the tangle of domestic intrigue, the web of motives and allegiances, the chicanery that keeps them jawing for hours, throwing in jests and aspersions about their own spouses to raise a groan, a guffaw or a roar of assent from the assembled company. At times James wonders at himself, idling away his days in tavern talk but when it palls, it's not the meagre comforts of home he seeks out.

A Leith Cocking

There's a prickle of frost in James's nostrils, and the need to draw his muffler over his nose, but after a good pull of brandy his chest feels warm and his troublesome cough temporarily subsides. That he no longer aches is, in itself, a pleasure. It's a promising day for a walk down Leith Wynd. The sky is February pale with threads of cirrus, and a salty breeze blows up from the Firth of Forth. James's companion, Angus Burnside, silversmith, carries a pair of gamecocks in padded wicker cages. As they make their way down the brae, Angus talks to his birds more than to James:

A nip in the air, lads. And ye'll no be happy wi aw this jiggling aboot. But dinna fret, ye've pit up a guid spar ilka day and now's yir chance at the real thing. My money's on the baith o ye tae come oot victorious.

The birds flupp and fluster in their cages, beaking and tailing the bars, eyes glossy.

They're a spirited pair.

It's in a gamecock's nature tae fight. Yon are no yir barnyard cockerels that lord it ower the henhoose. They're a breed apairt. Even the females fight. In the wild they'll fight tae the daith. We're only adjustin nature a modicum for oor ain pleasure.

All the tavern drinkers know that Angus has lavished attention on his birds for the best part of a year. He's fed them on raw beef and maggots, on wheatbread soaked in urine. He's spooned brandy down their gullets, coddled them in blankets, sliced off their combs, wattles and earlobes so their heads are lean and sharp as gaffs. Before settling them down for the night, he's sung to them like bairns.

Wait till ye see them in thir siller spurs, says Angus, his voice glazed with pride. Only the best for Achilles and Genghis.

It's a man's right, James thinks, as he pulls at the brandy flask, to do as he pleases now and again. By absconding from the shop and leaving Helen and Katharine to attend to business, isn't he doing more good than harm, living according to his nature rather than bending to the will of God, the Kirk Session, or his wife?

About halfway down the hill, a small procession turns at Pilrig, thus beginning its gloomy trek to the Gallowlee.

Whit d'ye reckon? says Angus. The flames or the gibbet?

Either way it's a sorry misfortune.

We shouldna speak o fortune the day! says Angus.

Has fortune smiled on James? Not as much as he'd have liked. In his youth he'd fancied travelling to jungle, pampas, to alpine meadow and rainforest in search of new remedies for old ailments. He'd imagined spending weeks at sea contemplating a tilting horizon. He doesn't think about any of that now. He doesn't think at all now if he can help it. Because when he does, all he thinks about is debts and the impossibility of clearing them.

From all directions men converge on the circular pit, their paths like spokes on a cartwheel. All ranks of men are drawn to the hot thrill of the cocking: those with time on their hands and money in their purses, and those who can't resist the temptation to write promissory notes they have no hope of honouring.

On the thatched roof, attracted by a rich mix of scents, crows hop to and fro until a man brandishing a sharpened pole shoos them away.

James is cheered by the meeting and greeting, the backslapping, the craik. Angus, chary of agitating his birds, covers his cages.

Shouldna get their blood up ower soon, he says. They need tae save thirsels for the ring.

The cockpit is already crammed when James and Angus squeeze in and search for a space. Even by the unglazed windows where there's more light and air, the crush, the din, the hum of sweat and bloodlust is intoxicating. Angus straps the silver cockspurs on Genghis; they glint like stilettos. He lovingly laces the leather anklets.

A gaff can kill a man, says Angus, niver mind anither cock o the game.

He wears a protective glove and works with the same care and attention to detail he gives to his silversmithing, all the time crooing terms of endearment, stroking feathers, kissing his bird like a man about to take his new wife's maidenhead.

My, my, Aikenhead. Learnin the tricks o anither trade? Ower tardy, I fear, should ye wish tae reverse yir ill fortune.

Hepburn of Blackcastle stands over them, a spurred bird wedged under an arm in the manner of a henwife about to chop off its head. But of course Hepburn is taller, straighter and much better dressed than any henwife. James's head thumps. His chest is tight. It's nothing to worry about; no more than having to endure Hepburn lording it over him as usual.

Time will tell, he says.

Time tells aw, says Hepburn. Maister Burnside, we'll meet in the ring. And I'll wager my bird will mak a boiling fowl o yours.

Ye were aye ane for a jest, says Angus. My bird will mak *your* bird lick the dust. Will ye no, my lovely?

Angus's bird paddles his tail furiously.

Bide yir time, Genghis. Bide yir time. Weel now, Maister Hepburn sir, be kind enough tae leave us be until oor numbers are ca'ed.

By aw means, says Hepburn. I've better things tae dae than pass the time in chatter. But mind, Aikenhead, he says, elbowing a gap in the press of bodies, yir rent's been wanting ower lang. And now the College o Physicians has barred ye and yir guild-brethren frae dispensing lozenges for love, custom is like tae decrease.

As ye ken, says James, the real faut lies wi the procurer o the lozenges, and how they were administered, no wi the dispenser.

Folk believe whit they wish tae believe, says Hepburn.

Out of loyalty to Angus, James places a small bet on each of Angus's birds, as well as a couple of others he fancies, though all that he wagers is already spoken for several times over. Before their numbers are called, several other fights take place.

Each is fleeting and brutal, a squawking blur of feathers, beaks, spurs. Each is fatal. Between fights, fresh sawdust is thrown into the ring to soak up the blood and conceal the gouts of gristle, the eyes and beaks, the petals of coxcomb come adrift. The carcasses of the losing birds are thrown in a heap.

It is customary for the gentry to have their men present their gamecocks in the ring but Hepburn likes to get his own hands bloody. His bird is a glorious specimen, with black and white plumage and a lush, plum-coloured tail. Angus's bird is long and lean, with copper plumage and eager eyes. As soon as the pair are released they are at each other's throats, whirling in a deadly embrace.

Get tae it, Genghis! James roars. Show them whit ye're made o! And then his chest tightens, his jaw locks, and he crumples onto the muddy floor.

It is only after Angus's second bird has been dispatched that Hepburn's coachman, a slight, wiry man who, from the window, has been trying in vain to glimpse the fights, pushes through the crowds to inform his master that James has been taken poorly.

First things first, says Hepburn, and goes to collect his winnings.

Bystanders have propped James against the wall, as much to make space as to make him more comfortable. He is by no means the only man to have been overwhelmed by the crush, the excitement, and the taking of strong drink. All he can see is a wall of close-pressed rumps. He gasps and wheezes and cannot shift the fist of pain in his chest. Beside him, oblivious to James's condition, the ensuing bustle and the continuing activity in the cockpit, Angus rocks back and forth, head in blood-streaked hands.

Once all the listed fights have taken place, butchers pluck the dead birds and offer them for sale. Cheap. Very cheap. Only the hungriest will eat fightkill. The crowd begins to disperse and Hepburn approaches. In a rare gesture of magnanimity, he instructs his coachman to drive James home, along with Angus Burnside and his rattling cages.

Plum Cake & Attar of Roses

The sun is shining. The sky is blue. Birds twitter. Daffodils nod cheery heads. Children whoop. Women plash and laugh as they tread linen in tubs of water. Masons hammer and chisel and joke with each other. A horse whinnies. Pigs snuffle and squeak. The breeze, pushing through gaps in the kirkyard wall, croos like a pigeon. How can the day be so merrily full of life?

Thomas's neck itches from his new jacket. His shoes pinch. He has climbed onto the wall to see better as six men carry the mort kist into Greyfriars churchyard. It contains the body of his father, wrapped in a shroud knotted at the head and feet. The kist-bearers are neighbours who have carried the body from the house, through the streets and beyond the city walls, to its final resting place. Unbeknownst to his mother and sisters, Thomas slipped out of the house and followed the men as they walked in silence, without pause or a backward glance. Some but not all are men he knows; it does not matter; what matters is that they are proceeding, with slow heavy steps, to where two gravediggers lean on shovels beside a heap of freshly turned earth.

Still in silence, the men lower the mort kist part way into the ground. There is a clank as bolts on the kist are withdrawn, a creaking as the bottom swings open and a dull thud as the body of Thomas's father drops into the grave. His father, who knew so many plants to heal a body; who helped ladies beautify themselves with liquorice root and eyebright; who encouraged decrepit old men to alleviate their ills with carpenter's weed or camomile – his father, who was neither decrepit nor old, is dead. God rest his soul. As the men once more secure the bolts on the lower panel, raise the now empty kist, set it on the ground and bow their heads in wordless prayer, Thomas turns and runs. All the way home.

There is so much black fabric around him it is as if night has crashed into the middle of the day. Such a roomful of people. As if all the people his father has ever known were gathered in the house like some kind of charm – but a charm against what? And yet there's plenty of talk, laughter even, albeit muted. The funeral meats and ale are laid out on his father's workbench and the neighbour women who helped his mother wash the body now serve food. They smile at him. Everybody smiles at him. Too many want to pat his head. His mother sits with Anna pressed tightly to her chest, staring at nothing. Katharine, red-eyed, bewails her loss to Uncle Thomas, the Minister of Duddingston, who purses his lips, nods his long, narrow head and presses a bible into the small of his back like a close-kept secret. Uncle Thomas was not called upon to carry the mort-kist.

His father's tavern friends form a tight, smoky knot near the refreshments: stroking chins; sucking on pipes; keeping up a low rumble of talk. Thomas recognises Angus Burnside and two or three other men. When the kist-bearers arrive at the door, the tavern men break ranks, welcome them into their company and charge their glasses. Helen rises to her feet, passes Anna into Katharine's care and shakes hands solemnly with each of the men.

A lavishly dressed woman and a tall man with a streak of silver in his heavy dark beard enter the already packed room. They pay their respects to the widow then, without partaking of food or drink, take their leave. Through the open door Thomas sees them climb into a fine scarlet carriage and drive off. He does not know or care who they are. Archibald Pitcairne, who has said repeatedly that he can't stay, though he has charged his glass several times, is deep in conversation with James Armour. Whichever way Thomas turns he hears his father's name couched in kind words and compliments: James was a stalwart family man, a great teller of tales; James had big ideas, a big heart, an indomitable spirit.

A piece o plum cake, lad. Hae a piece o plum cake, a sup o

ale, tae keep yir strength up. Ye're the man o the hoose, now, Lord have mercy.

Peg Lorimer's bosom tips towards his face, exuding a dizzying whiff of attar of roses. She pats him on the head, her eyes soft and indulgent.

Leave me alane, says Thomas, meaning to shout it, at Lucky Lorimer, at all those filling up his home with their black clothes and their rumbling voices. Leave me alane! He wants to yell it so loud that the bottles rattle on the shelves but all that comes out is a faint little gasp, so faint Peg Lorimer bends even closer:

Whit is it, lad? I ken ye're grieved aboot yir faither, awbody is, weel them as has a charitable bane in thir body, but the Lord gieth and the Lord takketh awa, yon's the way o things and whit are we but worms crawlin ower the face o God's earth and mercy me ye're jist a poor laddie who's lost his faither...

The only way he can escape the drench of babble and the odour of attar of roses is to accept a piece of cake, bolt through the black forest of skirts and breeches, drop down behind his father's workbench, draw his knees to his chin, take the biggest bite of plum cake a seven-year-old boy can manage, and hold the sweetness in his mouth for as long as it lasts.

Man With a Bay Horse

Wild winds and driving rain have kept them indoors much of the day. Katharine has been hoping fervently that the foul weather will deter the expected visitor.

There's nocht for it, Katharine.

Ye ken Jeremiah will tak ane look at me and turn his een elsewhere.

Has he no looked lang enough tae mak up his mind?

The time's no richt for makkin a pledge. His faither needs him tae travel in the interests o his business.

And whit o yir widowed mither's needs, Katharine? Whit o her business? It may no be thrivin but it's yir mither's business pits food on the table.

Some o the time.

I dae my best, Katharine.

Aye, says Katharine, without conviction.

Three or fower year hence and then—

Three or fower year! Where d'ye think we'll aw be then, says Katharine. We'll be in the debtors' prison or the workhoose. That's where.

The sums don't add up. They never have added up for as long as Helen can remember, though not, on her part, for want of trying. Whatever James died of – some say the rising of the lights, others tissick, stone and strangury, the pipe, the brandy, the ingestion of one of his own remedies – she is convinced that he died from abandonment of hope. He left behind heavy debts, mostly owing to Hepburn of Blackcastle and George Borthwick, another apothecary with premises in the Canongate, who have since been appointed executors of his estate. That Hepburn did not evict James's widow and bairns straightaway had little to do with kindness of heart.

The children need to eat and the generosity of neighbours

and friends is waning; there's only so long anybody can expect help, only so much to go round. Too many nights she lies awake, her head jumping with sums. The more children grow, they more they need. Like leaky jugs she fills and fills them but they never stay full. If only James had spent less. If only he had sold more. If only.

Ye've sae little faith, Mither.

And ye have ower much. Can ye be sure, say, that Jeremiah's een dinna stray? Sure that when he's in Rotterdam or Leiden, or wherever else his faither thinks fit tae send him, he disna let his gaze roam ower the yella-heided Dutch lasses?

Dinna speak o Jeremiah like yon!

Whit way then should I speak o him? He kens the pickle we're in, kens the debts yir faither left behind. The haill toun kens the length and breadth o oor indebtedness. Wid he see us hirple roond the Grassmarket wi beggars' badges on oor coats? Tae tell it plain, we're worse off than beggars. Beggars have nocht but we hae *less* than nocht.

Wid ye accept charity frae onybody, Mither?

Beggars canna be choosers.

Do we no hae family tae look tae for charity?

D'ye see ony family forthcomin wi assistance?

If ye dinna ask, ye dinna get… Pride's a sin, mither.

And so, Katharine, is vanity.

The room is steamy, scented with infused herbs and oils of orange and almond, along with black spleenwort. Only the best ingredients. And hot water, plenty of it. Thomas has been sent three times to the well and each bucketful has been heated over the fire then poured into the tub. Stripped to her sark, Katharine is bent over the foaming water. Helen works her fingertips into Katharine's scalp, as she did when her daughter was small. She is now sixteen and her childhood is well and truly past.

Wid ye dig holes in my skull?

If it wid mak ye see sense, I widna hesitate.

It's *you* who needs tae see sense – for pity's sake, Mither, yon stuff stings!

If ye'd shut yir een like a sensible lass—

If ye'd open yours like a sensible woman – Aaagh, my een are on fire! Have ye pit stuff in the water tae turn my hair yella?

Dinna be daft, Katharine. The wash for yon is made wi ashes o ivy. And wi hair as dark as yours ye'd need a barraload.

No awbody's in thrall tae yella hair.

And whit a blessing that is.

Anna and Thomas sit by the window, wrapped in a blanket. Thomas is reading a book about Indian flora and fauna which his dominie has loaned him. The window seat, though draughty, is the brightest spot. As well as English and some Latin, he understands a little Dutch; so many supplies are brought into the Port of Leith by way of Holland. His father told him that the great minds of the century reside in Holland and Thomas would dearly love to meet the owners of great minds. He imagines them as tall, angular men with high, broad foreheads, alert eyes and agile brows. He imagines them in periwigs and many-buttoned jackets, lace collars and velvet breeks, in rich greens and browns; nothing too ostentatious or distracting. Scientists, philosophers and artists, they'd sit together for days on end around a table, conferring and demonstrating discoveries to each other – only pausing in their search for knowledge to take sustenance and sleep.

Anna is stitching a sampler. When she stitches letters she is more at ease than when she reads or writes them and the dame has even praised her once or twice for her efforts. With a needle she can make the letters stay in place more easily and this pleases her. Since her father's death she has become withdrawn, speaking only when required, retreating from her surroundings to some private place only she has access to.

Helen, who has finished washing Katharine's hair, combed and dried it and checked for nits, glances at Anna, whose thin braids swing as she sews. Anna's hair is too wispy, she notes. But perhaps in a year or two...

Dress yirsel, Katharine, says Helen. Mak yirsel respectable.

If ye pursue this, ye'll ruin my life!

Aw oor lives are already ruined.

I'll help mair wi the business. I'll gaither herbs we can sell. I'll cajole Jeremiah's faither intae gien us mair credit...

I havena sacrificed such costly ingredients for the benefit o Merchant Skaill.

Does the wig man hae a bay horse? asks Thomas, his nose pressed to the window.

Aye, says Helen.

And cheeks like radishes? And an auld dame's rump?

How d'ye ken?

He's here.

The now? At the door?

Aye. Did ye no hear him chappin?

Flustered, Helen drags the tub of slapping water to the corner of the room.

Let me kaim yir hair ane mair time, there's a guid lass.

Tell Maister Unwin tae get back in the saddle, I beg ye, Mither.

Efter travellin in this weather, d'ye think the man'll be for gaen hame empty-handed? He'll come in, Katharine, and he'll leave wi whit he came for, sae help me.

I'll be ashamed tae gang ower the door.

There's shame, Katharine, and there's disgrace. Shame fades like a blush on the cheeks. But disgrace, there's nae shaking off disgrace. Now be douce. And mind on how far a guinea will gang.

Accompanied by a blast of rain-laced wind, Solomon Unwin brings in with him the smell of saddle and horse sweat. In his quest to find the best materials he is reputed to cover great distances and drive his horse mercilessly.

Sit ye doon, Maister Unwin. Ye'll hae a stoup o brandy to revive ye efter yir journey?

Unlike maist, he says, I dae business wi a clear head.

For a stout man, Unwin has incongruously slender-fingered hands, which flutter as he makes a slow circuit around Katharine, who has seated herself stubbornly in the gloom at the back of the house.

Move ower tae the licht m'dear, says Unwin, where I can better observe yir crownin glory.

Must I, Mither?

If ye wish us tae eat the morra, ye must. Thomas, Anna, gie Maister Unwin room tae cairry oot his inspection.

Displaying a snaggle of teeth in a greasy grin, Unwin ushers Katharine to sit by the window. He grasps a hank of her still-damp hair and holds it up to the light. Katharine humphs and glowers.

Braw, he says. Silky but strang. Wi a glimmer that'll please the gentry. Mind, if the colour had been yella like the bairn's – but wha dares question Providence in such maitters?

Whit, sir, says Katharine bitterly, does God care aboot periwigs?

God cares aboot aw and sundry. The sma and the muckle. As ye ken.

Unwin strokes Katharine's hair with his soft, fluttering fingers, presses his belly against her shoulders, breathes hotly in her ear. Katharine is stiff as a corpse. Unwin turns to Helen, who has been hovering behind him.

So, Mistress Ramsey, we are agreed, are we no?

Aye, says Helen.

Unwin takes a pair of shears from his pocket. He gathers Katharine's hair into a mare's tail, presses his fist against her crown then briskly snips off the lot.

A Charge of Riot

It is not a rap on the door but a prolonged battering that shakes the windowframes and sends the cat straight up to the rafters, tail stiff and bristling as a bottle brush.

Awa wi ye! Helen shouts from her bed. Whit time d'ye think this is tae be makkin such a disturbance?

The battering on the door continues. The children stir, grizzle. Helen draws a blanket around her, gets out of bed and lights a candle.

The ten o'clock bell rang lang syne! Awa wi ye! Helen shouts through the bolted door.

This isna whit ye'd cry a social call, comes a voice from the other side. Open the door. Or I'll brek it doon.

I'll dae nae such thing unless ye tell me wha I'm speakin tae.

D'ye no ken, woman? D'ye no ken wha'd pit hissel tae the inconvenience o callin on ye at such an hour? It's no as if ye possess the kinna attributes a man might seek oot efter dark. Mind, yir eldest dochter has some chairm…

And now Helen does know who's calling from the ice-house timbre of the voice. She throws back the bolt.

Keep yir filthy thochts tae yirsel.

Or whit? says Hepburn, pushing the door open and stepping over the threshold.

A pair of hounds slip past him, leaping and snapping. Two sturdy, sullen manservants, resentful of being dragged on an errand at such a late hour, follow their master inside.

Clinging to each other, Thomas and Anna shrink back into the bed. Katharine is already on her feet. The hounds yowl and sniff at her petticoats.

Ca' the dugs! Ca' the dugs or ye'll lose an ee, I sweer! Helen yells.

She picks up the poker. One of Hepburn's men wrenches it

from her and twists her arms behind her back. Hepburn claps his hands and the dogs slink back to his side, their milk and liver coats gleaming.

Now, Mistress Ramsey, ye ken I am a patient man. Ower patient for my ain guid.

I ken ye for a leech that bleeds a poor widow woman dry.

When he slaps her face, Thomas springs out of bed and pushes between Hepburn and his mother.

Ye're nocht but a bully! he squeals. And a coward.

Restrain the brat.

I'm no a brat. A brat is dirty and unruly. A brat is—

Wheesht, Thomas! his mother screeches.

Dae as yir mither bids, says Hepburn, for awbody's sake.

Ye've nae richt tae force entry, says Helen. Leave us in peace, ye bloodsucker.

Hepburn clouts her around the head.

Ye'd be weel advised tae tak yir ain coonsel, woman, and hush up, if ye dinna wish tae find yirsel in a scold's bridle.

Blood flows from Helen's nose. Anna whimpers. Katharine goes down on her knees and mumbles a prayer.

Hepburn sighs, lights a candle and takes a leisurely turn about the room, noting with disdain the paltry furnishings, the dented pots, Katharine's heavily-repaired dress, her shorn locks.

Whit d'ye wish o us, Hepburn? Whit maks ye forsake yir feather bed at this time o nicht?

Did I gie ye permission tae speak?

Since when dae I need yir permission?

Ye willna learn, will ye? I used tae think ye an admirable woman, and passin handsome intae the bargain. The young Helen Ramsey, aye, she wis nimble o foot, shapely o haunch and fiery o nature but now – now ye're a shrivelled auld hag.

It was you and yir damned rent pit the wrinkles upon my brow, you, wha disna lay awake at nicht, conjurin ways tae mak ends meet. And if ye happen tae find yirsel short o siller, ye can aye trade yir horse or yir hounds, or send a brace o servants packin.

At this, one of the men drives his knee into the base of Helen's spine. Thomas kicks out at the other man and receives a clip round the ear. The room once more erupts with clamour. Hepburn remains impassive until the commotion subsides.

So, he says, yir spendthrift dolt o a guidman wis blameless? The faut lies wi his generous, patient creditor, who, oot o the kindness o his hert, turned a blind eye when the wastrel wid raither fling his siller on a gamecock or a thraw o the dice than pit it in the haunds o a creditor? But this is aw ower and done wi. The man's in his grave – and no a moment too soon, if ye ask me.

I didna ask ye. And I widna.

It's a sin tae speak ill o the deid! says Thomas. Ye should be ashamed o yirsel!

Wheesht, Thomas, for pity's sake, says Helen, pressing his face to her skirts.

Weel now, says Hepburn, tae the maitter in haund. Ye ask whit I wish o ye and yir brood. I wish ye oot. O my hoose. This meenit.

Whit? Ye'd pit us oot in the middle o the nicht?

Tak whit you can cairry and awa tae hell.

Ye canna dae that. Ye've nae richt. Ye think ye can push us aboot on accoont o me bein a widow woman but ye canna!

Ah but I can. Here, he says, holding up a stamped and sealed notice from the City Chambers. Here is my decree. Ye've been warned time and again that if ye didna mak amends, I'd tak measures tae reclaim my dues. Which is whit I'm daein. Taen back whit's mine. For aw concerned, it wid gang better if ye dae my biddin douce-like.

Douce-like? We've tae mak oorsels destitute *douce-like?* And where d'ye suggest we gang at this time o nicht?

That, Mistress Ramsey, isna my concern. But it's mild and pleasant ootby. Why no tak a moonlit turn by the Nor' Loch and ponder on life's possibilities? There's nae mair than an oor or twa till dawn, when the birdies will commence tae sing thir wee herts oot and the irksome auld world will seem fresh and new.

A curse upon yir hoose and aw that bide in it.

Mind yir tongue, woman, if ye dinna wish tae be tried for a witch. But enough o this pitiful banter. Gather up yir belangins, the lot o ye. And be quick aboot it. For mysel a mair attractive assignation awaits.

Hepburn instructs his men to release mother and son. Helen flings a stool at Hepburn, striking his shoulder a glancing blow. Thomas butts the servant who'd restrained him. An even greater uproar ensues: Anna and Katharine wail; the hounds growl and snap; and Helen curses her landlord to eternal damnation. Hepburn stands complacently in the thick of it all, massaging his bruised shoulder, when there is a second volley of door-rapping.

On the doorstep stand six of the Town Guard. One holds aloft a flaming torch; the remainder bear pikes and expressions of grim determination.

Whit time o nicht is this tae be causin a public disturbance? says the torchbearer, a stooping, sour-faced man with a withered arm.

Greetings, gentlemen, says Hepburn. A fine nicht tae be oot keepin the peace. Does the scented stock no mask the stink o shite wondrous weel?

We're no here tae discuss the quality o the air, says the torchbearer.

I dinna doot it, says Hepburn. The Gaird has better things tae concern itsel wi than oor triflin squabble.

Whit's triflin aboot rousin folk frae thir beds on the cusp o midnicht? says a sturdy, bull-headed man. Step ootside, sir. And them o yir pairty forby.

With a loud, long-suffering sigh, Hepburn signals to his men to follow him, with the dogs, onto the street.

On whit grounds can ye justify such a breach o the peace? says the bull-headed guard, whose assertiveness singles him out as the leader. Ye ken a workin man needs his sleep.

And whit o yon bairns, adds the torchbearer, as Thomas and Anna, tear-streaked, peep out from behind their mother.

Whit grief have ye caused them?

Emboldened by Hepburn's exit from the house, Thomas pipes up:

The mannie wis gaen tae pit us on the street! In the dark!

Aye, says Helen. Wratch that he is.

Gentlemen, says Hepburn. If a tenant disna pay the rent, I am within my richts tae evict her, bairns or nae bairns. Ye ken as much.

That's as may be, but no in such a manner. And no at such an ungodly hour.

Whit maitters the hour?

Ye can see for yirsels how mony God-fearin folk ye've inconvenienced, says the torchbearer, angling his torch to illuminate a clutch of bleary neighbours who have foregathered to grumble and glower.

By the power that is invested in the Toun Gaird, says the bull-headed man, we hereby chairge ye, Hepburn o Blackcastle, wi riot and order ye tae quit the vicinity forthwith or be escorted, by force, tae the Tolbooth.

Riot? says Hepburn. Ye ca' this riot?

We dae indeed. Yir behaviour is neither appropriate nor seemly.

I dinna need a bunch o superannuated donkeys tae approve my behaviour.

Ah but ye dae, Sir. And if ye dinna dae as yir telt, ye'll suffer the consequences.

Amid much clamour and indignation, Hepburn stalks off, hounds and men in tow. Helen and the younger children huddle on the doorstep, glaring at their backs.

Come awa in. The neebors have seen and heard enough for ane nicht, says Katharine.

When she ushers them inside and closes the door, the neighbours drift back to their own homes. The Guard continues on its nocturnal perambulations, to seek out further hurly-burly and apprehend the perpetrators.

The Minister of Duddingston

Katharine turns into World's End Close.

Mind yir feet, she says. And yir heid.

Two floors up, a bog house has been built out from the wall and just as Thomas is about to pass beneath it, a bare arse descends, for the purpose of evacuation, towards the gap. It is too good an opportunity for a boy to miss. He picks up a pebble, flings it upwards where it hits its tender target then slithers down the steep wynd after Anna and Katharine, to the accompaniment of a stream of curses from on high. When they reach the Cowgate, Katharine affects a stern expression but before long all three of them are hooting with laughter.

Hurry! says Katharine. We dinna wish the owner o yon fat arse tae come seekin retribution. We'll mak a race up the Pleasance.

Whit's the prize? says Thomas.

Glory says, Katharine. Everlastin glory.

Can it no be a piece o the cake in yir basket?

Yon's for Uncle Thomas.

The haill o it?

Aye.

Why does Uncle Thomas need aw that cake?

Just tak my word for it. For once.

Anna is given a head start but as soon as Thomas has counted to ten, he's off like a hare from a trap. Katharine hitches up her skirts and follows them. They make a curious sight, tearing up the Pleasance in the mourning clothes their mother insisted they wore for the outing. Thomas wins. He usually wins, when it comes to races with his sisters: Katharine never fully enters into the spirit of competition and Anna, even with a head start, is no match for him. They leave the Pleasance and join the track which borders the King's Park.

Katharine has been instructed to continue on the path to the village of Duddingston but Thomas insists that it would be better sport to scale the hill and come down the other side: the ground is dry underfoot; the grass is new and soft, and think of what they might see from the top! On and on he goes. Then Anna chimes in with *Please Kathie, please, please*, until it's easier to let the bairns have their way than not. Besides, Katharine is in no great hurry to reach their destination.

But you must promise tae dae nae foolhardy thing or I'll tell Uncle and he'll thrash ye, see if he willna.

Katharine has no idea what Uncle Thomas might do or say. She has not seen him since their father's funeral.

In spite of its purpose, it is a pleasant outing. The grass is lush and springy underfoot, the sweet-scented gorse is a blaze of yellow. Meadow pipits fly up, wheeping in alarm, looping and darting to divert the walkers from ground nests. A breeze blows through the long grass: cool, salty, with a whiff of somewhere else in it. In Katharine's basket are a dozen pomanders. Not long after James died, Doctor Pitcairne called round with a bag of oranges, saying that the children should eat them, that they were good for growing bodies. Helen cut a couple into segments and shared them out but once the doctor had taken his leave insisted that the rest be made into pomanders. James had bought in surplus dried cloves – what better use for them now that they also had oranges.

Katharine and Anna had driven the cloves into the peel of one orange after another until the tips of their fingers were numb and the aromatic dust had them sneezing. With blue ribbon Katharine fashioned decorative baskets. The ribbon, a gift from Jeremiah Skaill, had been intended for her hair before Solomon Unwin's visit made a mockery of that. Although customers of the apothecary admired her handiwork, sales were slow and unsold pomanders shrank and shrivelled, the skins of the oranges growing dark and tough as old leather. A minister can niver hae ower mony aromatics tae freshen up a kirk, their mother had insisted. Mind and acquaint him wi how weel Thomas is doing at the school. Mind and say this and that and the next thing. Katharine is also carrying a seedcake, a bottle of a bilious-coloured emulsion – a purge, as Uncle Thomas is prone to digestive problems – and a letter.

I'm at the tap! Thomas shouts. I can see forever!

So can I! Anna shouts. Forever and ever, Amen!

I can see three tall ships.

I can see five, says Anna.

Where?

Yonder, says Anna, pointing into the distance at what, to Thomas, are little more than dark specks.

How d'ye ken they're ships? They might be whales or sea monsters.

I can see the riggin.

Ach… says Thomas, peeved that he can't see any rigging. Whit's yon rock, settin oot in the water?

The Bass, says Katharine. The most terrible jail in the country. Where they pit the warst fanatics and leave them tae rot until thir spirits are brak and they confess. And once they confess, they hang. If they willna confess, and some are stubborn as ye like, they pit them tae the boots and tighten the thumbikins—

Whit maks it sae white?

It has a special cloud o ice tae keep the prisoners cauld and mak thir punishment worse. Even on the hottest days, the Bass is surroondit by a cloud o ice.

How could a cloud jist hang in the same spot forever?

I'm only repeatin whit I wis telt.

Well it's a daft thing tae repeat, says Thomas. Clouds move aw the time. Look, he says, pointing up at the sky. See for yirsel.

Weel, Maister Ken-it-Aw. Keep on as ye're daein and ye'll find oot for yirsel why the Bass is white.

They stand for a while, taking in the view then scramble down the hill to where the church and manse perch at the head of the loch.

The loch is a deeper blue than the sea and stars of sunlight shoot off the surface. At its edge is a silvery frill of waterlilies, their round leaves glinting like coins. Without once flapping its wings, a heron glides above the loch from one side to the other, then settles on a tree studded with tall, cone-shaped nests. Stands of reeds sway, dry and whispery.

The manse sits above a well-tended garden. Tidy rows of vegetables and herbs run down the gentle slope to the lochside. Hens and ducks pick about. The minister's horse, an old grey mare with dappled flanks, stands by the water's edge. The breeze sifts through its mane. It snuffles and nods, as if confirming an important point.

Are ye a guid horse? Thomas asks.

The horse nods.

D'ye believe in original sin?

The horse nods.

Even for horses?

The horse nods.

D'ye believe ye should be punished for yir sins?

The horse nods.

Even tae the daith?

That's enough, says Katharine.

Can we hunt for frogs?

Perhaps later, if ye behave, and we get whit we came for.

Whit've we came for?

Charity, says Katharine, spitting out the word. Mither says ye've tae inspire pity. Sae dinna grin, Thomas. Look dulesome. Mind yir poor faither deid in his grave. Look dule and thochtful. And cliver. Ye haveta look cliver.

Thomas tries what he thinks is a doleful, serious, clever face.

He looks like a deid fish, says Anna.

Just be guid and douce, says Katharine. Speak when ye're spoken tae.

Whit aboot me? says Anna. Whit am I tae dae?

Be complaisant. The minister will no be seekin a bursary for a dunce, will he?

Anna's no a dunce! says Thomas. It's them that cry her ane

who're the real dunces. That maks *you* a dunce, Katharine. Duncie, duncie, dunce!

And ye're a bladderskate!

Weel, weel, says a voice behind them. Whit hae we here?

Thomas Ramsey stands at the church door, a crummock of a man with a broad head and bristling brows.

It's Katharine, sir. And this is Anna and Thomas. We're—

I ken. I ken ower weel. Sae my sister's brood have come tae brawl at the kirk door?

No, Uncle. Sorry, Uncle, says Katharine.

And whit, pray, might be the nature o your visit?

Our mither sends her best wishes for yir guid health. And some sma gifts forby, Katharine continues, doing her utmost to sound bright and confident, as a token o her sisterly love and enduring esteem—

Dearie me! Fancy phrases as weel as gifts frae the impecunious. Ye'd best come in. I'm engaged in some extraordinary kirk business but it will dae my sister's bairns nae hairm tae look and learn. He ushers them into the small church. Sunlight streams through the windows casting bars of gold on the flagstones. At the far end of the aisle, a lass in sackcloth kneels on the floor. Bare-headed and bare-legged, she is midway through a lengthy, snivelling confession.

Louder! the minister insists, his voice bouncing from one rough wall to another. Just think o the shame if ye'd had tae mak yir repentance afore the haill congregation!

The lass sighs deeply, raises her head and continues, endeavouring to make her words travel the length of the aisle:

…I regret the sins I hae committed I truly regret them wi aw my hert and promise as God is my witness that as lang as there is braith in my body I willna resort tae such filthy wickedness iver again nor consort wi them as wid lure me intae bein pairty tae thir sinful desires. Though it wisna me that sought tae engage in carnal knowledge and I protested agin it wi aw my might it wid've been better I had expired than submitted tae such wicked urges. I beg forgiveness frae the Lord God

Almighty makar o aw things seer o aw secrets detester o aw sins that I willna be cast oot o the warm beam o His mercy that He will hear my words and look upon me wi pity an errant misguided saul…

At a sign from the minister the lass advances down the aisle on her knees. The penitent is young, buxom and comely, the kind men sniff out no matter how she might cover herself or attempt to slip past a tavern door unnoticed. To spare her further humiliation rather than to shun a sinner, Katharine lowers her eyes.

Whit did she dae? Thomas pipes up.

Sins o the flesh, says his uncle.

Whit are sins o the flesh? Thomas asks Katharine, who pinches him.

When he squeals the woman glances up and Thomas could swear she gives him a wink.

At the door, the minister signals for her to rise, remove the sackcloth and make herself decent. Her knees are scraped and bleeding. She thanks him effusively, drops coins into the poor box and leaves. Anna points to the trail of blood down the central aisle, lit from the window by splashes of sunlight.

The minister's housekeeper, Bessie Begg, is plump and flustery. She smiles indulgently at the poor mites in their mourning clothes until she learns who they are, at which point she clucks and claiks but offers refreshment all the same: a sup of foaming goat's milk, a heel of bread, a hunk of kebbock. The children don't need to be asked twice.

The house is plain but tidy and clean. A generous fire burns in the hearth; the Reverend Ramsey toasts his bony buttocks.

Yir gifts, Uncle, says Katharine. Ye havena opened yir gifts. There's a letter tae.

A letter? Penned by my sister?

Thomas helped. He's cliver. And diligent. But since Faither wis mert and Mither has managed the apothecary she has learned tae read a bit and mark up figures in the ledger.

That surely must be a blessin in itsel. Though if my sister could only mak her figures tally, the blessing wid be magnified.

Mither hopes we might bring back a reply.

Rejoice in Hope, he says, raising his eyes to the ceiling. *Be patient in tribulation, be constant in prayer*: Romans 12:12

He fetches Katharine's basket and returns to the fireside. Bessie Begg sinks onto a nearby stool.

A cake, Bessie! says the minister. Does my sister think ye dinna feed me?

Bessie clucks again, like a great roosting hen.

A medicament! But will it dae mair hairm than guid? And a dizzen pomanders, tricked oot in ribbons like painted jades! Does she think I havena herbs and flooers on my ain doorstep tae sweeten the kirk?

The pomanders might serve ye in the winter months, Reverend, says Bessie Begg, if they retain thir efficacy.

Cluck, cluck.

Thomas considers what sort of egg Bessie might lay – a huge, mottled pink one, he decides, the colour of her meaty cheeks. A giggle stirs in his belly, pushes up past his ribcage, bubbles into his throat and bursts from his mouth. He tries to disguise it with a cough but that only makes him spray crumbs of bread and cheese over the table.

Bessie Begg humphs and shifts on her stool.

Somethin wrang wi the kebbock?

No, no, says Thomas, hiccuping now until Katharine dunts him between the shoulders.

Once Thomas has composed himself, the three clear their plates in wary silence as Uncle Thomas reads the letter. His eyebrows arch steeply then flatten out again, a frown knots then burrows into the bridge of his nose, a long tschhhhh of disapproval escapes his lips...

Hah! he says. Once mair my sister leans upon my charity. Weel now... as ye've come aw this way—

Thomas is a guid lad, Katharine says. And cliver. The dominie says—

Let me guess, says their uncle. The dominie says young Thomas is the apple o his ee!

Aye! says Katharine. How did ye ken?

I didna! And doot the veracity o such a statement. I've met a score o dominies in my time and niver heard reference tae ony pupil in such glowin terms.

Maister Armour niver said ony such thing, says Thomas. But he does say I'm ane o the brichter lichts in his firmament, and that's the truth.

Dis he now? And dis he no inform his pupils that pride is a deadly sin?

Thomas is a guid lad, Katharine says again. He's aye at his lessons.

Yir loyalty tae yir brither and yir poor feckless mither is commendable, lass, but I'd be a fool tae tak awbody's word for that. If ye're done wi yir bit and sup, the lasses can accompany Mistress Begg tae the gairden. Ye can fill yir basket wi produce tae tak hame. In the meantime, I'll pit young Thomas through his paces.

As his sisters skip out of the door and into the sunshine, Thomas struggles to contain his annoyance.

A Curious Reek

Their mourning suits flecked with seeds and burrs, Thomas, Anna and Katharine arrive back in town in the late afternoon. Katharine's basket contains a salty cheese, an oaten loaf, dusty purple beets, lilac and white swedes and tender peapods. Thomas carries a sheaf of kale and bundles of garden herbs, and Anna a spray of wildflowers, picked on the walk home. As they pass through the Canongate the luckenbooths are closing up and market sellers packing away their wares. The more fastidious traders sweep up their debris and toss it onto the midden. Others let the filth lie.

Beggars, on the lookout for scraps from the fleshers, the fishmongers, the bakers and cheesemakers, cautiously circle the stalls. The fleshers' dogs, having dozed much of the afternoon, are now on their feet, hungry and fearsome, as eager to sink their teeth into a human shin as a sheep shank. Their viciousness is notorious and after complaints to the Privy Council, some of the worst offenders have been tethered and muzzled. But they are essential to the fleshers' livelihood; without the dogs, the fleshers insist, their meat would walk, dead or alive.

Of the beggars many are maimed or suffer disfigurements of birth, but it is not their aspect which disconcerts Thomas: he is familiar enough with customers seeking remedies for unsightly sores and swellings. It is mostly the ranters and ravers that make his heart hammer in his chest; they seem so intent on being heard yet what comes out of their mouths is no more than a bleak, angry yawl. And yet it is a silent shilpit woman with a matted thatch of white hair that disturbs him the most. Her eyes are wide and dark, as if she is witness to some frightful horror. He remembers her: she is one of the Borrowstounness folk who were taken to the House of Correction and thrashed. Is she still mad for God? And if he remembers her, does she remember him? As they pass through the Netherbow, she catches Thomas by the arm and turns her burning gaze on him.

My lad, she says, my ain wee lad—

He's nae *your* lad, says Katharine tartly. He has his ain mither at hame.

Katharine urges on her brother and sister but Anna darts back, hands the woman a poppy then hurries back to Katharine's side, her bouquet waving wildly.

Whit guid's a flooer tae a beggar? says Katharine.

It's bonny, says Anna.

Aye, but whit's its purpose?

Tae be a flooer. Tae be bonny.

Weel, it's no bonny the now, says Katharine. Yon woman's brak the stem and the bloom's aw droop-heided.

Thomas glances back and sees the woman thread the stem of the poppy through her matted hair.

She likes it, says Thomas.

Katharine nudges them on, keeping an eye on the contents of her basket.

And tae whit purpose wis oor trip tae the manse? Tell us, Thomas, as ye're the cliver ane, d'ye think oor uncle will oblige us?

We got provisions!

They'll nae last long.

We'll see whit purpose when Mither opens the letter. We canna brek the seal.

Mair's the pity, says Katharine. Traipsin tae his door in the hope o charity! Mither should have made the journey hersel, no sent us bairns tae dae her beggin and borrowin for her. She should be made tae wear a debtor's bonnet. See how pridefou she'd be then.

Since James's death, Thomas has come to know a deal more about his older sister: her monthly flows, her glooms and scalding tempers, her perpetual longing to be united with Jeremiah Skaill, her loathing of her short hair, to which she's applied ashes of doves' dung – a rumoured cure for baldness –

in the hope it might encourage faster growth; the results have been disappointing.

A meagre fire flickers in the grate and a curious, sweetish smell hangs in the room. It is not from the hops their mother stuffs into pillows and sells to those who can't sleep.

Helen is seated, gazing serenely at the flames. There is no sign of anything cooking.

See whit Uncle Thomas's woman gied us! says Anna. Kathie's basket is fou tae the brim! Mistress Begg let me eat her peas straight oot the pods and pu' up her wee pink radishes but I didna like the burny taste o the radishes—

It wisna really *Uncle's woman* that gied us the provisions, says Thomas. If it wis Uncle's hoose and gairden, it wid be Uncle's food. But if he bides in the manse and the manse is the Kirk's hoose, it's the Kirk's provisions, and the Kirk's woman.

See how he is, Mither? says Katharine. Aye workin that tongue o his.

They lay out their spoils on the table. Anna claps her hands at the plentiful array.

Uncle sent ye a letter forby, says Thomas.

Is that aw? says Helen.

Aye, says Katharine. That's aw.

Helen doesn't shift her gaze from the flames but passes the rolled paper, sealed with wax, from one hand to the other, as if trying to fathom its contents, then lays it aside.

Mistress Begg gave me comfrey and basil, camomile and St. John's wort, says Thomas. And I helped pu' the kale…

Helen's eyes drift towards the medicinal herbs.

And I picked meadowsweet, and poppies, says Anna, flag iris and forget-me-nots—

Grand, says Helen.

Pit yir flooers in water, Katharine tells Anna, or they'll wilt and ye'll have cairried them aw the way hame for nocht.

Aye, Helen drawls. Flooers need water.

And folk need food, Mither, snips Katharine, but afore I

prepare a sup for us, courtesy o Uncle Thomas, ye've tae open the letter he sent ye.

If ye insist, says Helen.

She breaks the seal, unrolls the paper and stares at it blankly.

Will I read it oot for ye, Mither? says Thomas, and ye can follow the letters. Will I dae that?

Aye, says Helen, still dreamy, distant.

Our uncle has a fine haund, says Thomas, and puffed up with self-importance, he reads:

Sister,

It was an unexpected pleasure to see your brood once again. Young Thomas seems, from my examination, to be a capable lad, though he has an inflated notion of his own ability and his leanings appear less directed towards the word of the Lord than they should be.

That's no true, says Thomas. And it wisna fair that Uncle Thomas gied me a test when he didna gie ane tae Katharine or Anna!

Get on wi the letter, says Katharine, or we'll aw gang tae bed hungry the nicht.

His mother continues to gaze at the flames.

Katharine is growing into a sturdy lass and my woman was charmed by Anna's prattle and her shy, modest ways.

In reply to your letter, I have no option but to be frank. The death of your guidman was a grievous and regrettable occurrence. My heart goes out to your beleaguered family and I sincerely hope that the Good Lord will see fit to bestow mercy on you all in your time of need. It behooves me, nevertheless, to remind you that a profligate such as James Aikenhead was, and even in his grave remains, a scourge on Christian society. Until you make good the damage to your name that his debts have incurred, I cannot in all conscience see a way to contribute to the upkeep of your family.

Who Goeth a Borrowing Goeth a Sorrowing.

Your brother, Thomas

A Key to the Door

Helen's inherited debts refuse to evaporate like morning mist dispelled by the warmth of the sun. Nevertheless there is some small blessing to be had from one item in the remaining stock: the sweet smoke of opium, as she has recently discovered, can rub the hard edges off most things: hunger, worry, aches and pains, the press of creditors, the clamour and grind of everyday life. Unlike wine, which can mask troubles but fuddles the mind and agitates emotion, opium subdues emotion and allows thoughts to drift – soft, weightless, calm.

One night, in a moment of seductive clarity, Helen conceives of a plan to keep the wolf and the creditors from the door, a plan which, in her detached state of mind, has a pleasing fittingness about it. In the early days, when Hepburn played the benevolent landlord and she and James the grateful tenants, Hepburn began to use his cellar not only to store his canary and claret but also medicinal substances which keep better in the cool and dark. A dabbler in diverse business ventures, which include owning a one-tenth share in a ship, Hepburn bought imported herbs and potions, and sold them on to James and other apothecaries. In a gesture of goodwill, he gave James a copy of the cellar key, trusting him to take what he required, write him a chit and settle up in due course. James might have had his shortcomings but was honest to a fault.

Honesty is all very well for those who can afford it but what do you do, even if you are prepared to grovel – or send your children to grovel on your behalf – when no assistance is forthcoming, even from your own brother? When James died, Hepburn did not ask her to relinquish the key but it can only be a matter of time before he'll remember its existence and demand its return.

The cellar is tucked away down an ill-frequented wynd

which leads to the Grassmarket; due to an inexplicable red sweat which oozes from the stones, the wynd is reputed to be haunted and even vagabonds who might find shelter in a doorway, shun it. For the best part of two weeks, between the nightly rounds of the Town Guard, Helen has been letting herself into Hepburn's cellar and helping herself to flagons of his best wine. She is restrained in her decanting, only removing what she can conceal beneath her plaid. Her intention is to sell on to someone from out of town who wishes to stock his own cellar. She may have scant stock on the shelves but has plenty of empty jars and bottles. She is optimistic that she need not look too hard to find a buyer: everyone likes a good price and few are likely to brood on the provenance of wine. Besides, paying Hepburn his back rent with proceeds from his own wine appeals to her sense of justice.

She knows her crime could send her to the gallows yet the opium induces such a sense of equanimity that whatever might happen at some future point seems so distant, so inconsequential that she continues on her plan of action with few qualms. She is as soft-footed as the cat; not even Thomas, the lightest sleeper in the house, is wakened by her coming and going.

One night, however, she mistimes her trip and is apprehended as she is turning the key in the cellar lock. She insists that she is fetching simples and fully intends to pay for them but given the lateness of the hour, the Town Guard is suspicious and escorts her, amid vehement protest, to the Tolbooth.

The next morning Hepburn is informed of the situation. He reclaims the spare key and goes off to inspect his cellar. Helen spends an anxious morning awaiting his return. She'd dearly love a smoke of opium to calm her but nothing but water has passed her lips since she was brought in. What had seemed like a fair plan reveals itself as utter foolhardiness. But she has been careful in her pilfering and can only hope that Hepburn's wine consumption is such that he has a hazy estimation of his stock.

That she was not caught claret in hand might turn out to be a monumental stroke of luck.

She hears Hepburn before she sees him, his boot heels striking the flagstones as he makes his way briskly down the passage, followed by the heavy tread of the warden.

Guid day tae ye, Mistress Ramsey, says Hepburn. I hear ye've been visiting my cellar in the sma oors. Now why, I wonder, might a woman wi a year's rent due be trespassin on my property?

I wisna trespassin, says Helen. I wis in search o myrrh and barberry for the quinsy. She has had time to elaborate on the lie she told the guard and it comes out better than she expected.

Were ye, indeed. There's only *your* word for it and wha kens whit that's worth?

Helen and Hepburn face each other across the cell. They are within spitting distance. Helen holds her gaze as steady as she can; if she betrays the slightest hint of guilt, she's done for. Hepburn eyes her balefully.

I could detect nocht amiss, says Hepburn, but as ye ken, my stock is large, and it may be I've owerlookit an item or twa—

If ye dinna miss it, ye dinna need it.

But if at some later date I wis tae detect some signs o tamperin or pilferin, I'd ken the culprit, wid I no?

At some later date, says Helen, ye'd have nae proof.

My, my, there's gall in ye still. And how wid ye pay me for yon simples, had ye found them?

Frae the sale o the medicament.

Hepburn sighs, shakes his head.

D'ye credit whit pernicious stupidity I'm saddled wi? he says to the warden, a lardy man who huffs and puffs and rests his bulk against the wall. The woman wid need twenty folk tae purchase her remedy for quinsy tae recoup the cost o the ingredients. And I'd still be short o a year's rent.

Ye've income aplenty, says Helen. I'm a widow wi a failin business and three bairns tae feed.

Debts are debts, says the warden.

Aye, says Hepburn, and if the Toun Gaird had let me rid mysel o this chronic debtor and her bairns a saxmonth syne, I'd hae a new tenant and hauf a year's rent tae offset my expenses.

And whit expenses wid they be? says Helen. Yir wine and yir women?

D'ye hear this calumny, sir?

Mistress Ramsey, says the warden, restrain yirsel, if ye please.

I dinna please, says Helen. There's ane law for the rich and anither for the poor.

That's nane o my concern, says the warden.

Perhaps no, says Hepburn to the warden, but whit dae ye propose tae dae aboot my unpaid debts?

The warden does what he always does; he refers the matter to the courts. Helen is warded for thirty days.

Patriae et Posteris

Whit does it say? asks Anna.

For fatherland and... posterity? says Thomas.

As if buildin a jail wis a thing tae tak pride in, says Katharine.

Whit's posterity? says Thomas.

It's whit happens efter ye're deid. If ye're lucky.

When ye're deid, says Thomas, ye're deid. Nocht happens ither than the worms eat ye.

Ye dinna ken that, says Katharine. Naebody kens. And it's no whit happens tae the body but whit happens tae yir saul that maitters.

And whit does yon say? says Anna. She points to the motto, *sic itur ad astra*, emblazoned on the Canongate coat of arms set into a niche on the wall.

Such is the way tae the stars, says Thomas. Does it mean that prison's a way tae the stars?

Of course it disna, says Katharine.

Whit does it mean then?

I dinna ken, Thomas, and I dinna need tae ken at this pairticular moment.

Anna begins to cry. Thomas puts an arm around her but the sobs wracking her shoulders set him off and soon the pair of them are blubbing.

D'ye mean tae saut the bannock wi yir tears? says Katharine. We must bring hope tae oor mither, fool that she be. And sustenance, or she will surely starve. Things could be worse, she continues, despite the brittle edge to her voice, but as her haunds are no condemned as instruments o thievery, the hangman willna chop them off.

Anna wails.

Why no chop the hands off greedy landlords? says Thomas.

Because that's no thievin, says Katharine. But dinna fret,

now. Oor mither willna hang for no payin her debts and that's aw she's chairged wi. Thanks tae Bessie Begg and Lucky Lorimer, she willna go hungry. And nor will we. For the time being.

At the entrance to the Tolbooth, Katharine holds her chin high and her back straight. She is ordered to hand over her basket for inspection. She forfeits three pasties and a wedge of cheese as taxes to the prison warden, whose lardy dimensions suggest he might eat himself to death while his charges waste away. When, with groans and wheezes, the man eventually gets to his feet, he shambles off down the corridor. Agog at his vastness, Helen's three children follow him, in single file.

Since their mother was warded some two weeks past, Thomas and his sisters have had to endure countless visitors to their home: baillies, kirk elders, inquisitive neighbours, debt collectors, and the days have tumbled into each other like embers crumbling in the grate. From the first uninvited callers, the elders Mathieson and Morrison, who made a point of reminding the children of Helen's breaking of the Sabbath, Katharine has crackled with rage. Their mother did her penance for that. Who are they to cast aspersions once penance has been done? Does the Lord not forgive sinners who admit their sins?

They come tae gloat, she says bitterly. Thir charity is a sham, nae mair than a way tae big thirsels up in the eyes o the Lord.

Even Jeremiah Skaill, who has tried his best to offer consolation, not to mention all kinds of small treats, irks Katharine mightily. She has raged at her absent mother, as daughters do, for every wrong move she made, every careless action, careless comment, and finally for being unable to protect her children from the hazards of life.

Thomas is not angry with his mother. He longs to see her yet a creeping dread of who or what she might have become gives him pause. Apart from the orange pinprick of the warden's lamp there is no light in the corridor. Anna drags her feet and clutches at Katharine's skirt. Katharine covers her mouth and nose. The smells are foul. To suppress his urge to bolt,

Thomas repeats the words *Mither awaits us, Mither needs us,* under his breath. Thomas hates the dark but the scratching and scrabbling – of rats, or prisoners trying to dig their way to freedom with their bare hands – the rattle and clank of chains, the stream of low curses like a river churning mud from its bed, the sudden roars of terror and rage, the woeful, wolfish howls, make him grateful that he can see so little of his surroundings.

He cannot speak. He cannot move. He can barely breathe. The woman who roused him for school with a joke or a light slap, who sang love songs by the healing well, who cut down his dead father's clothes to make him a new suit, the woman who walked straight and tall and prided herself on neat, well-mended attire, is huddled on a bed of damp straw, filthy and dishevelled; one of her arms is shackled to the wall.

She wis makkin an accursed din day and nicht, says the warden. Yawling and sweerin, duntin the wa and haranguin me tae fetch her a smoke. I ken how needful a smoke can be and it's no for nocht the cooncil let only breid and tobacco be sellt on the Sabbath. So, frae the kindness o ma hert, I fetch her a pipe and a plug o tobacco. Wid ye credit it, the ingrate hurls the pipe back at me, curses me aw the mair and then, tae cap it aw, she bites ma haund!

He holds the lamp close to his hand and points to a snaggle of toothmarks.

She's a cur, yir mither. Keep yir distance, if ye ken whit's guid for ye.

How are ye, Mither? says Katharine in the sweet voice she usually reserves for Jeremiah Skaill. I've brocht some food – gifts frae Peg Lorimer and Bessie Begg. Bessie had a cadie bring a basket roond frae Duddingston.

Helen snatches the basket, pulls it to her chest and rummages through its contents; searching for something; not finding it. She crams one pastie after another into her mouth, drains a pitcher of ale in two draughts and continues to rummage in the basket.

Ye'll mak yirsel seik if ye dinna slow doon, says Katharine.

I'm seik as it is, says Helen, her voice ragged and coarse as straw. Nocht here but seikness and daith. But where's my blue bottle? Why did ye no bring me the blue bottle, the wee blue bottle wi the nick at the neck?

Part Two

Venice Treacle

Dinna look back, says Katharine, to no avail.

Thomas and Anna crane their necks and stare through the coach window at the retreating view of the city which until now has been the only place they've known. They stare hard, fixing in their memory the hump-backed contours of Arthur's Seat, the castle perched on a bluff at the top of the High Street and the Palace of Holyrood at its foot, the plentiful kirk spires and the tall lands huddled together like cattle sheltering from the elements.

The scarlet coach jounces as it turns out of King's Stables Road. With each turn of the wheels the city shrinks, the open ground and sky expands.

Why could we no bring the cat? says Anna.

Because the cat belangs tae Hepburn now, says Thomas. Like awthin else. But the cat'll fare weel, Anna. Dinna fash aboot the cat.

Where are we gaen?

Ye ken, says Thomas. Ye ken. Kathie telt ye.

Tell me again, tell me again!

Is yon bairn a gowk? barks the coachman from his padded throne.

How dare ye! says Thomas. She's dule. We're aw dule.

Oor sister wid've continued at the school, says Katharine, if we'd had siller tae pay the dame efter oor faither wis mert.

And now yir mither's mert tae. Ach weel. Wait and see. It may be a blessin in disguise.

Aye, sir, says Katharine. We'll wait and see whit way things turn oot afore we'll tak yir word for that, or awthin else.

Suit yirsels, says the coachman. If ye've nae a pot to piss in, aw kinds o circumstances can seem like blessins.

Anna whimpers. Thomas feels the hot prickle of tears but

squeezes his eyelids together and clenches his jaw, to appear brave, for Anna's sake. And his own.

Where are we gaen? Anna repeats through her tears.

Katharine sets Anna on her knee, wraps her in the clove pink plaid which is a treasured gift from Jeremiah. She hushes her with cuddling and crooning until, worn out by her own distress, Anna falls asleep.

Though it is early May, it is as if the season has turned back to winter. The world seems drained of its vital juices: there's no colour to the land, the sea, the sky; nothing but strata of dense greys; the firth is a band of lead, the sky dull bars of cloud. Inside the coach it is every bit as cold as it is outside. Thomas drums his feet on the floor, blows on numb fingertips. It is still early morning and frost glitters on shoots of barley, on turnip tops and purple-veined beet leaves.

John Barr – *Maister* Barr tae yous bairns – dunts the soles of his boots against the boards and whips the horses. He's a big, cussed man, with legs like logs and a proprietary air. He regards the coach as his own domain and when, as today, the maister is otherwise occupied, likes nothing better than to lord it over any passengers he has.

Just wait till we're past the village o Dene, he says. Till we're up by Ravelston, or Blackha'. When we're oot on the open road, there's nae tellin whit kinna ruffians might set upon us!

Onybody'd think ye'd be welcomin fisticuffs wi a highwayman, says Katharine.

Mair sport in it than cairryin greetin bairns tae the Big Hoose.

And wid yir maister be happy tae ken his coachman's opinion?

I ken ye ken the answer tae that, lass, says John Barr, grinning and baring long, pointed teeth. And I ken ye ken tae keep mum. If ye're for bidin awhile, that is. And where else might ye gang? Where else could three penniless orphans gang withoot the protection o yir guardian? Wi desperados on the highway and rumours o famished wolves in the woods? Naewhere.

The coach clatters past the flour mills and ovens that stand hard by the village of Dene. The sweet smell of fresh bread mingles with the sourness of fermented yeast. The Water of Leith is high and fast. It pours over the weir in a rippled curtain and gathers further downstream, foaming with effluent.

Mind when we went A-Mayin, Anna? says Thomas. Wi Mither? The wild garlic wis in bloom. And the bluebells. It wisna grey and cauld. It wis sunny and warm. A braw May day. A Sabbath.

No.

But ye must! We went tae the healin well. We douked in the river. Mither wis singin. And she made a wish.

I dinna mind.

Thomas does not know what his mother's wish had been but is sure enough that it didn't come true. She had been singing a sad song about a boy who grew up and everything happened too fast. One moment he was young and carefree, springing up like a new shoot, the next he was married, then father to a son, then dead in the ground with the grass growing over him. Was life so fast and short? Was that the last time he heard his mother sing?

Ye'll mind Mither bein punished for her Sabbath brekkin, says Katharine. Ye'll mind her bein stood on the stool o repentance, sax Sabbaths in a row.

Aye, says Anna, sniffling. I mind that.

When she was released from the Tolbooth, Helen Ramsey was as good as dead. She had crept and crawled home across the causey stanes, through the claich of fishbones and oyster shells, feathers and gristle, the steaming mounds of horse shit, the rivulets of human sewage, the gobs of tobacco spit. On his return from school, Thomas found her slumped on the doorstep: at first he thought she was a beggarwoman the worse for drink. It was only when she raised her head and he caught her blistering stare, so hot it might have scorched him, that he recognised the wretch at his feet.

He and Katharine dragged her indoors. The smell of dirt and disease swung about her like a fetid bell. They tried to make her comfortable, to feed and clean her but she would eat nothing, nor let them remove her filthy clothes. Thomas scoured Culpeper for a paste to soothe shackle weals, a poultice for pullulating sores, for any concoction which might induce an appetite, but all she wanted was the contents of the blue bottle. There was precious little opium left. Her hands shook so much that Thomas had to hold his dead father's pipe between her cracked lips and put a match to it for her. After puffing weakly, she retched but brought up only bile. Once the retching was over, she motioned again for the pipe. Thomas was wary of letting her smoke too much but how could he deny his mother the only thing she wished for? When the pipe's contents had turned to ash, she closed her eyes. Thomas is sure he saw the hint of a smile. Almost sure. Her fingers twitched, as if she'd wanted to reach out to him.

For a time she slept, surprisingly deeply, and while she slept, Katharine made Thomas write a letter to their uncle, begging him to come to their aid. Katharine hired a cadie to deliver the letter and bring back, if not the man in person, then at least a reply.

After being gone for longer than it would have taken to saunter there and back, the cadie returned. A gawky lad with bad skin and worse teeth, he feigned breathlessness, as if he'd run the whole way but the reek of the tavern was on him as was the flush of satiety which comes from a good feed at the Sheep Heid Inn. With a sly grin, the cadie pocketed his payment and handed over the minister's reply:

Dear children, it grieves me sorely to hear of my sister's condition. I will come, if and when the Lord sees fit to spare me from my duties towards my congregation. Please know that you are regularly in my prayers.
Thomas Ramsey

Katharine was beside herself. Were those all the words their uncle could spare? Was it more important for him to ponder the edifying passages of scripture with which he might assail

his congregation than pay his broken sister a visit? Katharine
burnt their uncle's letter and made Thomas promise that if she
ever became sick to dying, he would come to her directly, no
matter where he might be.

When they reach the Cramond Brig Inn, John Barr drops down
from the coach, tethers the horses and fetches them water.

How much further are we gaen? asks Thomas.

We're aboot hauf way, says John Barr. Mak yir ain estimation.

We've passed Ravelstane Dykes and I havena seen a single
desperado.

Mind whit ye wish for.

I dinna *wish* tae see a desperado. But ye said they were ilka
place and that's no true.

If ye dinna wish for owt, ye willna be disappointed. Dinna
be stravaiging while I wet my whistle, says John Barr, punching
his fists into his gloved palms and stamping up the pathway of
dirty snow which leads to the door of the inn.

A dozen packhorses, heads drooping, manes stiff with frost,
shift from one hoof to another. Denied the comfort of the
inn, left to keep watch on their maisters' drays are a handful
of carter lads, larking about and clashing the sharpened sticks
they carry against the threat of highwaymen. They're cold and
hungry but for as long as their masters are at their bit and sup
they're free from toil. When they tire of chaffing and mock
battles, they circle the coach, eyeing its occupants with a
mixture of suspicion and envy.

Where d'ye gang? says the biggest, boldest lad, screwing
his brows together into a dramatic scowl and dunting his stick
against the ground.

Say nocht, Katharine mutters. Thir maisters might be
highwaymen!

Dinna be daft, says Thomas. They're carter laddies. A
highwayman robs a body then maks off on a fleetfit steed. And
yon horses are no fleetfit steeds. They're auld nags. Onybody'd
catch a carter. And whit is there tae steal?

They dinna ken whit's in oor baskets, says Katharine. And this is Sir Patrick's coach.

I said, says the big lad again, pressing his mottled face close to the carriage window, where d'ye gang?

Anna grizzles. As if scenting blood, the carter lads move in closer.

Where d'ye gang?

We dinna ken, says Thomas, sae leave us be or yir maisters'll thrash ye for tormenting bairns.

Bold talk, says a quick, nimble lad, who leaps up and presses the point of his stick to Thomas's throat:

Yir claes o yir life! he roars, then drops down and prances around, crowing at his wit.

Hearing Anna's shrieks and expecting the worst, John Barr bursts from the inn door.

Can a man no hae a bite in peace?

The carter lads are back by their horses, smirking. Pie in hand, Barr curses at cutting short his break for nothing, wipes gravy from his chops, and, disgruntled, prepares to depart.

Promises make debts and debts makes promises, Hepburn had said, an appraising eye resting on the Culpeper the day after their father was put in the ground. Quality herbals were costly. He had business interests to consider, including investment in another apothecary, but couldn't put the Aikenhead widow and her brats out on the street, not straightaway at any rate and so, for the two years that remained of Helen Ramsey's life, *The Complete Herbal and English Physician Enlarged* – issuing from its author's residence in Spitalfields, London, next door to the Red Lion – remained on their shelves.

When Thomas could not sleep, and so that his father in heaven – or wherever he might be – would be proud of him, he set himself to memorise the ingredients in Mathiolus's *great antidote against Poison and Pestilence*, also known as Venice Treacle. Now, to postpone proper contemplation of what might lie at the end of this unfamiliar road for him and his sisters,

Thomas attempts to recall what he can of the receipt:

> *Take of Rhubarb, Rhapontic, Valerian roots, the roots of Acorus, or Calamus Aromaticus, Cypress, Cinquefoyl, Tormentil, round Birthwort, male Peony, Elecampane, Costus, Illirick, Orris, white Chamelion, or Avens, Galanga, Masterwort, white Dictamni, Angelica, Yarrow, Fillipendula or Dropwort, Zedoary, Ginger, Rosemary, Gentian, Devil's bit…*

Close to the end, when his mother could no longer lift her head to the pipe, Thomas took in the dreamy smoke then blew it into his mother's mouth. The kiss of poppy tears, of *lachryma papaveris*, might have dulled her pain but she did not die peacefully. Oh no, not peacefully at all.

> *…the seeds of Citrons, and Agnus Castus, the berries of Kermes, the seeds of Ash-tree, Sorrel, wild Parsnips, Navew, Nigella, Peony the male, Bazil, Hedge Mustard, (Irio) Treacle Mustard, Fennel, Bishop's weed, the berries of Bay, Juniper, and Ivy, Sarsaparilla, (or for want of it the double weight of Cubebs), Cubebs…*

With the children's mother dead, Hepburn wasted no time in getting his hands on anything of value: the herbal was the first item to go, followed by the scales, the mortar and pestle, the weights and measuring spoons, the scoops, phials, jars and bottles, the pots and sacks and baskets. He is surprised at the amount of wine turned to vinegar his men find in a cupboard behind the stairs but as it has no monetary value, he tips it out and saves the better bottles and flagons. Helen had never managed to run the business effectively: she didn't know enough about treatments; customers had less faith in her than they'd had in her husband; credit was hard to come by; her stock was depleted. At the end she had little more to offer than humdrum supplies for humdrum ailments. While Hepburn's men carted off the stuff and substance of their life, Thomas pocketed the empty blue bottle, as a keepsake.

...the leaves of Scordium, Germander, Champitys, Centaury the less, Stoechas, Celtic Spikenard, Calaminth, Rue, Mints, Betony, Vervain, Scabious, Carduus Benedictus, Bawm, Dittany of Crete, Marjoram, St. John's Wort, Schoenanth, Horehound, Goats Rue, Savin, Burnet, Figs, Walnuts, Fistic-nuts, Emblicks, Myrobalans, the flowers of Violets, Borrage, Bugloss, Roses, Lavender, Sage, Rosemary, Cassia Lignea, Cloves, NutElspets, Mace, black Pepper, long Pepper, all the three sorts of Sandres, wood of Aloes, Hart's Horn, Unicorn's horn, or in its stead, Bezoar stone, bone in a Stag's heart, Ivory, Stag's pizzle...

As from this morning, due to obligations undertaken at the baptism of James and Helen's children, Sir Patrick Aikenhead has become their legal guardian. He arrived at the door to oversee the children's removal from the premises. In mourning clothes once more, Katharine, Anna and Thomas, each with a basket containing their few possessions strapped to their backs, trudged behind him through the Grassmarket. Sir Patrick, a broad-backed man with thick black hair and a beard shot through with a streak of silver, thought fit for three recently orphaned youngsters to pause in front of the gibbet, for edification. The ground bore traces of blood, hair and excrement from the last execution.

Look, bairns, he said, and see where sin can tak ye.

On a stake near the gibbet was a woman's head, her face an arrested scream. Livid hack marks scored the neck. Beneath a cloud of flies, the grey flesh of her cheeks crawled with maggots.

That hellcat, said their guardian, murthered her husband wi his ain sword. She wis brocht tae justice and condemned tae daith. She wis hingit, then heidit, then rent limb frae limb on a chirurgeon's slab. Sae mind ye weel, bairns, he concluded. Ye can rin but ye canna hide frae the lang airm o justice.

When they reached the West Port, Sir Patrick instructed

John Barr to dispatch his charges to his estate and return for him the following morning; he had further unspecified business in the city.

> ...*Castoreum, Earth of Lemnos, Opium, Orient Pearls, Emeralds, Jacinth, red Coral, Camphire, Gum Arabic, Mastich, Frankincense, Styrax, Turpentine, Sagapenum, Opopanax, Laserpitium, or Myrrh, Musk, Ambergris, oil of Birtiol, species cordiales temperato, Diamargariton, Diamoscu, Diambra, Electuarij de Gemes, Troches of Camphire, of Squills, Troches of Vipers, the juice of Sorrel, Sow Thistles, Scordium, Vipers Bugloss, Borrage, Bawm, Hypocistis, the best Treacle and Mithridate, old Wine, the best Sugar, or choice Honey.*

The creator, Mathiolus, declared that this magnificent receipt, *were it stretched out, and cut in thongs, would reach round the world.* A receipt for kings and princes, Thomas's father would say, dragging a finger down the long list of ingredients. For the rest o us, there's garlic.

Close to the water now, they clop through the Royal burgh of Queensferry, with its solidly built houses, its churches and taverns, which cling to the ragged coastline. The firth is grey and choppy, whipped up by an icy wind. Ferries and fishing boats bob on the swell and out on the open water a fleet of sailing ships moves imperceptibly westwards. At the water's edge, a seal balances on a rock like a curved, polished stone. On the far side the soft hills of Fife are veiled in mist. The sight of the water and its attendant life lifts the orphans from their gloom. Eagerly they peer through the coach windows and take in great gasps of salty air. Anna indicates several small islands.

Are we gaen oot there?

No unless ye're terrible bad, says John Barr, and the Maister banishes ye tae Inchcolm tae bide wi the solan geese and the kittiwackes.

Whit's kittiwackes? asks Thomas.

Seabirds, says John Barr. And ken where they bide? At the tap o the cliffs! Thoosans awthegither. Ane big family. But dinna be deceived by thir smiley looks. Yon are fearsome hunters. When the firth freezes, a kittiwacke will hack through the ice tae catch a fish. I've seen it wi my ain een.

Are we tae bide in nests? says Anna.

Ye'd hae tae be a terrible scoondrel for the Maister tae pit ye on Inchcolm, John Barr replies, in more kindly tones than before. Besides, there's nae nests for the taen!

Is yon a kittiwacke? says Thomas.

Naw naw, says John Barr. Yon's a guillemot. D'ye nae ken ocht? Nae mistakin a guillemot.

All kinds of birds congregate on the stony beach and the water of the wide, misty firth. Many are species which the Aikenhead orphans have never seen in the city: dark, long-necked cormorants which skim the surface of the water; gannets which flash and plummet; wheeling, wheeping oyster catchers. They continue beyond the town. In places the road hugs the coast; elsewhere it cuts through sloping, ghostly fields and patches of woodland. Beneath the trees, garlic flowers are spread like a carpet of foggy stars.

John Barr tugs hard on the reins and the coach makes a sharp turn off the highway then rocks and sways onto a narrow track, to the children's alarm.

Ye'll hae tae find yir sea legs, says John Barr, if ye're tae travel by coach.

But the coach disna gang on the sea, says Thomas. Why dae we need sea legs?

Awbody needs sea legs, says John Barr.

The muddy track is deeply rutted and the coach advances at little more than walking pace. The constant tipping of the swell and the swaying of the coach puts the world on a tilt. Thomas and his sisters are journeying into the unknown and unimaginable. While they are in transit, nothing is fixed: not what has been nor what is yet to come; for now they are just rocking along, the mist fingering their faces like a cold dream.

They pass by a line of low cottages where coils of black smoke rise from chimneys then disappear into the mist. Men, women and children go about their chores: splitting and stacking wood, mending nets, tending to animals, spinning yarn. As the coach passes, the men doff hats, the children stare and the women dip into curtseys.

If they kent I wis cairryin three orphans they widna trouble wi such niceties, says John Barr.

Is Sir Patrick thir landlord?

He's thir breid and butter. Mair. He's thir life. And yours tae, frae this day forth.

Landlords are bad men, says Thomas. If it hadna been for Maister Hepburn aye efter his rent, we mightna be orphans!

Wheeesht, Katharine hisses in his ear. Awthin that man hears'll gang straight back tae Sir Patrick.

I dinna care!

Ye're a gowk, then.

It is near dinner-time when they turn off the track and clatter up the broad drive to their new home.

Netherstane

The new family to which Katharine, Thomas and Anna have been appended comprises: Sir Patrick Aikenhead, master of the household; his wife Hester, a plump, whey-skinned woman with a penchant for all things French; their daughter Euphemie, a willowy, hazel-eyed lass with flyaway hair and a habitually peeved expression; Malcolm, the first son and heir who shares his father's dark, craggy profile and possesses a precocious interest in matters of state; and Alasdair, the plump, spoiled, younger son, who takes after his mother.

As for resident staff, this includes: Zander Naysmith, tutor to the children; Matthew and Andra Fleming, Sir Patrick's manservants; Nan Shepard, Lady Hester's maid; Madge Boyd, cook and henwife; Aleen Shaw, housemaid; Ross Dubh, the groom; and, of course, John Barr, driver and coachmender. A score of other workers reside in cottages on the estate: gardeners, bakers, brewers, seamstresses, handymen, all of whom contribute to the household in labour or produce as and when required. To the Aikenhead orphans it seems less like a family they have joined, more a small kingdom.

Sheltered by a horseshoe of tall pines and set in the dip of a velvety lawn which rolls down to meet the shoreline, the house is squat and solid, with many windows and a turret room in each corner. The public rooms are lavishly furnished with silk-upholstered chairs and carved bureaux inlaid with nacre and bone. The walls are painted in the colours of earth and sky and several ceilings boast elaborate Italian plasterwork. Netherstane has its own brewhouse and bakehouse, with ovens large enough to roast an ox, or as John Barr has it, a good-sized man. The coachhouse, stables and kennels, which stand behind the house in a tidy row, are in good repair. Close to the kitchen garden is the henhouse and the doocot. Peacocks roam freely through the grounds, perching on turrets, gates, benches, settling on the lawn. They display their extravagant tails, assume proprietorial rights and keep all comers at bay with shrill cries.

The dining table can comfortably seat twenty persons. When in use it is covered with a linen cloth and laid with pewter plates, shining cutlery and all manner of pretty painted chinaware, jugs and decanters. Three ornate oil lamps hang low over the table and a dozen sconces are fixed to every wall but for the midday meal, except on the darkest of days, there is little need for lamps or candles to be lit as the curtains are drawn back and daylight floods in. The first time Katharine, Thomas and Anna sit down to dinner, brought to the table and served by Madge and Aleen, Anna is overcome by the sight of such plenty and can barely eat a thing. Katharine and Thomas at first attempt a proud restraint but soon give in to temptation and eat till their bellies ache.

It isn't long, however, before the new arrivals – *our city cousins*, as Lady Hester calls them, *the orphans* as most others do – become accustomed to rabbit, hare and venison; to chicken, duck, pigeon and woodcock; to all kind of fish; to peaches, pears, plums; to carrots, beets and greens pulled from the ground that very morning; to tart cheeses and creamy milk.

The orphans learn how the mistress expects them to comport themselves at table: to sit still and straight-backed; to wait until a dish is passed to them, or until Madge or Aleen has finished serving up; to cut their food without scraping metal on metal; to lay down their eating implements quietly when they have finished. They learn to value Malcolm's kind glances when they err on etiquette. They learn to say nothing when Sir Patrick, his wife and children are served bigger and better parts of the meat. They learn to sit patiently through Sir Patrick's fulminations on the state of the nation and Lady Hester's carping about the shortcomings of the servants and the extra mouths to feed. They learn to say nothing when Alasdair steals food from Thomas's plate, to say nothing when he pinches Anna or makes lewd faces at Katharine. They do not forget what it is to go to bed hungry.

Full Bellies and Feather Beds

A new life has begun. Every night, in the warm bed she shares with Katharine, Anna cries so hard that she wakes the next morning with eyes as red as boiled crayfish. She has frequent violent headaches and when they are upon her she can tolerate no light or sound, no food or drink. Even when the pain subsides, it is often a day or two before she fully returns to herself; she mutters in a dislocated way and is unresponsive to questions, like someone in a deep sleep, or a soul in limbo.

The Netherstane cousins have little time for the wee city cousin and her headaches and resent the exclusive, unfathomable terrain she inhabits. They view her infirmity as weakness, unwillingness to accept her lot, as arrogance, ingratitude. Their own father has taken in this contrary cherub and her shabby siblings out of the goodness of his heart. He has taken them from the squalid circumstances in which they were found, put food in their bellies and feather pillows under their heads. He has provided each with not one but two sets of clothes. Old clothes, to be sure, which Euphemie, Malcolm or Alasdair has outgrown and would normally have passed on to the servants' children, but better by far than what they brought in their baskets. Their own father has permitted Thomas and Anna to renew their studies under Maister Naysmith – what more could have been done for them? Isn't their father the soul of magnanimity and aren't they, his own begotten children, put upon in innumerable ways by having to share their home with distant, low-born cousins? The least the orphans could do is try to fit in and not make a nuisance of themselves.

Katharine grieves for her mother and pines for the life she left behind in the city, and for the rare, brief trysts with Jeremiah Skaill, though in her heart she knows her attachment to him is unlikely to come to fruition. Obadiah Skaill is a merchant through and through and one thing a merchant knows is that a marriage must bring revenue and status. If a man's strength is not to be sapped, he must not undertake the burden of a penniless spouse, no matter how agreeable she might be. Though she has neither seen nor heard tell of Jeremiah since they left the city, she continues to feed the flame of her affection by pondering each little thing he said or did, affording it a special place in her trove of memories.

In the house that would never feel like a true home, Katharine and Anna share a bed in Euphemie's chamber. With good enough grace Euphemie has accepted this imposition, on the condition that Katharine comb her hair every night and Anna carry out miscellaneous errands on demand. Euphemie is her mother's daughter. When she's in the mood, she enjoys having Katharine and Anna around, to pander to her vanity and, in Katharine's case, to furnish her with details of life in the city. Which fabrics are in vogue and which are shunned? How do ladies wear their sleeves, their collars? Do their curls hang about their face? Are they piled on the crown of the head or pinned at the nape of the neck? Do they favour ceruse or pearl powder to lighten the complexion? Is vermilion considered the best rouge or that made from the shells of boiled crabs? Where is the best entertainment to be had? Where might one see a play, where might one dance? And how do city women conduct themselves in matters of the heart?

Katharine can provide detail on the fabric and trimmings for gowns: black velvet, serge and stuff for winter; for summer, silk mixtures, paduasoy and prunell. She can list, though mainly from hearsay, delicacies which might grace a dining table but few of her culinary offerings are novel to Euphemie: Lady Hester endeavours to be as modish on matters of the table as she is on the cut of her gown. Katharine is conversant with ingredients which went into beauty potions sold in the apothecary, though her father, like many in the trade, would never impart the full receipt. As she has rarely been privy to confidences of an amorous nature, it is not long before

Euphemie's curiosity wanes.

Sir Patrick considers Katharine too old to educate. She is encouraged to keep her hands busy with needlepoint and embroidery, to act as chaperone to Euphemie when required and generally oblige his daughter and his wife in whatever ways they see fit. From Malcolm and Alasdair, she is expected to keep her distance. Katharine has little time for Alasdair and his brattish ways. As for Malcolm, who is two years her senior, he can become overly familiar when wine has been taken but has a gentleness about him that his younger brother entirely lacks. Anna, when she can escape Euphemie's errands, trails after Katharine like a small, woebegone shadow.

Zander Naysmith is less than enthusiastic about the new sleeping arrangements. Until the orphans arrived he had a room of his own at the back of the house: a small and scantly furnished room, to be sure, and lacking an open aspect, but warm and conveniently close to the kitchen and pantry. When Sir Patrick was not inclined to a game of chess or colloquium on matters of commerce and the housekeeping staff were too trachled to indulge in blether he has, until now, passed many a relaxing evening in his room, reading by the fire, toasting his toes and partaking of his employer's claret. He maintains his habit of reading and tippling, and continues to retire at his customary hour, but a child abed in the same room is limiting to say the least. The lad should have been put in Malcolm and Alasdair's bedchamber where there is ample space for another cot. Malcolm, with characteristic open-handedness, made little objection but Alasdair, the stoat, kicked up such a fuss that Lady Hester's entreaties on her favourite's behalf were followed by Sir Patrick's orders regarding the sleeping arrangements which regrettably Naysmith must, for the time being, endure.

For Thomas, the days are by no means all bad. With such a wastrel as Alasdair to contend with, who'd rather disrupt any lesson than learn, or let anyone else learn, Naysmith is obliged to be firm. But given the tutor's belief in free time for students and fondness for lengthy post-prandial naps, most afternoons the youngsters are left to their own devices. On the estate and further afield there is much for a boy to enjoy and, in the better weather, Thomas happily explores the coastline and the woods. Thanks to Malcolm he learns to hunt, to fish and to ride. Thanks to Alasdair's fondness for pranks, he learns to check his bed for a dead mackerel, a bloody rabbit's foot, the half-rotted carcass of a seabird, before saying his prayers.

For the first time ever, Thomas does not share a bed with his sisters and misses their cosy proximity, the soft rise and fall of their breathing. He misses the cat padding across the covers. He even misses his parents squabbling in the night and his mother mumbling in her sleep about debts and promises and mouths to feed. At night, his sleep is broken by Naysmith's stentorious snoring. Like Thomas's father, Naysmith is a heavy user of a Dutch pipe and everything in the room is impregnated with the smell of tobacco – the draperies, blankets, books, even the wainscotting and the furniture. Tobacco features in Thomas's dreams: he is often following a ribbon of smoke in search of his father but encountering, instead, a forbidding, faceless man.

Blubber and Baleen

Late in the year the weather turns rough and raw. Storms rip along the coast. Ropes of brine lash the shore where the tide has thrown up bottles and bones, knots of seaweed and broken baskets. There is tell of shipwrecks and rumours of continental vessels searching for a safe place to unload human cargo. Since Louis overturned an edict permitting freedom of worship, all kinds of unorthodox believers are anxious. If the Sun King has his way, there will be one faith in France and one only: Catholicism.

Towards any member of a household who refuses to convert to the King's faith, the *dragonnades* are merciless and Huguenots are amongst the first to be targeted. For any intent on preserving their faith, and their life, the only options are to go underground, live a lie, or flee. Like flocks of night birds, Protestant refugees pass through the ports of France. Any who possess the wherewithal to travel to the Americas gird themselves for the duress of an Atlantic crossing.

Those with fewer resources embark on more modest journeys: from France to Scotland entails crossing a short but treacherous body of water. Huguenots who wish to import their faith to Scotland, and their skills – silk-weaving, clock-making, gunsmithery, distilling – are not always welcome. It is an irony noted by those with long memories that the 'Protestant tide' took Covenanters from Queensferry to Holland: half a century later, the tide has turned.

One night the wind is particularly savage. It races down chimneys, worries the embers in the grate until flames revive and leap up in a wild dance. It tears round the horseshoe of clashing pines. It shakes doorframes, rattles windows, dislodges roof tiles. The hens fluster in their coop; the doos huddle in their cot; the dogs grizzle in their kennels, the horses snort and paw at the stable doors.

Katharine fears the wrath of God is about to descend on the house and its sinful, extravagant ways; she goes down on her knees to pray despite Euphemie's entreaties to cuddle up beside her. Anna buries her head beneath the blanket, presses her fists against her ribs. Her heart flaps like a trapped bird. Thomas, snug beneath a tobacco-scented quilt, is unaccountably thrilled by the nocturnal havoc. In the small hours, when the wind subsides, when the sound of the sea becomes no more than a soft swish and his tutor's snoring once again dominates the room, he is almost sorry that the storm has passed.

An hour before dawn Madge bursts from the kitchen and clatters up the stairs, hopping and craiking and clacking a wooden spoon against the walls:

Wake up, Maister, wake up!

Beside herself with excitement, she continues her spoon-banging until Sir Patrick emerges blearily, in night cap and gown.

Whit is it, woman?

Ye've landed the biggest catch ye'll iver see in yir life! Or else, Madge adds, cunning-tongued, yir neebor's landed it. Gien the lay the land, it's debatable whit side the cratur's on. But come quick, Maister, come quick. I wis doon the shore the morn. The henhoose roof wis tore off in the nicht and some o the hens were blawn clean oot the coop. I couldna see ony sign o them on the shore but whit I did see, Maister, wis a fearful sicht.

Whit did ye see, woman?

A monster, Maister, a sea monster. It's deid now but I saw the cratur braithe its last. Ane lang sigh and twa plumes o spray and that wis that.

Soon Lady Hester appears, her hair twisted in rags and her face devoid of any beautification. Naysmith and the children poke sleepy heads from bedchambers and bemoan the early rousing, though the servants have been up and doing for some time.

How mony hens have we lost? asks Lady Hester.

I'm nae sure, Mistress, a hauf dizzen or mair, but there's a sea monster on the beach! It's as big as a ship!

Reluctantly Sir Patrick pulls on breeches, boots and jacket – the man will happily spend all day in bedclothes unless he is expecting visitors. After having Matthew and Andra Fleming round up a dozen men from the estate, with a dishevelled Naysmith and a disgruntled John Barr trotting to keep up with his loping stride, the laird makes his way to the shore. The men are armed with swords, muskets and cudgels.

The dawn is slow in coming and there's a bone-gripping chill in the air. Sir Patrick regrets removing his nightcap, forgetting to don his rabbit-skin gloves, foregoing morning prayers and breaking his fast. Curiosity, nevertheless, has got the better of him.

In spite of his protests, Katharine insists that Thomas say his prayers before he joins the men. Anna refuses to get out of bed. With the exception of Madge, who has already skelped ahead of Sir Patrick to bear witness to her discovery, Lady Hester insists that the women remain within the house: there are hearths to be cleaned, fires to be lit, food to be prepared, ladies to be dressed, whether or not a sea monster has washed up on the beach.

The red, newly risen sun hangs between grey sky and grey water. The wind has dropped to nothing. The trees glitter with frost.

Sir Patrick is never an easy man to please but even on an empty stomach, with the cold air snapping at his extremities, he whoops and slaps his own, well-padded haunch.

A grand find, Madge. Weel done, woman!

Gled tae be o service, maister. See! Madge screeches, her scrawny shoulders jiggling in her excitement. A sea monster sure as day!

Yon's a whale, woman. D'ye no ken a whale when ye see ane?

It wis dark when I wis first here, Maister. Aw I spied wis yon great mooth on it.

The estate men huff and puff and lumber about, awaiting instructions. No-one is prepared for Madge's find, for the dimensions of the creature, its colossal head, cavernous mouth with its combs of baleen, the tail like an anchor driven into the sand.

Sir Patrick's party is not long alone in celebrating the whale's beaching and demise on that very patch of sandy shore. Bryce Lightfoot, whose estate borders on Aikenhead's, has brought a number of his own men who foregather on the far side of the carcass. Lightfoot is tall and lean, wedge-cheeked, with a blazing coxcomb of red-gold hair. A heated disputation ensues. As Madge and both lairds are keenly aware, if anybody were to draw a line from the beach to the woods, the whale would cut clean across the boundary between the estates. To whom, then, does the creature belong? On whose land does it lie?

Madge steps forward and draws breath deep into her lungs.

The shoreline belangs tae nae chiel. The shoreline is where awbody can tak whit they find.

Weel, we're awbody tae! says Lightfoot. But ye speak oot o turn. If I were yir maister, I'd hae ye disciplined.

I speak the truth, sir, says Madge.

She has a point, says Sir Patrick, though it's no her place tae offer opinion when nane is askit o her. Awa back tae the hoose, woman, and mak yirsel useful.

Madge is correct; the shoreline is free for all to use but neither laird pays this technicality much heed. If the whale does not belong to either of *them*, who else could it possibly belong to? A whale is a whale and both men claim it for their own. Voices are raised. Weapons are drawn. Both parties manoeuvre into lines of attack.

Thomas meets Madge as she's on her way back to the house. She's red-faced, clench-fisted and thunder-eyed, and marches off in the direction of the house without uttering a word. When Thomas arrives at the beach, the heated dispute is in full flow and both sides are close to blows when John Barr cracks his whip against the whale's back:

Is there nae mair than enough tae share o yon big ben o blubber? And if there's ony Catholics amangst ye, ye can saut awa the cauld meat tae keep yir bellies fou through Lent.

Lightfoot is, once more, about to chide one of his neighbour's staff for speaking out of turn when Aikenhead suggests a private word. The two men walk off towards the water, their boots leaving neat prints in the damp sand. Aikenhead matches Lightfoot in height, in straightness of back and broadness of shoulder. From their assembled men – the stocky, the gangling, the barrel-bellied, the whippet-thin, the halt or hunchback – the lairds are a breed apart. Only John Barr equals them in height and self-possession.

On the far side of the firth, the gentle slopes of Fife reappear. Overhead, seabirds coil and shimmer. The skin of the whale has the dark sheen of wet, scarred rock and is dotted with outcrops of barnacles and colonies of lice. Men run axe blades across their palms and wonder how they might ever butcher such a Leviathan. They are hungry and cold and who's to say what kind of eating might be in a whale? Would their tools have any purchase on that mound of flesh? Where would they start?

They are not whaling men. Some fish off the coast; they tend the fields; shear the sheep; fix roofs and dykes; oil coach axles and cartwheels; mend fences; shoe horses. They bring produce to their respective lairds – butter, cheese, bread, fish, meat, meal, seasonal fruit and vegetables, needlework, basketwork, woodwork, metalwork – as part payment for a roof over their heads. Their tools are small, domestic, unsuited to this scale of operations. Besides, the smell of the dead whale makes the men, Catholic or otherwise, doubt they'd relish eating it.

From the house, the beach is best observed from the first floor library. After checking that the kitchen staff are not being unduly distracted from their labour and requesting coffee and pastries to be brought up to her, Lady Hester installs herself in the window seat and, by means of her husband's telescope, observes the activity on the shore. The men are doing a great deal of striding about, gesticulating expansively: shaking fists, shaking heads, pacing around and coming to a sudden halt. There are a great deal of open mouths and furrowed brows. Altogether it is not unlike watching a stage performance in a vast, if empty, auditorium. She has heard tell of Galilean binoculars being employed in the French theatre. How she would love to see the French theatre for herself, were it not for the perils of a sea crossing and the inconvenience on her wardrobe and digestion.

The fire crackles merrily and the chill in the room is lifting. From the comfort of the padded windowseat the mistress of the house happily indulges in daydream: she is in a fancied Paris, bedecked in a black velvet gown which features extensive décolletage. A filigree of Normandy lace embellishes the neckline and wrists. Around her, flocks of elegant women and dashing men appraise each other's attire, coiffure and jewels in the silent but definitive language of nods and bows, snapped fans, of twirled moustaches and doffed hats. The space is bathed in the golden, tinkling glow of dozens of candlelit chandeliers. Every so often, deep male chuckles and high trills of female laughter emerge from the hubbub, in response to some jest. The perfumed air is as intoxicating as strong drink. To be sure there is as much drama on display in the stalls or the grand circle as there is on the stage.

When Lightfoot and Aikenhead conclude their parley, they raise brandy flasks and embrace stiffly. They order all weapons to be laid aside and carving implements to be taken up. From both sides a muted cheer goes up: no-one wants to fight on an empty stomach and certainly not over a great stinking carcass. The lairds dispatch men to fetch copper kettles, wooden tubs and flasks suitable for rendering and storing the blubber.

Malcolm and Alasdair approach the shore and Thomas races over to greet them:

Come and see the whale, he says, afore they butcher it!

Afore who butchers it? says Alasdair.

The men frae baith estates. They've agreed tae share it atween them.

Aw, says Alasdair. Sae there's tae be nae fightin?

No, says Thomas. It came close tae blaws, but no.

Shame, says Alasdair. I'd like tae have seen a guid battle.

No ye widna, says Malcolm.

I wid tae. And sae wid Forbes! says Alasdair, and charges towards Lightfoot's son, approaching from the other direction, and wrestles him to the ground.

Come and see the whale, Malcolm, says Thomas. It's… it's prodigious!

Aye, says Malcolm. And deid.

As the drama on the shore appears to have abated, Lady Hester slips the brass hood over the telescope's marvellous eye, licks crumbs of pastry from her fingers, savours her coffee and prepares to turn her attention to the household accounts.

Aikenhead and Lightfoot instruct those with the best knowledge of butchery to draw up a plan of action: given the scale of the task, the operation will require the organisation of many hands, equipped with saws, axes and long knives. The lairds' own part in the proceedings is to delegate and then to stroll, to set their haunches on one of the fallen tree trunks scattered on the shore, to oversee operations and exchange news, without getting their hands dirty.

Malcolm pays his respects to Bryce Lightfoot but once he has established that he is not required to assist in any practical way, excuses himself.

Where are ye gaen? asks Thomas.

For a walk, says Malcolm, kindly but firmly. Alane.

He means, says Alasdair, that he disna wish yir company.

I mean, says Malcom, that I dinna wish *ony* company. Yir ain included, Alasdair.

I widna wish tae join ye! says Alasdair. I'd fain be here, in the thick o things. Faither, can we help wi the butcherin?

Aye, says Forbes, turning a winning smile on his own father. Can we, please?

I dinna wish tae, says Thomas.

Naebody asked *your* opinion, says Alasdair.

I didna say ye did but—

Nae wranglin, lads, says Sir Patrick. We've already been close tae fisticuffs the day.

Butcherin is men's work, says Lightfoot.

Aye, says Sir Patrick. And nae the place o lads tae meddle.

Alasdair and Forbes badger their fathers to be allowed to help to no avail: there are sufficient estate hands to carry out the task; besides, proper procedure has to be demonstrated, on that both lairds are agreed.

Once the flensing is under way, fires are lit and the blubber is boiled down in kettles, set to cool in tubs then funnelled into casks. Throughout the day, maids from both houses bring bread and cheese, broth and ale, to sustain the menfolk at their labour and keep the kitchens free from blood and guts. It is not long before local people from outwith the estates catch wind of the goings-on and tramp along the beach to gather and gawp. Even a pair of raddled fiddlers, sensing an opportunity, hirple down the coastal path, scraping away at a jaunty tune. The smell in the air may be rank but the mood is a good deal merrier than it was first thing in the morning. The estate men are kept in good supply of food and drink and are beginning to enjoy the social aspect of this novel task.

Itching for amusement as the day proceeds, Alasdair and Forbes take it upon themselves to vex the local lads by charging at them with sticks until, undeterred, the lads find their own sticks – there is no shortage of driftwood after the storm – and begin to hit back. Aikenhead and Lightfoot, with a quantity of brandy under the belt, note the skirmishes with rueful indulgence: boys will ever be boys.

The work continues until well after sundown. The meat is divided amongst those who wish it and the tongue is the part most highly prized. All workers are also given a share of blubber for their lamps. The baleen is sawn off the whale's jaw, tied in bundles and wrapped in sackcloth, and set aside for the lairds. A prized commodity, particularly for its use in fans, corsetry and horsewhips, it will fetch a good price.

When they have dispersed the onlookers and sent home all but those required to continue rendering the remaining blubber, Aikenhead and Lightfoot daub their faces with whale blood and whoop as if they'd landed the creature with their own hands. Late into the evening, when the women and children are abed, fires still flicker on the beach and blubber still simmers. Downwind from the remains of the carcass, which will be left for scavenging birds, beasts and humankind to pick over, the two men, inured to the cold night air by countless stoups of brandy, clink goblets, toast their good fortune and drink the health of the King across the water. It has been a butchering to end all butchering. The beach runs red for days.

The Coat-tails of Another Family

Winter nights are long but to Thomas's delight there is no shortage of books to be read and candles to throw light on the pages; due to the stink of rendered blubber, Sir Patrick does not allow cruisie lamps in the library. The man has an aversion to the cold, and Lady Hester a fondness for gowns made of silk and lace, and so the house is kept warm, with fires lit in many rooms. Though hearth taxes are heavy, there is no shortage of fuel; besides, Aleen takes care of the laying of fires and the cleaning out of ashes.

Since the carving up of the whale, Lightfoot and Sir Patrick have discovered that sharing resources can be mutually beneficial and Alasdair has become thick with Lightfoot's son, Forbes, a fair, clear-skinned lad as indulged by his own mother as Alasdair is by his. Forbes and Alasdair have little interest in lessons, preferring to roam the estates, looking for adventure. If Thomas is invited along, it is usually as an afterthought. Thomas is not unduly concerned.

Sir Patrick has an extensive library but the man is less inclined to read books than to purchase them. He owns many books on foreign travel and customs, several manuals on plant propagation and crop husbandry but few works of religion or philosophy. His preference is for illustrated volumes and he reads more for entertainment than edification. For the sake of appearances, and guided by Naysmith in his purchases, he does hold several finely bound treatises on science and religion but rarely opens them. He is pleased that Thomas takes an interest, and once he has established that the lad treats his possessions with care, gives him the run of the shelves.

As for the education of his children, that is for Naysmith to attend to. Much to the delight of his mother, Malcolm is studying the law in France. To date, their firstborn has proven himself able and industrious. If he does not succumb overly to the fleshpots of Paris, and keeps himself free from the *French disease*, he will return home with a degree and a lucrative future. For Alasdair, there is time yet to turn the lad's lazy mind to learning, if he has any aptitude for it. If not, he can always help out on the estate, where an able body and a practical bent are of more use than book learning. Euphemie is as feather-headed as her mother, prattling on about fashion and gossip and eligible husbands but she's comely enough and will not struggle to make a match, when the time comes.

It is two years since John Barr brought the orphans to the door. Sir Patrick does not regret his decision. His generosity continues to stand him in good stead with the local community who view his guardianship as a demonstration of Christian charity, even if he is an Episcopalian. For themselves, the bairns are complaisant enough. The older lass is a mite pious for his taste and, like her brother, has a proud, stubborn streak. She would be bonny were it not for the self-righteous frown which snarls between her brows. The wee lass is slow with her lessons and a strange one: if you were of a superstitious disposition, which he most certainly is not, you might think her eldritch: she has a habit of appearing in the grounds at dusk, as if from nowhere, standing still and silent as a spectre between two crooked birches, frighting the servants.

The lad can be a puffed-up chiel when the mood takes him but he has a good head on him, knows when to mind his manners and is grateful enough for the opportunities he's been given. With the benefit of fresh air and good country fare, he is growing tall, strong and handsome. He has noticed his wife comparing Thomas to Alasdair and though partial as any mother might be to her own son's charmless mien, her gaze lingers longer on Thomas's thick dark eyelashes, his rosy cheeks, broadening shoulders.

Thomas does not regret that Alasdair has paired up with Forbes. It is less tiresome to be ignored than to be a perpetual target for pranks and ridicule. He enjoys his lessons, particularly when Alasdair feigns a bellyache or a fever and Lady Hester packs him off to bed, fussing and fretting and babying the big spoiled lump that he is. At such times Thomas misses his own mother, though she was never one for doting. When he sees Alasdair playing the fool or the invalid, he is more determined than ever to stick in at his lessons.

After a decade of dining at Sir Patrick's table, Zander Naysmith has grown podgy as an old dog which rarely leaves the hearth. When he is not engaged with his pipe, he has an old dog's habit of scratching his long ears. Having to take on two additional pupils was, initially, an irritation but Thomas's willingness to learn is some compensation for the loss of private sleeping quarters. As for the wee lass, she still has trouble with her letters though can bluff her way through some classes by memorising entire pages of text. He doesn't hold with the serious education of lasses: more often than not it serves little more purpose than to lead them to the altar but Sir Patrick pays his salary, when he remembers, and what Sir Patrick wants, he gets. And it has to be said that, since the orphans' arrival, the Maister has been more than generous with the contents of his cellar.

But if the lass continues to struggle, why persist in trying to dunt book learning into her pretty head? There's those that can and will, those that can and willna, and those that canna even if they will. She would be better served by the dame school in Queensferry where she might apply herself to spinning and stitching, dancing, playing the harpsichord and the speaking of the French tongue. If things keep on the way they're going, the speaking of the French tongue may soon, for some at least, become a distinct advantage.

Zander Naysmith, on a good day, though not as forthcoming with tales of adventure as James Armour, will tolerate Thomas's endless questions. And is patient with Anna, though it is only when Alasdair is absent from classes that she will dare to open her mouth and then no more than a cheep escapes her lips. Naysmith and Sir Patrick often sit up in the library, with pipes and brandy, long after the rest of the household is abed and Thomas, ever a light sleeper, is woken by rumbles of drunken laughter filtering through the walls. Where there are drunken men at night, there are crabbit men in the morning and after a late night's carousing with Sir Patrick, Naysmith clomps around, sighing and groaning and tamping down the dottle in his pipe. He sets long, dreary translations from Pliny's military campaigns and will not tolerate any questions whatsoever.

Thomas is beginning to notice changes in his body – hairs sprouting in his armpits and groin, strange nether stirrings, particularly when he is close to Euphemie, now fourteen, with her budding breasts, jutting hips and bold eyes which seem to drill right through to his bones. When he encounters her unexpectedly his prick stiffens, a hot flush surges from his knees to the tips of his ears and he becomes lost for words. For a lad who loves to talk, being tongue-tied is more alarming than the other more dramatic physical effects.

Katharine's body has taken on the curves of an hourglass, and on certain days she has a sharp, coppery odour. When Lady Hester laughs her bosom quivers like flummery and the cleft of cleavage can envelop a locket, a string of freshwater pearls. Madge's dugs are scrawny, her hips narrow: mannish. Aleen has a yeasty smell; her arse swells enticingly as she cleans out the grate. It is as if womankind had hitherto been invisible and only now that he's begun to pay attention, it is all around him, drawing his gaze. He learns the meaning of the word *lascivious*, relishes the sweet sibilance. He might have asked Malcolm for advice about the changes in his interest, and in his anatomy, but Malcolm is not expected to return from France until the end of the year.

For some time now life has been calm and ordered and without want. On the whole Thomas and his sisters have been treated well and adjusted to their new life: they no longer live in fear of a visit from Hepburn and his hounds, from the Town Guard or the bailiffs, and Thomas no longer lies awake at night, listening to his parents' quarrels. Except in jest, over who deserves the last sweetmeat on the plate, or whether Sir Patrick spends more time at Bryce Lightfoot's house than his own, or some other trivial concern, Thomas has never heard Lady Hester and Sir Patrick quarrel. But the house is so spacious, the rooms so plentiful, the walls so thick, and who can tell what muffled discontent is voiced behind closed doors?

He wonders how his own parents might have fared had such a place been their birthright, rather than cramped, rented accommodation in an overcrowded city. He finds it hard to imagine his mother and father emerging in bedgowns from separate chambers, padding down long corridors to a dining room where, on chafing dishes, awaits an array of food with which to break their fast. He can't imagine his father buttoning himself into a frock coat or powdering a periwig, or his mother spending hours of a morning at her toilet, aided by a maid. It is becoming hard to imagine his parents at all and when he can, they're not at their best: his father stotting in from the tavern, his mother a wretch on the doorstep.

The walls of the dining room are hung with old family portraits, some dating back more than a century. In the prime of their lives, decked out in the fashions of the age, Sir Patrick's defunct forebears gaze out from ornate frames with their swags and festoons, scrolls and volutes, gilding and gadrooning. Each subject has an air of assurance, an awareness of worth, of entitlement to display finery and jewels. The women, if not all beautiful, hold themselves proudly, as if to say: I may by now have been eaten by worms but see – my memory is immortal! No matter the grim or tragic circumstances of their demise, how comforting it must be to contemplate them captured at their best: to observe the blush on cheeks, to see in the set of a countenance some resemblance to extant kin.

By his own account Malcolm has written to the family regularly but only two letters have reached their destination: stormy weather has made the North Sea more treacherous than ever and wrecks are commonplace. Lady Hester regularly treats everyone – though now only the children and the maids feel obliged to listen – to the same reheated tidbits, from Malcolm's news:

> *There is little to match the Parisian salon for elegance. Conversation is at the highest level of sophistication and wit, and romantic intrigue is embarked upon at the doffing of a feathered hat or the snap of a fan.*

> *At the Comédie Française one can see plays by Poquelin and Racine, performed by the most dramatic of actors.*

> *The splendour of the court at Versailles is unparalleled. I hope one day to present my dear sister there.*

Each time her mother reads out this extract, Euphemie blushes and titters, and has to catch her breath, as if she has hastened through the Labyrinth of Versailles to a love tryst by a sparkling fountain. Madge and Aleen also croo their thrill, as if they too might one day join Euphemie at the French court.

The Ferry Fair

Like a woman who has spent hours, adding powder and beauty spots, bedecking her wig and gown with ribbons and bows, the town of Queensferry has been transformed. From one end of the main street to the other, stalls decorated with coloured streamers have been set up and all kinds of commodities are on sale, from staples to fripperies. Those who don't trust a cloudless sky to fulfil its promise have paid an extra four pound Scots for a covered stall.

The tempting aroma of freshly baked pastries overlays the salty pungence of the shoreline. Folk drift from one stall to another, pausing to browse, to peruse whatever takes their fancy, to haggle over the selling price. Children dart between the legs of the more leisurely adults in impromptu games of chase. Cats and dogs mooch around, keeping a keen eye, ear and nose on the activity around the meat and fish stalls. Tethered horses nod in the shade, tossing their manes from time to time to chase away the flies. Gulls wheel overhead, their cries somehow cheerful, as if they know that plenty scraps await when the day is done.

Madge and Aleen have been talking about the Ferry Fair for weeks, tempering their anticipation with scepticism: surely such an event can't live up to expectations? Queensferry is a thriving port and a hub for trade, with ferries transporting people, animals and supplies north and south, and a highway to the west. The town's cheesemakers, bakers and pastry cooks have been hard at work for days, preparing seasonal specialities, and fruitgrowers filling punnets with peaches and strawberries. But not only local vendors and victuallers hope to line their pockets. The fair was proclaimed in Kirkliston, Linlithgow and other nearby towns. All and sundry were invited to bring goods for sale.

Madge and Aleen push on through the press of people, enjoying the heat of the sun on their faces, casting a shrewd eye at what's on offer; comparing prices; admiring bonnets, plaids and petticoats.

There's Francie! says Aleen, waving in the direction of a covered stall where fish hang from hooks through open mouths and scales glint in the sunlight.

Could ye no have picked a spot nearer the ither end o the toun? says Madge, setting down her basket on Francie's table with relief. Mither Elspet's elderflooer wine disna turn my basket intae a feather pillow.

Aye but ye'll hae a lichter load on yir way hame, says Francie. Besides, we're in the thick o the traffic here. Naebody can miss us.

Seein is believin, says Madge. Now, Thomas, Anna, say guid day tae Maister Francie.

Guid day tae ye, says Thomas. Ye've caught mony fish. I can catch fish tae. Malcolm showed me how. I've caught bigger fish than thon. I've caught fish *this* big, he says, stretching his arms wide.

Weel, ye're a true fisherman tae be sure. Aye magnifyin the size o the catch!

It's true, says Thomas. I widna lee.

Tak the lad's word for it, says Madge. Or we'll niver get peace.

I hear ye, says Francie, winking.

He has sinewy brown forearms and the dry, salt-bleached curls and high colour of a man accustomed to being out in all weathers. His sleeves are rolled up to the elbows, his apron slick with slime. As he supplies fish to the estate, Sir Patrick has paid for the rental of the stall. In return, Francie will offer Madge's jelly and elderflower wine for sale, along with his catch of the day.

Anna is peering at the strange contents of a large dish of pearly shells.

Wid onybody care for an oyster? Beauties they are. Fresh as

they come.

Madge and Aleen don't have to be asked twice. They suck down the glistening knots of muscle then lick their lips.

Whit aboot the laddie? Or his sisters?

Thomas, Katharine and Anna decline Francie's offer firmly: their palates are not yet accustomed to all the curious fruits of the sea. A fish is one thing, a creature with a carapace another, but one without recognisable parts is flummoxing – what is the head, the body, the legs?

The weather has been settled and warm for days, the sky speedwell blue. Lessons at Netherstane are in recess. Zander Naysmith is visiting his sister in Peebles. Alasdair has joined Forbes Lightfoot and his father on a trip to Perthshire. Sir Patrick, ever keen to take advantage of the open road and attend to business in the city, has had John Barr drive him to Edinburgh, accompanied by Lady Hester and Euphemie, for whom a local fair couldn't possibly compete with the *divertissements* of the capital.

Katharine affects a measure of disinterest in the fair though it is evident that she has taken care over her appearance: her hair, recovered from the periwig maker's assault but nowhere near as long as it once was, sits on her shoulders in loose waves. She wears a butterscotch silk dress – a hand-me-down from Euphemie, two years her junior – and her treasured clove pink plaid. She has kept an eye out for moth holes and been assiduous in her darning.

Francie's stall is a stone's throw from the Hawes Inn. Nestled beneath a leafy hillock, the Hawes has the open, white-washed face of the best kind of country tavern despite its reputation as rough house. The full length of the town can be seen from the courtyard: the howffs and hovels, the churches, the manufactories and merchants' houses, the sliver of shingle beach, and, on such a clear day, the contours of the Fife coastline. And on this particular day the Hawes lays claim to a particular honour: it is the final stop for the Burraman.

In the courtyard, tradesmen raise their faces to the sun and their drinks to the holiday. In the shade of a flowering chestnut sit the burgesses, many already the worse for drink. Though the fair didn't officially open until noon, those upstanding members of the community had an early start. By command of the council, they were required to attend the baillies at seven in the morning and then proceed to ride the boundaries. Their civic duty done several hours ago, the burgesses are now a crass, unruly crew: spilling drink, roaring for replenishments, pissing haphazardly against the tavern walls.

So Francie, says Madge, whit's daein on the water these days?

No a great deal, says Francie.

Come now. Ye're no sayin that aw ye've clapped eyes on is a flicht o cormorant or a screech o gulls?

Perhaps so, perhaps no.

There's been talk, says Madge. A haill heap o talk aboot whit's been blawin up the firth.

I'm sure *you* dinna believe aw ye hear.

Unless I'm telt itherwise, I dae.

Francie grins but says nothing, and so Madge, with her master and mistress safely out of earshot, embarks on some loose talk about John Barr: it's been rumoured by Ross the groom – who got it from a pair of drystane dykers repairing a boundary wall between the Dalbinnie and Netherstane estates – that he's been seen driving a painted jade from the Cramond Brig Inn to the entrance to Lightfoot's estate, and on more than one occasion. John Barr swears foully and vociferously that no woman of any description set foot in Sir Patrick's coach – which he's as likely to refer to as *his* coach – on the days in question. But habituees of the Brig Inn say different. And, according to Madge, there's only one reason that sort of woman would be setting her heeled slipper on Lightfoot's Estate.

Ye may be richt, says Francie. And ye may be wrang.

I'm only sayin whit I heard, says Madge.

Once Katharine and Aleen have displayed the pots of jelly and jars of elderflower wine to Madge's satisfaction, they link arms and take themselves off on a tour of the stalls. They turn heads as they go, and attract seemly and unseemly comment. Katharine maintains an expression of noble perseverance, concentrating her mind on Jeremiah Skaill who, for all she knows, is at the other end of the earth. Not so, Aleen, who primps and giggles and casts her glance wide: she has no sweetheart, and can think of nothing more woeful than remaining unwed, like Madge, her whole life given over to service.

Madge would as soon Anna had run along with Thomas, who has wandered off on his own, but the bairn is daunted by the bustle and insists on staying close, transfixed by Francie's string of dead fish, reaching up when no-one's looking to stroke their silvery scales. Thomas relishes being in the thick of such a crowd; the sunshine has brought out a cheerfulness in all but the most curmudgeonly or infirm. The nearness of such bright-eyed young lasses is stirring enough but there's also the opportunity to indulge in another passion.

The very smell of books draws him. Half a dozen bookstalls have been set up and though the sellers would hardly offer a twelve-year-old choice titles for close inspection, he can glimpse amongst more modest publications a mottled leather cover, a spine embossed with gold leaf, an engraved frontispiece. When potential customers pause to make enquiries, by edging a little closer and listening hard, he gleans information on provenance of individual titles: *fresh in frae Amsterdam, prented in Leiden, Paris, Rome.*

The booksellers themselves are mostly unkempt, bespectacled men with inky fingers and unshaven chins who give the impression of being both scholarly and disreputable. Some regard him with disinterest – he has no money to buy books – others with suspicion, as if criminal intention were forever foremost in the minds of youngsters, and so he cannot linger as long as he might. At one stall, tended by a well-groomed man and a lively lass who move around each other with wordless ease, he is left to browse in peace. And to steal glances at the bookseller's daughter.

When a troupe of tumblers proclaims its arrival with fifes and drums, and puffs of dust, the lass claps her hands and begs permission to take time away from the stall to better see the entertainment.

As lang as ye dinna rin awa wi the raggle taggles, says the bookseller, and hands her a couple of coins.

So ye like tae read? she asks Thomas, who, without thinking, has fallen into step with her. They make their way towards an open patch of ground by the sea wall, where the troupe is gathering an audience before commencing its act.

Aye, says Thomas. And you?

I'd raither look at books wi pictures.

D'ye bide in the Ferry?

Linlithgow.

Is yir faither guid tae ye?

When he's guid, he's guid. When he's no, he's no as bad as some. And *your* faither?

The tumblers blast on their fifes again and kick up more dust.

The only other time Thomas has seen tumblers was when the elephant came to the Mercat Cross. It was a long time ago but the memory of the tumbling girls is sharp and clear: the jewel colours of their costumes, their tinkling bangles and bells, their cinnamon-coloured skin and dark, flashing eyes. *This* troupe does not resemble tumbling jewels: they are dusty and slipshod, and bungle several of their stunts though everybody around him, including the lass by his side, applauds heartily. When they pass a hat around, she drops in a coin.

Dae ye no care for the tumblers?

I've seen better, says Thomas. There wis an elephant forby.

A whit?

An elephant. A muckle great cratur wi a neb as lang as my airm.

Ye tell a lee.

It's the truth, I tell ye. Yir faither may hae a picture o an elephant in ane o his books, says Thomas. It's a mairvel!

But ye didna like the tumblers, she says, her voice dull with disappointment.

It disna maitter whether I did or didna. *You* liked them. That's whit maitters. I'm Thomas. And *you* are?

The lass gives him a drab look. Ye dinna need tae ken, she says, and turns away.

No sooner have the tumblers taken what coin they can than they move on down the street, blaring on their fifes, to find another spot and set up anew. Next to claim the audience's attention is a trio of travelling actors, in battered hats and horsehair periwigs. They present brief, satirical sketches about the deposed King, his allegiance to the church of Rome and the court of Versailles. They are slick and snake-tongued, their dialogue larded with viciousness, innuendo and downright obscenity. They prompt cheers and jeers and a few anxious frowns.

With arms folded tightly across his chest, Thomas stares fixedly at the actors but sees little of their performance, blinded as he is by a roil of shame and rage. The bookseller's lass liked him, he could tell: she was pleased that he followed her rather than annoyed. And he liked her – he still likes her – but now, due to some inconsequential thing he said, she won't even tell him her name. How could that be? How could it matter that he said he didn't care for the tumblers? With a hot prickle of shame, he drags his heels back to Francie's stall. The day has lost its shine.

The heat has made Katharine and Aleen thirsty and so they make their way back to Francie's stall, hoping that Madge will have saved them a drop of wine. In their absence, a makeshift table fashioned from reeds and branches has been set up to display a range of linen items. Behind the table, three women in plain caps and sober pinafores are busy with needles and thread. They appear ill at ease and make little attempt to attract sales.

Yon's lovely work, says Katharine, picking up a handkerchief, embroidered with tulips and edged with bobbin lace.

Aleen, who has little interest in embroidery, returns to the fish stall where she proceeds to relate to Madge, Francie and Anna every last detail of what and more to the point *whom* she and Katharine have seen on their perambulation. Aleen prattles and halfway through her interminable account, Madge excuses herself and, taking Anna by the hand, makes her way over to join Katharine at the embroidery stall, leaving Francie to provide an ear.

Two pound, says the older woman. Two pound one. Three pound two.

Ye'd get a better price in the city, says Katharine. She should know: Obadiah Skaill was – and likely still is – one of the chief importers of Dutch and Flemish linen. Similar pieces were displayed about his handsome house.

The older woman has a high, broad forehead and a steady gaze. The younger women have smooth complexions, soft lips and clear eyes. Bonny, very bonny, even with most of their yellow hair hidden beneath cotton caps.

Anna holds a piece of lace work up to her face and squints through a tracery of holes at the water.

Are ye Dutch? Netherlandish? Madge asks the women.

Two pound one. Three pound two.

Ye'll haveta learn the lingo, Madge says to the women, if ye wish tae mak ends meet. And whit are ye askin for yon cap? Dinna be gien me a price for twa, now. I've only ane heid!

When Thomas returns to the fish stall the women are slaking their thirst and Francie is sluicing his remaining fish in a pail of seawater.

Yon fish stink, he complains.

So wid ye, says Francie, if ye'd been deid since dawn!

Did ye see the tumblers? says Aleen. Were they no braw?

I saw them, says Thomas. They werena braw at aw.

Dear, dear, says Madge, somebody's oot o sorts!

I'm no, says Thomas, I'm no! but his fierce denial is lost in a loud cheer from the Hawes Inn.

Flanked by a brace of pipers, a stiff, queer figure approaches.

He is covered from head to toe in burrs and walks splay-legged, as if beneath his prickly exterior he is stuffed with hay rather than flesh and bone, muscle and sinew. Anna shrieks and hides behind Katharine.

It's only the Burraman, says Madge. He's blessin the toun. Tae keep us aw safe frae evil.

How can a walkin fricht-the-craw keep onybody safe? scoffs Thomas.

On accoont o he's the scourge o the deil.

But why wid the deil be feart o a mannie covered in burrs?

Wha kens, says Francie. But by the time the Burraman's drunk his way roond the toun, he'll be a richt fearsome sicht.

It's aw nonsense, says Thomas.

The merrymakers converge and buzz around the Burraman. Burgesses vie to ply him with drink which he can only consume by means of a reed straw. Children dare each other to reach out and touch him but none dares: a scourge of the devil is a force to be reckoned with. In the fuffle caused by the Burraman and his entourage passing Francie's stall, the lacemaking women pack up their unsold wares and make off along the main street in advance of the procession. Anna is first to notice their absence.

They didna say fareweel, says Anna.

Perhaps they didna ken how tae say it in oor tongue, says Madge.

It is time, in Madge's estimation, to start back. Aleen is loath to forego the dancing which is just getting underway on the green. She begs to remain a while longer and Katharine, though she'd as soon make tracks, agrees to keep her company. Madge is not a vindictive woman, nor the sort to thwart another's hopes of happiness but with all the merry-making, she couldn't possibly allow young women to find their own way home. Ever eager to please, Francie offers to accompany the lasses home.

It wid be my pleasure, he says.

It's a lang trek for ye, there and back.

Whit better way tae spend a summer's evenin than in the company o twa bonny lasses.

Ye'll haveta curtail yir tipplin.

Aw tae the guid, he says, if I'm tae be oot on the water first thing the morn.

They've tae be hame afore midnicht.

I hear ye, says Francie.

Madge, ye're a darlin, says Aleen. I'll mak it up tae ye. I'll muck oot the henhoose. I'll scrub the pots for a week—

We'll see, says Madge.

Madge, Thomas and Anna make their way along the main street, keeping their distance from the Burraman and his entourage. Some of the stalls have already been dismantled, including, Thomas sees with a jolt of disappointment, the bookstall where he met the russet-headed lass. Kinder now, he takes Anna's hot hand. As they pass the Bellstane harbour, the tide, as it retreats from the shingle, patters like genteel applause.

Once they leave the town behind, the noise of merrymaking fades though the strains of the pipes continue to follow them on their long, slow journey home. The air is balmy and sweet-smelling, the sky lilac with pink lozenges of cloud. Anna is still grizzling about the Burraman.

He's jist an ilkaday chiel, says Thomas. Until he puts on his costume. Just like Francie or Maister Naysmith, or John Barr. Perhaps Francie will be the Burraman next year. Ye widna be feart if it wis Francie, wid ye?

I'd be feart o John Barr, Anna replies. Or Maister Naysmith.

But they're no tounsmen, says Madge. Only Francie's a tounsman. Only Francie could be a Burraman.

I'd no be feart o Francie, Anna says. If I kenned it wis Francie.

But ye canna ken first, says Madge, or the spell disna work.

When they eventually arrive at the entrance to the estate the lush foliage darkens the path and clouds of midges swirl around their heads. It is the time owls begin to hunt and deer come down from the hills, to strip saplings of new growth.

Enchanted by the uncanny effects of the light, Anna stops and peers deep into the woods.

Look! she whispers. There! Atween the birks!

The birches are chalk-white, with slender trunks; their leaves flitter. It will not be completely dark for an hour or two but in the long summer gloaming the eyes can deceive.

Whit is it, bairn?

The sewin ladies.

Where? says Thomas.

They were ower there, says Anna, pointing straight ahead. They've gone now.

Surely they canna have been and gone as quick as aw that, says Madge.

They were rinnin, says Anna. Fleet as deer.

They could be fugitives, says Thomas.

Or figments o the lass's imagination.

A Game of Hell

Glorious my arse! says Sir Patrick, thumping his glass on the table and setting the many candles in the room aquiver. As if a Stadtholder o the Low Countries has ony richt tae the Croun.

And oor James incumbent on the hospitality o the King o France, says Lightfoot, from the head of his own sumptuous table.

Wha'd choose tae be indebted tae such a skittish monarch?

Or subject tae the whim o ane.

An indignity.

It's a mercy, mind, that he can still practise his faith. It wid be a sad day when a crounit King couldna practise his faith.

Ower the water, or itherwise.

Sensing controversy brewing, Lady Mary signals to her housekeeper for more dishes to be brought to the table.

Nae maitter he's a Catholic?

Nane at aw.

It's a sin agin God if a King canna practise his ain faith withoot fear o reprisal.

Nae cause tae bring God intae the talk. There's nae men o the claith at the table!

This last retort raises guffaws and renewed quaffing of Lightfoot's claret.

There's nae mony guid men o the claith in the kirks forby, says Sir Patrick. I hear frae my coachman that the minister o Duddingston Kirk wis thrawn oot. Taen pity on the man, the parishioners let him pack a bag and quit the manse unharmed. Then, on the highway he wis set upon wi staffs and cudgels and left for deid.

By the parishioners?

No, no. By fanatical Cameronians, accordin tae John Barr, and the man has a grand recall for whit's reported in the Sheep

Heid.

Some say the minister took shelter in a priesthole then set sail for France. Ithers that he's biding his time until the wind changes. Wheniver that might be.

We'll need tae inspect oor priestholes, says Lightfoot. Wha kens how mony outed ministers we might find!

Laughter ripples round the table, causing the candleflames to dance and shadows to play on the faces of the diners.

Whit happened tae the minister's woman? asks Thomas, his voice see-sawing between a boy's pitch and a man's.

Wha kens? says Sir Patrick. Why d'ye ask aboot the minister's woman when the man wis beaten wi staffs and cudgels?

The minister is oor uncle, says Thomas, but his woman has mair Christian charity in her.

Bessie Begg gied us kebbock, says Anna. And beets and peas.

I'd hope it tae! says Lady Hester. And talkin o food, she continues, in a somewhat brittle tone, I hear the French King has the maist marvellous dinners. As well as the quintessence o entertainments, wi musicians at his beck and ca' frae dawn till dusk. Even on the hunt, the royal trumpeters follow the King on horseback, tralooin as they gang.

My dear, says Sir Patrick, there's mair tae bein heid o state than makkin music.

Indeed, she continues, jewels glinting in the shivering candlelight, décolletage as moist as the slices of roast swan on her plate, King Louis is ower fond o dancing forby. At Versailles, I hear he has his ain ballet maister tae instruct him in pliés, jetés and arabesques for an hour ilka morn, and then there's boating on the lake in a Venetian gondola – how splendid tae ride in a gondola! she continues breathlessly, in the hope that an unbroken gush of verbiage will forestall the conversation sinking into the gloom and tedium of political debate.

Lady Mary surveys her table and continues eating. She too appreciates a fine piece of swan. And of partridge, pigeon and quail. She considered serving peacock this evening; when presented complete with head and tail it does make a fetching centre-piece. But this is not the occasion for such ostentation.

Though it's a dreich April night with rain battering against the windows, the curtains are thick and the dining room cosy and well-lit. The glass and silverware gleam. Lady Mary basks plumply in her role of hostess and wife. Her husband would rather have a woman with meat on her bones than a scrawny old boiling fowl. This evening, before taking his seat at the head of the table, he demonstrated his enduring fondness for his wife's ample dimensions by cupping her breasts and putting each in turn to his lips. This prompted uproarious appreciation from the dinner guests and set a jolly tone for the evening.

Lady Mary finds such public display of cupidity more flattering than demeaning: how many wives could lay claim to excite her man's carnal desire after twenty years of marriage? If on occasion he seeks out other amusements, far be it for her to concern herself over any such peccadillos. She is content with her lot: if she can sit down each mid-day and evening to a good meal, she has little complaint. She has birthed two hale sons and two fair daughters and considers she has done her wifely duty.

The only children present are her own and the orphans. She has placed her daughters, Rhona and Mysie, midway down the table, one on either side, and directly beneath the Italian chandelier which casts a golden glow on their fresh, open faces. Euphemie sits next to Rhona, and Katharine, with her dark charm, next to Mysie. Euphemie, as voluble as her mother – and as lavishly attired – is holding forth, as much for the lads further down the table as for her immediate neighbours.

As for the older lads, Forbes, Alasdair and Thomas, her husband has been plying them with wine and already they are flush-faced, gluttonous and loose-tongued. Colin, her youngest, and the orphan Anna, who has barely touched her plate, are showing signs of tiredness: drooping heads, slack pouts. She would have had the servants tend to the bairns in the kitchen but her husband believes in accustoming children to adult company as soon as they can sit at the table, no matter how reckless and indiscreet the company might turn out to be.

The arrival of William of Holland may be no cause for celebration but rather than brood over bad news, Bryce Lightfoot has thrown a supper party for a number of men in the area whose sympathies, religious and political, lie with the exiled James. At least he believes this is the case, but if he is mistaken it does no harm to know one's enemies as well as one's friends. Tomorrow, or the next day, or perhaps the day after that, he and those who share his sympathies will begin to hatch plans; tonight is for eating, drinking and making merry.

Lady Hester wholeheartedly approves of Lightfoot's hedonism: life must go on and it might as well go on comfortably. She enjoys a good supper party: it's an occasion to display her jewels and her velvet gown before fashion, if not the capricious weather, demands that she don less sumptuous fabrics. Besides, Euphemie is at an age when she should be demonstrating her charms in the right circles. It is a pity Lightfoot insisted they bring the orphans. She would have happily left all of them at home to be fed by Madge. But their host is adamant that the more young minds know of the folly being perpetrated at Westminster, the better it bodes for the future of their ilk.

When it comes to strategy, Thomas is more likely to waste time on debating the whys or wherefores of a situation than pledging himself to any cause. The lad will never let a thing lie and why her husband indulges him as he does is beyond her. Nocht wrang wi an inquiring mind, he says, as lang as thochts dinna turn tae deeds. But there's the rub; thoughts do turn into deeds. And if thoughts turn into deeds and trouble were to break out close to home, to what useful purpose might Katharine and Anna be put? Surely more women around means more folk to be defended against marauders?

As for her own children, Euphemie needs to be thinking of making a match, not worrying her head over matters of state. Skellum that he is, Alasdair will always be her favourite; he may lack Thomas's intellectual acuity but does he ever question his parents? He does not, and that's why, as she keeps saying, he's altogether as good a son as Malcolm, who is still studying in

France and, it would appear, still attempting to gain access to court. She has not received a letter in many months and even though she hangs on Malcolm's every word, she has to admit – if only to herself – that all he relates about the court is second-hand: *He has heard tell… People say… Rumour has it…* But has he ever witnessed anything of note with his own eyes?

She wonders, too, what kind of a man will return in the place of the steady, warm-hearted lad who went off waving until the coach was round the bend in the track. Will he begin to disdain all things not French? Will he sing the praises of its women over his own mother and sister? Will he favourably compare their beauty, wit, accomplishments, sagacity – as if sagacity matters – to that of his own mother and sister? Will she and Euphemie become a source of chagrin *when* – she will not say *if* – he eventually returns from France? She misses Malcolm's calm containment, his sweet habit of kissing her hand while looking deeply into her eyes. Her eyes glaze with fond tears at the memory, but the table has been cleared of the meats and the desserts are on their way.

Patrick Aikenhead is not a Catholic, like James Stuart, but has no truck with being told how to worship by anyone: religious observance is one thing, life another, and he has precious little time for the Kirk's avid intrusion into the private lives of the populace. On the night after the beaching of the baleen whale, when only he and Lightfoot remained on the shore, a black-coated clergyman appeared on the strand. He marched right up to them, then, quoting copiously from the bible, launched into a tirade about their drinking and singing of bawdy ballads. The bawdier the better, is Sir Patrick's opinion: who wants to sing about lost love and lost battles, about shipwrecks and drownings, storms and hauntings, about lives cut down in the first flower of youth, when you can sing about a buxom wench raising her skirts with a smile on her face? Lightfoot was for gentle remonstrance but no, he sent the sanctimonious anatomy packing with a kick in the arse and a warning to mind whose feathers he ruffled.

After the French macaroons, the fruit fools, the jumballs and candied rosemary have been served and all the men have taken brandy in the drawing room, about half the men and all the women depart. Lightfoot's groom is at hand to ensure that guests are secure on mounts or safely inside carriages before they set off into the night. John Barr, who has spent the evening in the stables with bread and ale and an ample portion of estate gossip, is charged to escort Lady Hester home, along with Anna, Katharine and Euphemie. Alasdair and Thomas have been invited to stay over. Sir Patrick tells his wife not to wait up for him. Noisy farewells echo round the courtyard. The rain has stopped and the moon is round and bright as a new florin.

Restless in adult company and reckless after wine, Forbes persuades Alasdair and Thomas that they should try some night hunting. Lady Mary protests, afraid that in such an inebriated state they might do themselves a mischief but her husband airily dismisses her fears and hands over the keys to the gunroom: young lads need escapades to keep their blood up. The remaining guests, all men by this point, gather round the gaming table. Lady Mary instructs the servants as to what should be saved of the leftovers, what they may eat and what should be thrown to the dogs, or the hens. She would as soon all the guests had left by now but knows better than to cross her husband when he's in his cups, so graciously bids the company goodnight and retires.

Lately Thomas has been invited more often to join Forbes and Alasdair in their exploits. They claim his bookishness amuses them. Though Thomas suspects there is more behind their new-found camaraderie he does not mind why they choose to include him. He is hungry for the company of boys his own age. Though he has made the acquaintance of some lads on the estate, his privileged position of residing at the big hoose is a barrier to any real closeness. Besides, estate boys his age are already doing the jobs of grown men while he is still at his books.

The air is fresh and clear after the rain. In the distance, waves swoosh against the shore. Due to dense foliage and a carpet of leaf mulch, the woods are dry underfoot, though drips splash down from the trees and startle them.

Shhhhh! says Forbes, we'll nae catch a thing if ye dinna hush up!

Whit if we see a wolf? says Thomas.

There's nae mair wolves, says Forbes. They're aw deid.

That's whit they say, says Thomas, but whit if they're wrang?

If we see ane, we'll shoot it, says Forbes. And thraw it tae the dugs.

But whit if there's a pack o them? We couldna shoot a haill pack.

Shh, says Alasdair, shhhh. Can ye hear howlin? And somethin movin through the brush? Look, Thomas, look! I think it's a wolf!

Where? says Thomas, spinning round and accidentally discharging the gun.

The shot ringing through the darkness is followed by Alasdair's peals of laughter.

Fooled ye! he says. Fooled ye.

The servants eat in the kitchen once the mistress is safely upstairs. They fill their bellies with the scraps allotted them and purloin a few choice morsels as well. They drain what remains in several flagons of wine before feeding the dogs and the hens. In the drawing room, the men continue to play cards and avail themselves of the decanter. When the dogs have stopped barking, and the servants ceased clattering pots and ashets, and are bedded down for the night, Lightfoot, with exaggerated appeals for hush, invites his remaining guests to follow him through his office door and make their unsteady way to the back of the house and into the cellars.

In the grounds, the three lads careen around, pausing to steady each other whenever a twig snaps or urgent scrabbling disturbs the undergrowth but the only wildlife they encounter is a pair of mating frogs, their four eyes gleaming like gold buttons in the moonlight. At first they are entertained by their own erratic progress and aiming at imaginary targets but after a while Forbes and Alasdair grow bored: they need event, incident. Thomas is surprised by their lack of patience: doesn't a good hunter know how to stop still and wait?

Where's aw the rabbits? says Forbes. I'm for bed.

Aye, says Alasdair. Where's aw the rabbits?

The deid wolf has eaten them aw!

They retrace their steps to the edge of the wood. On the far side of the lawn, the house stands, large and dark.

When the thud of their footsteps has faded, Thomas remains alone on the damp lawn, gazing at the sky. The moon is startling in its brightness. His head has cleared and he no longer feels inclined to sleep. He picks his way round the exterior of the house, mulling over the conversations at dinner. Could a king really have direct communication with God? And if so, wouldn't God be consistent in the mode of worship he preferred? Could a Protestant and a Catholic king both lay claim to having direct access to the divine?

At the back of the house, the air is rich with smells from the kitchen, the stables, the henhouse, doocot, the alehouse. The horses snuffle, shifting straw crackles, the groom snores. From the cellar come faint but distinct whoops and guffaws. They are followed by cracks, groans and shrieks, as if folk are engaged in some riotous game that elicits both pleasure and pain. What kind of game of hell has folk whooping one minute and shrieking the next? And who punishes wrongdoers or madmen in the dead of night?

Part Three

Bajans and Billiard Halls

The bajans stream through the gates and settle in a loose skein against the wall. They have just completed their first morning as students at the College of Edinburgh and survey the city laid out before them with greedy eyes.

I dinna ken aboot *you*, says Thomas to the lad next to him, but my heid fair pains me frae such a superabundance o the Latin. Readin and writin is aw weel and guid but haein tae converse in it at aw times is wearisome.

Quod me nutrit me destruit. We should be speakin in the Latin still, my freend. Have ye no acquainted yirsel wi the regulations? Inside and oot o class students are tae converse solely in the Latin... Quintegernus Craig, says the lad, offering his hand. But for ilkaday occasions I go by Mungo.

Mungo Craig? The same as had lessons wi auld Bernard Armour?

In name at ony rate.

I didna recognise ye!

Naw? I kent *you* straightaway. Nae mistakin yir vauntie swagger.

It's jubilation maks me swagger, man... I didna think on meetin ye here.

Aye weel, ye learn somethin new ilka day.

How richt ye be. I hope that this time we shall become freends. I hope, tae, that we can dispense wi the Latin when we're oot o earshot o professors and regents.

Ah, Tam, there's lugs at ilka wa. This verra wa, at this verra moment, has fowerscore o young lugs eager for whitiver intelligence they can garner. And some willna concur wi yir sentiments.

Propped against the wall are forty-odd young men: each is taking the measure of the other; noting who exudes an air of confidence; who has the ear of whom; who is well-dressed, whose heavily patched garments speak of subsidies and scholarships; whose attention lies beyond the college gates and their own inchoate community.

But Latin at aw times? We're no Romans. For readin and writin I grant the advantage but a man should be free tae speak in a manner felicitous tae his ain hert. We are here tae learn mair, no tae abandon whit we've already maistered.

Ye were aye a blether, Tam. And now, I note, the owner o an incendiary tongue.

No in the least. I widna set a match tae the beliefs o ithers jist tae see them burn.

Is that a fact? Wid ye pit a wager on it?

I'm no a wagerin man. My faither—

Aye. Yir faither.

Mungo Craig is a stunted youth, with a pocked complexion and eyes which flicker like dismal fish. By contrast, Thomas is tall and dark-haired, with what his sisters enviously call a strawberries-and-cream complexion, and glitter-eyed, as if all he sees before him is a new-minted marvel.

Whit'll we dae for meat? says Craig.

I hadna thocht on it.

Shall we treat oorsels tae a tuppenny dinner and a game o billiards?

The ancients, says Thomas, believed a man has as much need o sport as he has o exercisin his mind.

The ancients believed that God dwelt in a cave and disguised hissel as a swan.

Should we invite some classmates tae join us?

Craig strokes a chin from which sprouts a clump of colourless whiskers. He surveys the bajans; gaze settling on none; taking note of all.

Is it no wiser tae refrain frae profferin the haund o freendship ower hasty than be compelled tae withdraw it at a later date?

I havena pondered upon the subject, says Thomas, but as ye've raised the question, I commit tae gien it due consideration.

A wise decision, says Craig.

Although, on the subject o choosin one's freends, is it reliable tae judge a man by appearances? Wid that no increase the likelihood o misconstruance? Are we no ower apt tae mak hasty assumptions based on insufficient evidence?

Ye talk like an advocate, man. Aw prevarication and qualification.

Craig draws himself up to his full, if inconsequential, height. Imitating the rasp of their old dominie, he addresses the line of bajans relaxing against the wall:

Question Twenty Two: How did Christ, being the Son of God, become Man?

As if a shot had been fired into a flock of pigeons, the bajans take off in a flurry and disperse themselves over the High Street.

Ha! says Thomas. Ye'd think they aw had auld Armour for dominie.

Their day of study is nowhere near done. When they return from the dinner break, the regent will examine them on what they have learned from morning lectures and who performs well on an empty belly?

Tempus fugit, says Craig, linking arms with Thomas and ushering him in the direction of the Canongate. Thomas feels a flush of pleasure. He has just matriculated as a student at the College of Edinburgh. He has been set up in his own lodgings, thanks to Sir Patrick's financial support. The September sun streams down the High Street from the Castle at the head to the Palace at the foot.

Are there nae college rules forbiddin students tae enter the taverns? says Thomas.

I expect there are rules tae prevent us pissin and shittin. But where else is a man tae eat?

If we're caught, we'll be punished.

We've already brak ane rule by neglectin the Latin, says Craig, we might as weel brek anither.

Hanged for a sheep as a lamb.

Or thrashed for ane.

I've heard tell, says Thomas, that Cunningham is a hard taskmaster.

I willna tolerate a public thrashin. I will refuse it! If need be, my parents will intervene on my behalf.

That's guid assurance.

Thomas does not remember Mungo Craig's parents but the weals on his calves were not caused by the dominie; Armour might have made plenty song and dance about thrashing delinquents but he never struck bare skin and his stroke was light.

Aye, says Craig. We're bajans and shouldna be subjected tae bodily degradation at the haunds o regents. And you, Tam? If ye're hauled oot for a thrashing, wid yir faither or mither intervene on yir behalf?

They couldna. They are in thir graves.

So they are. But have they no been mert for years? Ye'll be ower grievin, surely.

I miss them still. There's scarce a day when—

So Tam's a poor wee orphan laddie – a bursary boy? Wi guid connections?

I am greatly fortunate tae hae this opportunity tae expand my mind.

Is yon the reason ye're at the college, Tam, tae expand yir mind?

I hope tae find employment after laureation but the opportunity tae reach an understanding o the world we live in is my prime objective.

Mercy, says Craig. Are ye no a chiel o exceeding high principles, no tae mention a lang-winded turn o phrase? A guid position is my chief goal. I'll dae whit's required and keep oot o mischief. In the meantime, stew and ale. *Fabas indulcet fabes*.

Lucky McCloud's is down a steep wynd leading to the Nor' Loch. Thomas hasn't been in an Edinburgh tavern since the days when his mother sent him to fetch his father home. On occasion, after an interminable wait in the reek and clamour, his father might grudgingly consent to stumble home with him. More often than not he'd refuse to budge, and box Thomas's ears for his persistence. But his father is dead and Thomas, at fourteen, is no longer a child.

Above the door, a sign depicting a pair of jolly, periwigged advocates creaks and sways in the breeze, giving the impression that the painted figures with drinks in hand are toasting each other. As they make to enter the tavern a beggar woman insinuates herself between them and the threshold, and thrusts out a dirty hand. Poverty has made its marks on her, not to mention the scourge, but beneath old scars, ingrained grime and fresh lesions are remnants of ruined beauty. She gives none of the usual rigmarole about how honest and God-fearing she is, how never in this life has she committed a sin in the eyes of the Lord, how misfortune has been cast upon her to test the charity of others and so on and so forth. She says nothing at all at first, just shifts her gaze from one face to the other and her weight from one bare foot to another, then intones in a cracked voice: *As fire consumes the wood, as flames do mountains set on fire! Chase and affright them with the storm and tempest of thine ire!* and Thomas remembers her shock of white hair and her fierce, dark stare: she's the Sweet Singer of Borrowstounness who screamed those very words at him before the dragoon kicked her back into that sorry, straggling line on its way to the House of Correction.

Here, says Craig, handing her a merk. Now shift yirsel.

Thomas fishes in his purse. Only the other day he took possession of his allowance and feels magnanimous. Craig stays his hand.

I've gien sufficient. Mair and the wretch will become emboldened by greed. He turns to the woman. I've gien once, he says, and willna gie again, sae mind my face. If we cross paths anither time, keep yir distance.

She nods and scuttles off, ragged skirts brushing against the walls of the narrow wynd.

The tavern crackles with supping and jawing and conviviality: merchants and burghers, garbed in expensive, imported fabrics, recount tales of travel and business; chirurgeons and physicks demonstrate new tools and devices; advocates expound the intricacies of recent court cases; goldsmiths and hammermen, their cheeks and aprons gleaming with metallic dust, exchange talk of trade.

The tavern-keeper, Ishbel McCloud, is tall and lean, with the narrow, shaggy head of a wolfhound and an unwavering, inquisitional glare. Between serving drinks, she ladles mutton stew into bowls from the kettle simmering on the hob.

Will she no ken us for students and turf us oot?

No fear, says Craig. Lucky McCloud kens whit side her breid is buttered on. The students o today are the physicks and advocates o the morrow.

And the preachers tae. I've heard tell that since the Glorious Revolution, the kirk has a great need o new preachers.

That's as may be. But mair than maist, a man o the claith must mind whit way the wind blaws.

Thomas does not challenge the point. He has mixed feelings about the fate of ministers.

This is where the real education taks place, says Craig. This is where they aw come, sooner or later.

Where *wha* comes?

The firebrands. Demagogues. When John Toland studied in this city, McCloud's wis his chosen hostelry. And for guid reason. Aw manner o topics are chewed ower on these premises. Look aboot ye. Whit d'ye see?

I see a roomfu o chiels at thir bit and sup. Whit mair should I be seein?

Ah weel, says Craig, I mustna be pittin ideas in young Tam's heid, for fear he might act upon them.

Whit use are ideas if they remain unvoiced?

Some ideas are best concealed in the dark nooks o the cerebellum.

When I wis a bairn puzzlin ower a conundrum, says

Thomas, my faither wid say an idea wis aye better oot than in. Mither and Katharine were less convinced but Anna—

Ye're nae langer a bairn, Tam. Nor yet a man, unless I'm mistaken. Ye're a hobbledehoy, Tam, a bajan and a hobbledehoy!

As they push through the close-packed bodies, Thomas recognises one or two faces he hasn't seen since his parents were alive, including that of Archibald Pitcairne. The man has grown stouter and ruddier of complexion and his attire is more ornate and ostentatious: satin and lace, velvet and damask, pearl buttons in serried rows. He is holding forth to a cluster of advocates who hang on his every quip, and titter or bray when occasion demands.

Craig hands Thomas a tankard of ale and drinks deep from his own.

Yir health. I see ye've spied oor celebrated Doctor. Lately returned from Leiden, on accoont o a woman! Jacobite, Episcopalian, worse – *atheist*, if whit's said on the street is true.

I mind him as a generous man.

In his cups ony man is generous. And Pitcairne is mair in his cups than oot o them.

He wis a customer o my faither's. He has a kind hert.

Ony man has a kind hert tae those he favours.

I'm sorry ye disapprove o him.

Awa! How could I disapprove o ane whose acquaintance I've yet tae mak?

Then let me introduce ye! *Carpe diem.*

Anither time, Tam. *Festina lente.* We're here for meat. And billiards, at which I intend tae troonce ye!

After a hearty bowl of stew, which both declare to be as good as their mothers ever made, they take their ale through to the billiard room.

Anither rule brak afore oor first day as bajans is oot, says Craig. With a thin, lopsided smile, he reveals a set of small, pointed teeth.

Indeed, says Thomas. And wha kens where oor already lang acquaintance will tak us?

Climbers on a Stair

By Gassman the Goldsmith's shop at the head of St Mary's Wynd
November 1692

My Dearest Sisters,
   The nights being long in this season, I venture abroad and return home in the dark but the scant daylight makes our dinner break all the more delightful as we can step into the light. When we have the funds, Mungo Craig and I hasten to Lucky McCloud's where we have become regular if not extravagant customers. If you recall the name you'll mind Craig was no friend in my schooldays but time and circumstance has changed us both. Now he goes out of his way to enhance our acquaintance; it would be churlish to rebuff him.

   In these winter months I am spending more on coal and lamp oil and am grateful for my woollen coat. During these last weeks I have rarely gone over the door without it. I must write to Sir Patrick and thank him again for such a useful gift. I am well set up on the top floor of a respectable land, hard by the Netherbow. It is novel to be a climber on the stair rather than living at street level and my new neighbours are admirable folk. Directly beneath my garret is an outlandish fellow from Holland, a man brimful of new ideas for manufactory and a most ingenious and hardworking individual. I hear him tapping away at his models when I am burning the midnight oil and find it comforting to know that I am not the only soul awake at such an hour.

   Others with whom I have a passing acquaintance include a writer to the signet, a goldsmith whose workshop is on the street level, a sober hammerman, his wife and their brood of shock-headed bairns. In spite of limited means, this is a family which laughs more than it greets. When I am in low spirits – which, be assured, is rare – I think that, had our own faither been of a more sober disposition we might not have become the sorry orphans we are. Though we are told that all is the Lord's will and we cannot but accept it, I wonder why He would deprive bairns first of their faither and then of their mither if He truly wished them to thrive. That He might wish any bairn not to thrive is a matter on which I still ponder.

Such thoughts aside, I consider myself extremely fortunate at this period in my life. With the help of some new acquaintances, in particular Mungo Craig, who has become as willing and obliging a confidant as one might hope for, I am learning to manage my living expenses and eke out my allowance so a little remains for entertainment. Earlier in the autumn, when the weather was still mild and there were more hours of daylight, a man called Beck put up a concert of music which I was fortunate enough to attend, thanks to an invitation from Doctor Pitcairne, who is also a resident of the Tron Parish. By the bye, he tells me that his wife's family and that of our late mother are connected!

The doctor is heartier and more outspoken than ever – with a big voice, a big wig and a big purse! I am fortunate to be acquainted with a man who proves that wearing one's erudition lightly can be as instructive as any solemn lecture.

The concert to which I accompanied him – his wife was indisposed that afternoon – was a most diverting counterpoint to my studies. Observing the audience alone might have been entertainment enough! Many were in extravagant garb, despite endless remonstrations from the pulpit equating sober attire with godliness and frills and fancies with an errant soul. To expend energy on the merits or demerits of apparel, or any other outward show, is needless. Fallaces sunt rerum species: the appearance of things is indeed deceptive, as any thinking person must realise.

There was great glee surrounding the erection of the musical concert. When the man Beck requested permission to set it up, the Master of the Revels pursued him for a hefty licence fee. The council, to its credit, rejected the Master of the Revels's right to the said fee, declaring firstly that his licensing powers extended only to 'plays and gaming and the like', and secondly claiming the man used the fees to fill his own purse. In short, he failed to attend to the reason for his *having the licence in the first place, which is to restrain immorality. Where, you might ask, could a man find immorality in music? And I would reply: if it's in a man's mind to find a thing, he will seek it out and convince himself he beholds it, when in truth all he beholds is his own fancy. It is high time that such a rank monopolist as the Master of the Revels be held to account.*

But to the concert itself. I enjoyed the music greatly though would struggle to recall its composer or the style of tunes presented. I have an untrained ear but found its lilt most transporting and easeful. When the music was done and the audience put its hands together I felt my spirits wonderfully lifted. Dr Pitcairne declared the music was no match to the compositions of a Mr Henry Purcell, whose work he'd heard in London and whose vocal melodies brought tears of joy and sadness to his eyes. He was most enamoured of a piece in which Dido, after falling on Aeneas's sword, begs him to remember her but forget her fate. The good doctor even sang the refrain, though his bass voice and portly frame made it hard to envisage the tragic queen of Carthage! He is adamant, however, that given the present turn of the Kirk, we should be thankful for any music at all.

I will conclude by saying what I intended to say straight away, viz. that I miss you both terribly. I hope and pray that things go well with you.

Your loving brother, Thomas

The Blue Firth

Now there's a bonny jade, says Mungo Craig. Her wi the fern green plaid and the chestnut hair.

Aye, says John Potter. Braw. Whit say ye, Middleton?

Dinna ask Middleton, says Adam Mitchell. A lass wid tak ane keek at him, pick up her skirts and mak for the hills.

And once she'd got tae the hills, says Potter, like as no she'd choose a rag-tag hill preacher ower Middleton.

And why wid that be? says Patrick Middleton, straightening up to his full height and towering over his classmates. Why wid I scare a lass awa?

Ye're ower lang and ower lugubrious. A lass widna wish tae crick her neck tae spy yir gloomy phiz.

The Lord made me as I am, says Middleton, uttering each word as if it cost him.

That He did, says Mitchell, and it's the cross ye haveta bear.

It's nae a burden, says Middleton, it's a blessin. I can see things ithers canna. Like the taps o yir heids and the louses lowpin!

At the head of College Wynd, Thomas and a handful of classmates idle against the wall and watch the world go by, in particular the young women who, freed from domestic chores, are taking the air, and making the most of the longer summer hours of daylight and the mild temperature. At the foot of the High Street, behind the palace of Holyrood, the firth is a bar of intense, cobalt blue.

Whit a heavenly hue, says Thomas. Ye could lose yirsel in the depths o it.

I could lose mysel in the folds o yon lass's skirts, says John Potter. Her there, wi the tilt tae her chin and the spring in her step.

Potter is slight and slope-shouldered. An incorrigible nail

biter, the indeterminate features of his face are half-obscured by his hands.

Ye widna ken where tae pit yirsel, Potter, says stocky, block-headed Mitchell. Ye could ask, mind, if she'd let ye. Fortune favours the brave. *Carpe noctem*!

The colour blue, Thomas interjects, signifies eternity. It is revered by maist religions o the world.

Now why wid we concern oorsels wi religion, says Mitchell, when we've lasses tae revere?

Why wid we concern oorsels wi ither religions, says Middleton, when we ken the ane true religion?

Surely, says Thomas, aw believe thir ain religion tae be the true religion?

Then maist are wrang, says Craig. And it's oor duty tae enlighten them.

Are ye for startin a crusade? says Mitchell.

Are ye for joinin ane?

No me, says Mitchell. Wi the lang shanks on him, Middleton's yir man for a crusade. He could walk aw the way tae the Holy Land on breid and water.

Naebody could walk *aw* the way, says Middleton. There's a sea tae cross. At least ane.

And a desert tae, says Potter.

True, says Craig. And even Middleton wid need the assistance o a fower-leggit beast tae traverse a desert.

In Tibet, Thomas continues, mony statues o the Buddha are blue. And in Constantinople, the great Sultan Ahmed Mosque is blue.

Wha telt ye that? says Craig.

The same as telt *you*, says Thomas. Oor auld dominie.

Is that so? says Craig. I dinna mind. Armour wis aye harpin on aboot far-flung pairts and heathen ways. The mair far-flung and heathen, the better for him.

He wis a guid man, says Thomas. And aw his tales o dervishes and djinns taught me there's mair tae life than whit's under oor nebs.

Whit's wrang, says Patrick Middleton, wi acceptin yir lot?

I accept my lot, says Thomas, and wi gratitude. But whit hairm is there in entertainin ither possibilities?

So, says Potter, gnawing a fingernail, Craig and Aikenhead have kent each ither since they were bairns?

We kent each ither for a year or twa, says Thomas—

We werena close as bairns, says Craig. That's aw ye need tae ken.

Perhaps, says Mitchell, that's for us tae decide.

Bairns will be bairns, says Thomas airily. I'm no ane for bearin a grudge.

It isna Christian tae bear a grudge, says Middleton.

Ye're aye statin the obvious, Middleton, says Mitchell. But perhaps, he says slyly, Craig wishes tae keep oor regent's favourite tae hissel.

Aye, says Potter. In the hope some advantage will fa' intae his lap.

I'm no his favourite! Thomas protests.

Aye ye are, says Craig. But let this be noted by ilka ane o ye: I seek nae advantage frae *ony* regent. And certainly no a vicious, intemperate ane like Cunningham. But it will be dark soon, I am low on candle and must attend tae some readin afore I say my prayers.

A Knowledge of Simples

The gates of the Hortus Medicus Botanicus are unlocked but there is no sign of anyone around. Without straying too far from the entrance, Thomas picks his way down the narrow paths between plant beds, stopping to admire specimens and to identify what he can. It is a mild clear day in late spring and the beds are lush with new growth. Bees slew from one bush to another, butterflies flitter about like petals on the wing, worms drill eyeless heads through the soil; a few slugs, which have so far escaped notice, munch holes in tender new leaves.

After yet another wearisome morning of Latin, Thomas is tickled to find himself alone in such a fragrant, orderly space, where colour and birdsong rule and even the air quivers with vitality. What a wealth of flora is contained within these well-dressed walls! Each has its own unique structure: the silvery lanceolate lavender leaves fan around the stalk; the leaves of the deep green rosemary are similar in shape but the structure of the bush is altogether different. Every plant form is so particular, complex, so perfectly designed. For some – for many – such abundance is proof of the existence of God. But why, if the true purpose of life is to conform to God's will, would He need so many different species, such endless variety?

I trust ye've been treatin my plants kindly.

On my life, sir, says Thomas, straightening up and knocking earth from the knees of his breeks.

So ye're Aikenhead's lad?

The same.

Yir faither wis an ill-luckit man.

James Sutherland is long of limb and straight as a rake, with wayward brows and shrewd blue eyes; he scrutinises his young visitor, as if, Thomas thinks, for imperfections.

Yir gairden is in admirable condition.

It didna get like it is by itsel. A gairden requires care and close attention. And a prayer or twa intae the bargain. In these pairts we canna tak clement weather and guid growin for granted.

Thomas follows as Sutherland conducts a tour of the plant beds. The Keeper began his working life as a common gardener, caring for the plants in Robert Sibbald's Botanical Gardens. Through diligence, God's will and green fingers, he is now considered an authority on medicinal plants. Students do not normally embark on medical studies until they have completed their general degree, but Thomas, already nurturing the hope of studying medicine at a later date, requested an early introduction.

Valerian, digitalis, monk's hood, briony, belladonna – ye've mony poisonous plants here, says Thomas, pleased to be able to identify them.

And an apothecary's lad should ken frae the teachin o Paracelsus, says Sutherland, that whit maks a man seik can also cure him.

The deil's in the dosage, says Thomas. As my faither learned tae his cost.

Oors is a perilous trade. And ye'll note that the maist baneful floo'ers can be the maist bonny forby.

As they stroll slowly down the narrow paths, Sutherland comments on the condition of plants, their provenance and, in the case of exotic varieties, the cost, pausing to nip a withered stalk, flick off a pest, offer up a bud for close inspection.

My faither aye wanted tae concoct Venice Treacle, he says. Some say it draws poison frae the saul as weel as frae the body.

Some believe aw kinds o hocus-pocus.

So ye dinna believe that whit cures the body can also cure the saul?

That's anither maitter awthegither.

I used tae ken the receipt for Venice Treacle by heart.

Well dinna be recitin it the now, says Sutherland. Life's ower short! A guid memory can be an advantage in the medical profession. But dinna confuse compilin facts wi learnin.

How richt ye be, sir. In class we must commit tae memory vast tracts o information already kent and spend little time assessin its veracity or its value. I wonder – is the function o the brain the same as a blottin pad? Is it no wasteful tae ingest information then regurgitate it undigested? Is it no wasteful tae merely repeat whit's already kent?

Yon are questions for yir tutors, says Sutherland. No for a simple man like mysel.

Wi respect, sir, ye're no a simple man.

I'd raither be ane, says Sutherland.

A swift skims the plant beds, swoops off then repeats its looping so frequently that it might have been a toy twirled on a string. Sutherland stops in front of the sundial, planted with different varieties of thyme and comprising hourly segments of a clockface.

Ye'd best mind yir time, he says, with a dry laugh. I widna wish tae incite the ire o yir regent.

Indeed, says Thomas. And oor regent's a man wi scant patience for tardiness. I'm indebted tae ye, sir.

He offers the standard fee but Sutherland waves away his florin.

Ye'll learn mair frae the earth itsel than frae ocht I can tell ye. Yir een, yir neb, yir fingers and yir tongue are the best teachers. But afore ye gang back tae yir books, there's somebody ye should meet.

At the bottom of the garden, fruit trees – apple, peach and plum – stand close to the high wall. At the back gate, secured by a stout chain, is a rowan.

D'ye believe in the power o the rowan, sir?

I neither dae nor dinna. If the power is true, we're protected. If it's fause, we hae a braw tree tae look upon nanetheless.

As they approach, a lad darts behind a peach tree.

Ye ken we can see ye, says Sutherland indulgently. Come oot, ye loon! And meet young Thomas. He's a mitherless and faitherless bairn, like yirsel.

A shaven head pops out briefly then is withdrawn.

Peekaboo, says Sutherland.

Peekaboo.

The lad inches out from behind the tree. Small, with a twist to his shoulders and a face as bland as an acorn, he holds out both hands and advances with trepidation.

Meet Zeno, says Sutherland. I cry him Zeno because he is a paradox. Aye approachin zero, niver gettin there.

Guid day tae ye, says Thomas.

The boy waggles his head, seeming to agree and disagree at the same time.

Zeno's no much o a conversationalist but he has a way wi plants. He can haundle a seedlin as gentle as if it wis a woundit sparra.

Sparra, says Zeno. Barra. Marra. Yarra.

Aye, says Sutherland. Show Thomas yir new seed frame. I'm sure he'll be maist impressed.

Head still waggling, Zeno pulls Thomas towards the end of the wall where glass panels have been set at an angle. Below them, seedlings stand in neat, even drills.

Whit a fine haund ye must hae, says Thomas.

Fine, shine, mine, dine, wine, wine, wine! says Zeno, breaking into a grin.

Ay, we'll hae a drap at the day's end, says Sutherland, if ye behave yirsel!

Dine! Wine!

Yon seedlins hail frae Brazil and the East Indies, says Sutherland. The frames protect them frae frost and when the sun shines, the gless increases the heat. Oor exotics, fancyin they're in warmer climes, respond accordinly.

Zeno squats on his haunches, nose almost touching the frame. He is beckoning Thomas to come closer when a commotion breaks out on the far side of the wall. Zeno springs to his feet and lollops off up the path.

We'd best gang efter him, says Sutherland.

From the top of the sloping garden they can see the cause: outside the grounds of the adjacent Trinity Church, a dozen or so young men are haranguing the minister who, staunchly ignoring the disturbance, remains stationed at the gate, distributing gruff blessings to members of the wedding party as they depart. That this is the wedding of some notable Presbyterians can be ascertained by the sober garb and austere demeanour of the guests.

The auld minister might support the King ower the water, says Sutherland, but he wis held in affection by his congregation. And see wha they've pit in his place – a dour auld fanatic.

Dae ye no support thir protest? asks Thomas.

I dae not. Yon's nae way tae behave. Holy matrimony is holy matrimony. As mony ken, I'm o the auld faith but whit transpires atween me and my Makar has aye been and will aye remain a private maitter.

Thomas has limited sympathy for the new arrivals in the pulpits, loudly proclaiming themselves right and their precursors wrong. And outing has not been confined to the pulpits: college professors known to sympathise with the deposed monarch's Catholicism, and the old, Episcopalian ways, are being hounded out of their posts and replaced with those whose beliefs are in line with the tenets of Presbyterianism. Unless, like Archibald Pitcairne, their social standing carries sufficient clout to protect and preserve them.

When Thomas was a child, in the year of the great comet, students got up protests against the papists and a hooded procession, bearing an effigy of the pope, tramped from the Canongate to the foot of the High Street. When it reached Holyrood Abbey – to beating drums and chants of *Doon wi the papists!* – the students set the effigy alight. The tables may have turned, but bigotry remains hale and hearty.

Doon wi toadies tae King Billy! Nae mair calumny agin the true King!

With the hauteur of one who believes himself inviolable, the minister strides through the gates, staff raised, and lashes out indiscriminately until he is overpowered and forced back inside the church grounds. Raising his voice above the ruckus, the minister sends for the Town Guard.

Some hate the Roman Catholics, says Sutherland, shaking his head. Some hate the Episcopalians. Some hate the Prebyterians, the Jews, the Mohammedans. There's aye plenty hatred tae gang roond.

Roond. Crooned. Wound. Drooned, whimpers Zeno, burying his face deep in the smooth, comforting leaves of a bay laurel.

House of Curiosities

St Mary's Wynd
November 1693

My Dearest Sisters,

Though my studies take up many hours of each day – bar the Sabbath, of course – and one day becomes another in the blink of an eye, there are many possible diversions if one has the time for them. Recently I was introduced, again by Mungo Craig, who has his finger on the pulse of the city, to the House of Curiosities, in Grange Park. For those willing to venture beyond the city gates, it offers the opportunity to witness some singular marvels of the age. You might, for example, be afforded a demonstration of the Magical Lantern in which images of Scaramouch, Acteon or Diana, only a scrimp broader than a ducatoune, are magnified to the size of a man, or a Humbling Mirror, which shrinks and flattens a full-sized man to the squat compactness of a dwarf. The Automatical Virginal, a combination of barrel organ and a clockwork device, plays tunes without the aid of a human hand and the Manifold Writing Engine has the capability of making several copies of a text at the same time! It is thrilling to consider how this might facilitate the production of printed matter of all kinds. I hope very much that this prototype might in my own lifetime become a functioning machine. The more folk who have access to the written word, the better a society we must surely have.

I must not ramble on for fear I will bring envy into your hearts for not being able to witness such curiosities with your own eyes but I also saw a Diving Ark, a contraption which takes a man deep down in the sea and allows him to observe all manner of creatures never seen on land, and David Dun's machine gun which can fire repeatedly.

Finally, I must mention one more item: Kircher's Disfigured Pictures. This is not a machine but a clever trick, at least until its workings have become common knowledge. When one looks at the canvas, board or block, all one sees is a confused mass of colours but when a sheet of perforated metal is placed over the chaos, a delightful and comprehensible composition is revealed. Mungo Craig says, with some considerable disdain, that this enjoys great popularity with those loyal to the King over the water, as it enables them to contemplate likenesses of their beloved monarch while escaping the attention of the Lord Advocate!

I could continue at greater length on what this House of Curiosities contains but as I am not certain this letter will reach its destination, I will keep it brief. Did you know that on the highway south there has been a spate of assaults on the post boy, and armed robbers made off with the mailbags? Who knows what has already gone astray.

I will conclude by saying that I still miss you both terribly and my heart leaps ahead to when we will once more be united.

Your loving brother, Thomas

The Naked Eye

The city is chock-full of men of the cloth. Every widow who has rooms has let them out, installing additional pallets where possible, cranking up the price to double or triple the going rate. Ostlers too, struggle to accommodate the abundance of horses left in their charge. Blacksmiths work longer hours than usual. Milliners, haberdashers, tailors and cobblers are doing a brisk if sombre-hued trade. Even the goldsmiths are unusually busy. Though the kirk representatives are here on solemn business, many have travelled long and hard to reach their destination and wish to make the most of provisions and services only available in the capital.

The taverns and coffee houses offer food and refreshment from early morning to the ten o'clock bell. Ballad sellers stroll, stot or hobble from one establishment to another, promoting the latest broadsides, many of which – pious, satirical or scurrilous – have been penned and printed hastily for the occasion. Booksellers and printers, with whom the city is well-provided, have rearranged window displays to feature a selection of bibles and pious publications. Less conspicuously, an altogether different range of titles can also be obtained, for a price. Concealed beneath plain covers, or false covers pertaining to wholesome interests like the propagation of cucumbers and marrows, their contents are designed to whet very different appetites. As many in the book trade are all too aware, the pious and the salacious have long been bedfellows.

It's a filthy day. The March wind blows in riotous gusts and the rain pelts down, turning the streets to sluices of muck and making it impossible for anyone to keep clean or dry. The taverns, coffee houses and assembly rooms smell of damp wool, of rabbit-skin hats steaming above fireplaces and whatever foul matter that clings to bootsoles, of ale mulling and coffee brewing, of stew simmering and whatever else the proprietors deem best to cheer the spirits of those seeking refuge from the elements. The city's black-clad visitors, a veritable shoal of them who further darken the aspect of the city, interpret the weather as a sign that the city's heart and soul are also foul, and resolve to purge the foulness therein.

Ministers foregather for the first General Assembly in several years. To the ire of many of the clergy, the Assembly has already been twice postponed; having the event coincide with such portentous outpourings from the heavens strengthens their resolve to reinforce ecclesiastical authority in the face of the reigning monarch's disinterest in its proceedings. The Assembly generates no revenue for the crown and, by all accounts, King William considers it to be of little service in his continuing war with France. It is widely believed that he considers the entire nation of Scotland to be of little service; after four years on the throne, he has yet to make the journey north.

Despite the weather, for students under the regency of Alexander Cunningham, the latter part of the morning has been given over to football. Regent Cunningham, whose raddled appearance belies his youth, nurses a thick head and is thankful that the window glass muffles the noise his students make as they charge around the courtyard. He might regret the previous night's excesses but it's a small price to pay to have been part of such colourful and invigorating company: alongside other freethinkers, including Archibald Pitcairne and David Gregory, he passed a most stimulating evening of copious imbibing and setting the world to rights.

Most of the students enjoy the football game for its own sake and a bit of mud is a small price to pay for a break from Latin dictation. It also provides a welcome reprieve from the harsh discipline meted out by their regent. In recent months Cunningham has become increasingly brutal, boxing some in the face to the effusion of blood and caning others with a severity which has resulted in septic weals, permanent scarring and complaints being lodged with the Privy Council. Though these complaints have resulted in a general ban on regents carrying staves to class, Cunningham persists in flouting the ruling.

Thomas, who has been excused games, is in the library, seated at a window table that overlooks the courtyard. For all Cunningham's harshness, if a student has an active desire to study, far be it for him to stand in the way: there is more, he believes, to be gained from books than from chasing after an inflated pig's bladder. From time to time the sound of shouts and running feet draw Thomas's attention to the game in progress. John Potter is quick and nimble. Mungo Craig, who has assiduously sought out his companionship since matriculation, is an enthusiastic if inelegant player. His shortness of leg can be a disadvantage yet there are times when he can get the better of bigger, stronger lads, like lanky Patrick Middleton or sturdy Adam Mitchell – today in the opposing team – confounding them with feints and bluffs more than with deft footwork.

Thomas's fondness for books is, in part, physical: he loves the look of them, their smell, the crackle as he turns a page; he loves the feel of covers, bindings, the grain of paper, the slickness of print. The works he has in front of him, Andreas Vesalius's *De humani corporis fabrica* and Maria Sybilla Merian's *Raupen wunderbare Verwandlung und sonderbare Blumennahrung,* are particularly exquisite publications. He is comparing human and animal structures, noting the marriage between composition and functionality. He is turning around the notion that each discrete entity might not necessarily fit into some overarching plan or design but might, instead, simply exist alongside other discrete entities – all complete and perfect in their own way – when the dinner bell clangs across the courtyard.

So, says Craig, appearing outside the library, flushed and muddy. Did ye see me strike?

I did. Ye're the verra deil o a player. I widna wish ye as my opposition.

A deil, ye say? Bold words, my freend. *Exitus acta probat.*

The opposin side might no agree that the result validates

the deeds.

Wha gies a fig aboot them! But if we stand aw day debatin the whys and wherefores, we'll miss oor dinner!

Should we no wait for the ithers? says Thomas.

They ken where tae find us.

The two dash up College Wynd, cross the High Street and hasten down the hill, weaving between groups of ministers equally intent on securing shelter from the elements.

Sae mony clerics in toun! says Thomas.

If only Toland were here, says Craig. He'd set squibs aneath thir sententious arses. Did I tell ye I met the man hissel? I wis but a green lad, sneakin intae McCloud's for the craik but whit craik there wis when Toland wis in the toun! Kent the length and breadth o the land for the fettle o his tongue. Ye widda been on yir country estate when Toland wis here, baskin in the comforts o the big hoose.

I'd raither a guid mind than a big hoose, says Thomas. Look at the sons o gentry that bring thir ain tutors tae assist them in thir studies. Thir minds canna be as keen as oors – *ex nihilo nihil fit*.

I widna baulk at a private tutor, says Craig. In pairticular ane wha'd tak Cunningham's lash in my stead.

Surely, says Thomas, we should suffer oor ain punishment, even if it be unjust, than mak anither suffer?

My, my, Tam, whit high-minded principles ye haud! By the bye, I hear ye passed the morn wi the works o Vesalius and Merian.

Wha telt ye that?

It's nae secret, man. Onybody can see frae the register wha signs for whit. But here we are, at McCloud's, and whit a drouth I hae upon me! I thank the Lord for the delights o the tavern.

★★★

Another who thanks his good fortune – if not the Lord – for the tavern, in particular Lucky Lorimer's tavern, which refuses to serve students, is Alexander Cunningham. His students irk him aplenty. Not for their youthful high jinks; that's a fact of life and what would life be if everyone behaved with wisdom and propriety? It's the slackness he can't abide, the mental slackness which makes expressions go blank and gobs drop open whenever he attempts to introduce new ideas. In such protean times there is so much to ponder: natural philosophy and its correlation with scripture; God's hand in the workings of the world; whether a monarch from Holland could be considered the true envoy of the Lord when a crowned King was forced into exile; the clergy's authority over the nature of belief and the manner of worship.

And yet most students just soak up his words without question; or worse, crib from bought or borrowed notes. Do they think he's as lacking in mettle as some in the college, repeating the same lessons year upon year? Do they think they can satisfy him, and themselves, with short measure? Do they think the great philosophers of the age – who, to his mind, include Baruch Spinoza, René Descartes and Thomas Hobbes – devoted their lives to study, and often risked their necks into the bargain, so sluggards who didn't know one end of a syllogism from the other might amble through their own unexamined lives?

He is in little doubt, too, that some of the most fearful or vindictive will have spread calumny about him. Perhaps he's already been put under surveillance. No matter; the college censors are clop-footed, drawing attention to themselves by affected nonchalance, loitering at popular rendezvous, intent on witnessing some piddling misdemeanour. As if there were nothing better to do than apprehend pranksters and broilers, swearers and cursers, lads who let their hair grow long to show support for the Cavaliers, those whose gaze is drawn by a winsome lass or a painted jade. At this moment, he couldn't give a damn.

Whit'll it be, Maister Cunningham?

A restorative, Peg, if ye please.

Hair o the dug that bit ye?

There ye hae it. And how's business for ye?

Brisk! The ale's barely had time tae settle afore it's doon some loon's gullet. I've heard tell some are addin a bunch o broom tae the barrel tae fortify young ale sae they can sell it on mair quickly. Ye ken that's no a practice I favour. Ishbel McCloud, now, she's no averse tae tampering wi her drink when she's got a rush on. Sae if ye dinna wish tae meet faerie folk or worse on yir way hame, stick wi Peg Lorimer's ale, sir.

I'll keep that in mind. Nocht like deliberatin on the spiritual welfare o the nation tae gie a man a drouth!

Bar poondin the pulpit, says Peg, leaning towards him, as eager to pass on gossip as to sell him another dram: I hear this and that. They've passed an Act agin Profaneness. In the main it's the same as afore: cursing and sweerin, Sabbath brekkin, fornication, adultery, and, as ever, drunkenness.

Cunningham begins to feel the soothing effects of warm brandy almost immediately. He savours the plumpness of Peg Lorrimer's powdered breasts and the lilt of her voice as she warms to her theme: There's a new clause tae. A minister frae ower the west, efter he'd drunk hissel mortall quoth it thrice sae I ken it by hert: *To stem the impiety and profaneness that aboundeth in this nation, the mocking of piety and religious exercises.* Aye and *horrid blasphemy* is tae be rooted oot.

Weel, weel, he says, we'll hae tae bridle oor tongues.

When the dinner break is over, Cunningham surprises his class by introducing an impromptu debate on the newly approved Act of Profaneness. He quizzes the students on what they consider to be the definition of profanity then poses the question: Dae ye consider this act tae set the cat amangst the doos, or tae cast pearls afore swine?

As one after another student struggles to provide a reasoned response – and give proper regard to the principles of debate – their regent's gaze drifts to the window. A faint, private smile flits across his face and for the remainder of the day he does not abuse a single student.

★ ★★

Ye canna gang hame, Tam. No the nicht. Bein oot and aboot while the Assembly's in toun is an essential pairt o yir education!

Though the dark sky continues to churn and threaten further cloudbursts, the rain has stopped and the wind has died down. In spite of the inordinate amount of blackcoats abroad, the city has a festive air. The luckenbooths are open late, making the most of the new street lighting and the increased opportunity for commerce. Young women selling oranges and lemons move through the busy street, their bold eyes and swaying hips arousing interest and disapproval in equal measure.

Some ministers from nearby market towns make a mental note to raise, at the first opportunity, the question as to how in truth these young women earn their living. Others, who have travelled from desolate parishes, where such temptations are only to be found within the pages of a forbidden book or the secret chambers of the imagination, find it possible to convince themselves, temporarily at least, that it is no more than a pleasing coincidence that lemon sellers wear more lavish and alluring garments than one would expect from a street hawker.

There is even some music. A lad with a viol – a sorry-looking soul with a shattered leg – sits by the Mercat Cross. His delicate airs float above the street like feathers of melody. Passersby, charmed by the plangent cadences and stirred to charity by the player's infirmity, slip the lad a coin. Thomas, too, is about to contribute when Craig distracts him:

Tam, Tam, look who's a-buyin lemons!

He gestures towards St Giles Kirk where a number of ministers have congregated. They have just attended evening prayers and are exchanging ecclesiastical gossip: who has been outed; who has been transferred to a grim, outlying parish; who has been reinstated. They compare travellers' tales; appraise the quality of the service; deplore the extent to which the fabric of the building has deteriorated since they were last in the city;

debate the likely cost of renovation.

I see nae lemon seller amangst the ministers.

Naw, naw. There, by Jackson's Entry. It's Cunningham, clear as day, and the jade is drawin him doon the wynd! Come on, he says, tugging on Thomas's arm. Let's see whit we can see!

They reach the entrance to the wynd just in time to see their regent follow a red-headed woman into the doorway adjacent to Lucky Lorimer's.

If we gang roond the back, says Craig, we'll see whit they're aboot.

I ken Cunningham is a hard man, says Thomas, and unjust tae ye mair than maist, but I willna spy on him. As Maister Sutherland says, a man's conscience is a matter for hissel and his Makar.

Whit does a papist gairdener ken? Sinners must be brocht tae accoont, ye ken as weel as I.

I willna spy on Cunningham.

Suit yirsel.

With misgivings, Thomas bids Craig a curt goodnight.

Craig continues on alone past the tavern entrance to where the wynd opens onto the dark expanse of the Nor' Loch. Moored boats knock against the pilings. The area is deserted. The Nor' Loch is not a place to go after nightfall unless you need darkness to conceal your business.

Due to the lie of the land, the cellar on the lochside is on ground level, with wooden shutters on the lower portion and windows above, overlooking the water. Crouched down, with an eye pressed to a gap in the shutters, Craig locates where the woman has taken her quarry and the orange glow of a lamp allows him to view the scene in vivid and astonishing detail.

The shapely jade unlaces the bodice of a sea-green gown, cups her breasts and offers them up to Cunningham as if they were fruits. He flicks his tongue over one and then the other, licks at a raspberry nipple then catches it between his teeth. She pulls away, surprised, then laughs. She continues to laugh when he turns her round, bends her over a cask and raises her skirts, exposing the pale moons of her buttocks.

Craig's eyes are fit to pop out of his head. He forgets to breathe. Cunningham slaps the jade's arse. She laughs again. He unbuttons himself. Craig's heart knocks between his ribs. He has never before seen the intimate parts of a woman from this or any other angle and is only just beginning to make sense of what he sees when his tutor, breeks about his knees, throws himself upon the woman and vents his lust with a ferocity that Craig, in another context entirely, is familiar enough with.

What he sees appals him, and yet his body rebels from the dictates of his brain: his groin throbs with such intensity and insistence that, while he spies on the pounding gallop of the beast with two backs, he thrusts himself against the rough stone wall until he too is spent.

When the twist of shame has dissipated and self-righteous disgust resumes, his first thought is to slink off into the night, with no-one any the wiser. But what use is it to witness sinful behaviour unless it can be put to advantage? He raps on the glass. The jade is first to notice him. She's brazen at first, but not for long. When Cunningham, in the process of making himself decent, recognises the peeper, his face becomes a seethe of fury. With vengeance coursing sweetly through his veins, Craig makes off up the wynd and into the throng moiling on the High Street.

Thomas has been drifting up and down the street, aimless and out of sorts. There is plenty to divert him, had he a mind for it, but the contretemps with Craig still gnaws at him. As he passes the Mercat Cross, a sturdy, able-bodied clergyman, calling on the Almighty for validation, is berating the viol player for seducing citizens from the true path of sombre worship of the Lord. With a heavenward tilt of the chin the lad plays on, as if to say: What else can I do? The clergyman, incensed by the lad's intransigence, wrenches the viol from his hands and strikes it repeatedly against the Cross. When the neck cracks he lets it fall to the ground: a heap of mute, useless wood.

Ezra's Fables

I'd ken yir faces onywhere, at ony time.

And we'd ken yours. We'd ken yir face at the ends o the earth.

Katharine, Anna and Thomas stand at the West Port, breathless, drinking in the sight of each other like an elixir which must be drained to the last drop.

Ye've grown, Anna! says Thomas. Ye're as tall as Katharine and ye're… ye're a young woman now.

And I'll soon be an auld crone! says Katharine.

Awa, says Thomas. Ye're in the prime o womanhood. I'll be fendin off the gallants.

It is nearly two years since they've been together and there is so much to say and so many questions to ask. They leave the West Port with the odours of horse dung and saddlery drifting over from King's Stables Road. Katharine and Anna have promised John Barr, who has already made himself scarce, to be back at the coach by the 8 o'clock bell. They cross the Grassmarket, talking hard and fast, darting from one topic to another, mindless of the direction they take or where they place their feet – they are fortunate that the ground is dry – and oblivious to everyone and everything around them: even passing the gibbet and its regularly replenished display of heads on stakes does not douse the flare of joy they share at being once more reunited.

Thomas has a sister on each arm.

How wis the journey?

Uneventful, says Katharine. Mercifully uneventful.

We didna meet ony highwaymen, says Anna, but there were dizzens o faimished folk on the road.

I pity them, says Thomas. The city is already chock-fou wi thir ilk. And wis John Barr his usual crabbit self?

At first he grumped aboot drivin us, says Katharine, as Lady Hester and Sir Patrick were bidin at hame.

But efter wettin his whistle at the Brig Inn, says Anna, he wis mair douce.

Civil, says Katharine. John Barr's niver *douce*.

And whit o life at Netherstane?

We dinna gang hungry, thanks be tae God. Even in these stricken times.

If looks are ocht tae reckon by, ye're the picture o health! Wi yir skinklin een and rosy cheeks. How blessed I be tae hae such hale and fair sisters! Are the Maister and Mistress kind tae ye?

As lang as Euphemie's content, says Anna, they leave us be. And Euphemie's plenty content since she's betrothed.

Tae the son o a Perthshire judge, says Katharine.

Lady Hester must be pleased! Does she still pine for Paris?

She pines mair for Malcolm, says Anna. There's been nae word from him for mony a month.

Is Alasdair still a rogue?

Worse than ever, says Katharine. He's fallen foul o Forbes Lightfoot. Ower a lass, accordin tae Madge – wha kens aw there is tae ken – and even Lady Hester is sair tried by him.

And how fares Madge, Aleen?

Madge prays for deliverance frae aches and agues, says Katharine, and Aleen prays tae mak a guid match afore the year is oot.

Ye must send them my best regards. And auld Mither Elspet?

Mert, says Katharine. Francie found her a month past on the path tae the ice-hoose, which wis as far as her spindleshanks wid cairry her.

When he brocht her tae the big hoose, says Anna, Francie wis greetin like a bairn. He says she taught him aw he kens aboot the tides.

Shame, says Thomas. She taught me a thing or twa aboot the ways o the water tae. And how tae predict the morn's weather by the evenin sky. Whit wis the cause o daith?

Naebody kens, says Katharine.

She wis ower auld, says Anna.

And ower trachled, says Katharine.

Aye, says Thomas, for once lost for words.

They stop at the Bow Well, at the east end of the Grassmarket, where a handful of women and children wait their turn to collect water. Three roads lead off: Candlemaker Row, which curves upward to Greyfriars Kirkyard; the Cowgate, which cuts clean through the underbelly of the city; the West Bow which leads to the upper end of the High Street and on to Castlehill. Katharine and Anna wish to see their old house, to visit their parents' last resting place and, of course, they long to see Thomas's current lodgings.

Thomas suggests they begin with the kirkyard so that their mood may lighten as they proceed; their visit is, after all, an occasion for celebration. Yet when the breeze blows down Candlemaker Row and the reek of tallow brings tears to their eyes, he directs them instead towards the West Bow. As they clamber up the steep, curving street Thomas indicates coffee houses, bookshops, booths selling gloves and shoes and bolts of linen. He refrains – but only just in time – from pointing out a wigmaker's shop: Katharine's hair has grown as long and luxuriant as it was before her encounter with Solomon Unwin and could easily fetch another guinea.

When they turn onto the High Street the sisters pause, clutch at each other and gaze around them, in silence.

Ye'll see changes since ye were last here, says Thomas. New establishments openin up, old anes closin doon. Developments and renovations. Some guid, some ill—

We ken ye ken whit we'll see when we gang further up the street, says Anna, but—

But let us see for oorsels, says Katharine.

I'll dae ocht ye wish, says Thomas. For my darlin sisters, I will even bite my tongue!

I doot it, says Katharine. Should ye live tae be an auld man.

They stand across the street from their former home. Gone

is their father's name from the shop sign; gone the blue letters on a black background, the painted yellow mortar and pestle, decorated with the staff of Asclepius.

When George Borthwick took over the apothecary, he repainted the sign, says Thomas, addin his ain name, in crimson.

But look, says Anna. The crimson paint is fadin and the blue o faither's name is pushin through!

So it is! says Thomas. I miss yir sharp een sorely.

Hae ye been inside? says Anna.

No, but I've stood at the hatch a time or twa, on an errand for Doctor Pitcairne. Borthwick does guid business. Better than faither did.

That widna be hard, says Katharine.

Oor faither had little luck, says Thomas.

And whit little he had he squandered in taverns and gamin ha's, says Katharine.

We shouldna speak ill o oor deid faither, says Anna.

It's no a sin tae speak the truth, says Katharine.

If ye canna say fair, be silent, says Anna.

Please, says Thomas, dinna bicker! No the day.

At the gate of Greyfriars Kirk, Thomas buys a bunch of gillyflowers from a clam-eyed woman who takes his coin with neither word nor sign of acknowledgement.

How will we find the heidstane? says Anna.

I ken where they lie, says Thomas.

Silent, they walk in single file along the narrow paths between the graves. Even for Thomas, who has visited the kirkyard much more recently, only isolated and incongruous detail remains. Of his mother's burial, he recalls rain dripping down his neck, his chin scraping on the churchyard wall. Of his father's, he minds the breeze cooing through gaps in the stone wall, the itch of his new jacket.

Though dwarfed by its larger and more elaborately decorated neighbours, the headstone is modest but well-finished, with names and dates for both James and Helen cleanly incised and a mortar and pestle signifying their father's trade. Anna lays the flowers against the headstone and only now Thomas wonders who paid for it – Sir Patrick, Uncle Thomas, Hepburn? As they are paying their respects, a band of vagabonds, who find sleeping in the kirkyard more amenable than the streets, approaches. In the pursuit of alms. Or entertainment. Thomas and his sisters are not inclined to linger.

We'll stick tae the high roads while we can, says Thomas, pressing on in the direction of the Pleasance. It is a warm, close day. Storm clouds gather above the sandstone crags in the King's Park.

D'ye mind rinnin up there in oor mournin claes, says Thomas, on oor way tae Duddingston?

I dae, says Katharine. Ye won the race, as aye.

Did we climb yon rocks? says Anna.

No, says Thomas, but further roond the park we climbed a hill tae the tap. We could see aw the way tae the Bass.

So we did, says Anna. I saw ships in the firth!

Where the Pleasance meets the Cowgate they cross the busy thoroughfare and make their way up St. Mary's Wynd.

The lands o the Coogate are sae tall! says Anna. And the streets sae fou o folk!

D'ye miss Netherstane? says Katharine.

I miss bein close tae my sisters, says Thomas. And I miss the clean, salty air. But city life has much tae offer a thinkin man.

D'ye excel at yir studies?

I dae weel enough, by aw accoonts.

Are ye the aipple o yir regent's ee? says Anna.

That's no how it works, says Thomas. College isna school. Though the regent is fair tae me.

Are yir college freends fine fellows? says Anna. And yir neebors?

I believe so.

D'ye no bridle at the nearness o neebors, says Katharine, the lugs at the wa, the busybodies noting yir ilka coming and gaen?

Only a man wi something tae hide, says Thomas, is fearful

o whit the neebors see or say. He opens the street door with a flourish. Here we are. Onwards and upwards! And upwards!

Katharine and Anna eagerly climb the many flights of stairs. Despite Katharine railing at busybodies, she and Anna would dearly like to catch a glimpse of Thomas's neighbours but they are disappointed: they pass no-one on the stairs and the house doors remain closed.

In advance of their visit, Thomas has tidied his garret accommodation, sorted his clothes and papers into piles, and arranged his writing implements in a neat cluster on the table. With some difficulty, and considerable cost, he has procured some meat pies, cake and preserved fruits. He has laid out his offerings in as appealing an arrangement as his limited kitchenware permits. He has cleaned candlesticks and trimmed wicks – though he hopes, as ever, that there will be enough daylight to spend little candle. Remembering Lady Hester's attention to the niceties of entertaining, he has placed an arrangement of hedgerow flowers on the table.

When he opens the door to his lodgings, his sisters marvel at the spread before them and he congratulates himself on his forethought. Of course they would not for the world have come empty-handed and once they have been shown around, peered out of the small window, been taken aback by the nearness of neighbouring buildings and awed by the long drop to street level, they present him with cheese, a dozen eggs, a bottle of claret and two dozen cured swan quills.

The claret's wi compliments o Sir Patrick, says Katharine. The quills are frae Maister Naysmith.

Such grand gifts! says Thomas. I shall write a letter o thanks tae Naysmith. In my best haund, of course! And ane tae Sir Patrick and Lady Hester for the victuals.

It wis Madge sent ye the eggs, says Anna. Lady Hester wis loath tae pairt wi them.

In that case I'll write Madge a note.

Best no, says Katharine. We'll pass on yir thanks tae her.

I concede ye ken best on such maitters, says Thomas.

Katharine tells him that Naysmith's days at Netherstane will soon be over. Schooling for Alasdair and Euphemie has been completed and he must find some other family with children to educate.

While they eat, after Katharine insists on saying grace – a practice Thomas has let lapse since he has lived alone – they mull over how they'd like to spend the afternoon. Should they take a trip to Leith to visit the glass manufactory, or venture over to Bruntsfield links where they might see folk at the golf? Or should they remain in the city centre, strolling at their leisure and dipping into the luckenbooths as they go?

Katharine cuts him short. She should perhaps have mentioned it earlier but needs some time to herself, an hour or two, and Thomas should not press her on this: there are some things a woman is not obliged to divulge.

I willna stand in the way o yir hert, says Thomas.

I didna say it wis a maitter o the hert! says Katharine.

Ye didna need tae.

They part company at the Netherbow and agree to rendezvous later in the day at a coffee house near Parliament Close. Thomas and Anna decide that they don't want to hike the long road to Leith or even to venture over to the links. They are content to maunder, arm in arm, to enjoy an idle afternoon and each other's company. With Katharine temporarily absent, they skip, whisper, giggle, exclaim at unusual sights and eccentric characters, poke around the luckenbooths and discuss the curiosities on sale.

One booth offers an array of magnificent seashells. The vendor, a lame, lantern-jawed man draws Anna's attention to a large conch shell with its smooth, flesh-pink lip. It has a special property, the vendor tells her. If she were to hold it to an ear, she would hear the sea. He presents the conch to Anna in the coarse, chapped hands of a man who has worked around boats and brine for many a year, and encourages her to try it out for herself.

It's true! she says, then laughs in delight. I can hear the sea!

And it's no just ony sea, says the vendor, but the verra sea it came frae.

Thomas offers to buy the shell for Anna as a memento of her visit but she won't hear of it:

I want for nocht, Thomas, ither than yir company.

Fine sentiments, says the vendor, but if aw the lasses said the same, I widna hae a merk tae my name.

Weel, weel, says Mungo Craig, appearing from nowhere with Patrick Middleton at his side. A lass that seeks the company o Tam Aikenhead!

Ye refer, Craig, tae my younger sister, says Thomas. He has the niggling impression that the pair have been close by for some time.

My pleasure then, Craig replies, making a low, sweeping bow. Quintegernus Craig, also kent as Mungo, at yir service. Once Craig has introduced Middleton, in equally histrionic manner, he suggests that all three take Anna on a tour of the college grounds. Thomas is torn between keeping Anna to himself and showing her off. Showing her off wins the day and Craig leads the way towards College Wynd. As they pass Hutchison's bookshop, he declares Thomas to be an inveterate bookworm, extolling his appetite for learning in such a hyperbolic manner that the result is ridicule.

Surely, says Anna, measuring her words, if a man disna love learnin he widna be a student?

Thomas laughs off Craig's ragging and reassures Anna that this kind of harmless badinage is standard amongst the students.

Ah but mony a true word, says Craig, is spoken in jest!

And mony a fause word tae! says Thomas.

Anna nods but says nothing until, emboldened by her reserved demeanour, Patrick Middleton engages her in conversation. Stooping to bring his long, craggy face closer to the level of her pinkish, elfin one, he asks about her journey, how she spends her days on the coast, her interests and accomplishments. In the art of conversation Middleton might lack wit and brio, but not persistence. When he has finished quizzing Anna about her life, he invites her to take a turn around the perimeter of the courtyard. He adopts the role of guide, indicating architectural features of college buildings and commenting on them at some length. Anna listens politely, allowing her gaze to be directed to a rose window, a trefoil arch, a niche containing an intricately carved coat of arms.

Pricked by an unexpected barb of jealousy, Thomas interrupts Middleton's monologue: Ye're in fine voice the day. That must be the maist words tae come oot yir mooth in a month.

I'm only bein hospitable, says Middleton.

That's as may be but dinna monopolise my sister.

Of course, Middleton continues, addressing himself once more to Anna, man's achievements are nocht when compared tae the works o the Creator—

And dinna feed her cant intae the bargain, says Thomas. This constant schism atween the works o man and the works o God – they're ane and the same, are they no? God is pairt o the faithful and the faithful are pairt o God. And as for Him creatin the world, that canna be mair than Ezra's fables.

Rash words! says Craig.

And tae utter such statements in the presence o yir fair sister, says Middleton, is mair rash still.

Thomas scoffs at their objections and puts an arm around Anna.

Am I tae presume, says Thomas with a sly grin, that Maister Middleton is sweet on my sister?

Ye're tae presume nocht, says Middleton, who flushes deeply and affects sudden interest in passing clouds.

Ah Tam, says Craig, smirking, ye've abashed Middleton grievously. And him daein his utmost tae be hospitable tae yir sister.

It wis but a jest! says Thomas. *You* ken and *he* kens it wis but a jest. And my sister kens tae. Am I richt, Anna?

Anna declares that she may not be clever enough to detect

when a student at the college of Edinburgh is jesting but must mention that she and Thomas have an appointment elsewhere and cannot, regretfully, tarry longer. She omits to mention whom they are meeting or where their rendezvous will take place and Thomas, for once, refrains from elaboration. She thanks Craig and Middleton politely for their time and patience then, taking Thomas's arm, whisks him onto College Wynd before Craig or Middleton – though it would ever be Craig – might volunteer to accompany them to their destination.

The enticing aromas of tea, coffee and chocolate greet Thomas and Anna as they enter the long, bustling coffee house. Tall windows let in a fair amount of daylight and the benches set around the trestle tables are fully occupied. On a stool near the door, rocking to and fro, Katharine stares up into the rafters where a coil of smoke turns sluggishly.

It isna guid news, says Anna.

Corpus Vile

The corpse is ashen and beaded with moisture from having been washed in advance of the doctor's arrival. At his request, it has been left uncovered. The head is shaven. The eyes are closed but the mouth gapes. As well as consuming an ear, the rats have left tooth marks on the genitals.

The cause o daith wis a seizure, says Adam Block, Keeper of Paul's Work. The man wis aboot tae say his prayers when he wis taen by a violent shudderin. He yowled like a beast haein its throat cut, crashed tae the floor and braithed nae mair.

As it is a Sunday, the looms are silent and the residents recline on their pallets, conversing quietly amongst themselves or reading their bibles. A small fire burns at each end of the dormitory to little effect.

It's cauld, says Archibald Pitcairne. But when it comes tae the deid, the cauld is a physick's freend.

His two robust assistants manoeuvre a canvas sling mounted on poles into what little space there is beside the body.

Easy does it, says Pitcairne, pressing a kerchief drenched in chypre to his face. Mind how ye go. We widna wish for brak banes the day, neither o the quick nor the deid.

Aye, Doctor, his assistants reply in unison.

Callum and Magnus Fairweather are burly, identical twins. Pitcairne is fond of saying he employs them because they think and act as one but have the strength of four. With Callum at the head and Magnus at the feet, they ease the body onto the sling.

A blanket at least! says Block.

Guid sir, says Pitcairne, the deid dinna care if they are draped in silk and velvet or left on a high plain for carrion tae strip the flesh frae thir banes. The deid are insensible. It is only the livin wha crave the nicety o a mort claith.

For the sake o modesty and in respect for ither residents, wid it no be a kindness tae cover the corpse? The man may lack family but dinna think there's nane that laments his passin. For mysel, I wis fond o the chiel. A quiet saul. God-fearin. Industrious.

Aye, aye, says Pitcairne, the pauper's trinity. Keep mum, fear the Lord and get on wi yir work.

Whit richt hae ye tae mock?

I dinna mock, sir. Certainly I mak a jest but mock neither yirsel nor the deceased. A simple play on words. Aw scriveners – and I admit tae bein ane o thir number – employ word play as pairt and paircel o thir craft. If only readers could comprehend, par exemplum, the function o metaphor, they'd fret less and chuckle a deal mair.

That's no for me tae contend, Block bridles, but this isna the time for a jest. O ony sort.

How richt ye be, says Pitcairne. Nor the time tae waste a sheet on a cratur no yet bound for the grave. I've nae wish tae offend ye, man, but unless ye can vouch for the cleanliness o yir bedding – as I doot ye can – I canna transport a blanket frae here tae my chambers. I'm sure ye're aware o the dangers o bedbugs and fleas. But dae ye ken forby that Antonie van Leeuwenhoek, the great and *unschooled* Netherlandish innovator in the field o lens-making, has demonstrated that animalcules, ower sma tae be spied by the nakit eye, can lurk in soiled claith? It wis Leeuwenhoek's ain clarty hose alerted him tae thir verra existence. We can but hope that efter such a momentous discovery the man laundered his apparel a deal mair!

So I've tae gie ye caller claith? Block grumbles. Is that whit ye're sayin? Quality linen frae oor manufactory?

Is it no a sma price tae satisfy yir sense o propriety?

Scratching his scalp, as if the mention of bedbugs and fleas has caused them tae bite, Block clomps off through the dormitory.

Had it not been for Sir Patrick taking them in, Thomas and his sisters might have been chapping at the door of Paul's Work, offering up their orphaned selves as slaves to the looms.

The labour is hard. The lint clogs lungs and shortens lives. Everyone coughs in the Work.

Ye're ower wan, Thomas, says Pitcairne. Ye're no aboot tae boak, are ye? I canna be haein an assistant wi a mutinous gut.

I'm grand, Doctor. Just thinkin.

Dinna owerburden yirsel.

Pitcairne casts a magpie eye around the dormitory, assessing the general health of the residents.

Are we for off?

Aye, sir, say Callum and Magnus.

Wait! says Block, hurrying down the long dormitory, brandishing a roll of cloth. Here's some caller claith for ye. Ower choice for the purpose but as ye insist on cleanliness—

Block tosses a length of meal-coloured stuff over the corpse. Pitcairne sighs theatrically.

That's better, is it no?

If ye say so.

Afore ye go, Doctor, if it please ye tae sign the dispensation?

A pleasure, says Pitcairne, taking up the quill and writing in a loose, flamboyant hand:

I, Archibald Pitcairne, certify that I am removing the body of John Smith, pauper, mert, for the purpose of medical investigation and undertake that after dissection and subsequent inspection of the innards has been carried out I will, at my own expense, effect a proper Christian burial of the remains.

Archibald Pitcairne, Professor of Physick, College of Edinburgh, October 31, 1694

All Hallows' Eve, nae less! Will this suffice?

Aye, and thankin ye, sir.

Thank *you*, Mr Block. I'll be back midweek for tendin tae yir sick but mind and alert me *posthaste* if ane o yir folk passes.

Aye sir.

Posthaste, man. Ye dae appreciate the need for a caller corpse?

The men exchange long glances. Pitcairne's is arch; Block's intransigent.

Perfectly synchronised and betraying no sign of strain, Callum and Magnus raise the covered corpse and await intructions.

We hae a fascinatin day ahead, says Pitcairne to Thomas. We will begin oor study with the peritoneum, omentum, stomach, intestine, mesentry and pancreas. On the morrow we will progress tae the liver, spleen, kidneys, ureters, bladder and pairts o generation, and so on for the remainder o the week. I hope ye've a strang constitution.

I hope the same, says Thomas.

I will ask that ye be excused frae yir studies for pairt o each day. Time is of the essence. We must strike while the corpse is caller!

As they proceed through the dormitory, drawing gloomy looks as they go, a frail, ancient man begins to sing in a breathy tenor: *The Lord's My Shepherd, I shall not want. He maketh me down to lie. In pastures green, He leadeth me—*

Onward! says Pitcairne breezily.

It's a raw morning. A wind peppered with grit buffets the tall lands of the High Street. As they continue in the direction of the doctor's rooms in the college, the citizens of Edinburgh, brushed up for Sunday service at this kirk or that, cast sideways glances. And aspersions.

Afford the Lord's Day tae the Lord!

Have ye forgotten the teachins o Hippocrates?

I believe, Pitcairne retorts, I'm as familiar wi the Hippocratic oath as ony chiel: *I will be chaste and religious in my life and in my practice. I will not cut, even for the stone* – but yon refers tae the quick, no the deid—

Chaste! Religious!

Cartin a body through the streets on the Sabbath – they should pit ye in the jougs!

Pitcairne pauses and strikes an imperious pose: stout legs planted wide, arms akimbo.

Guid people! he declares, loud as a town crier. I've been granted permission by the Court o Session tae cairry oot investigations which I undertake for the benefit o ilka ane o ye.

Can ye no wait anither day for anither corpse?

Dae they no drap lik flies in the Work?

Next he'll be requesting permission tae dispatch a pauper wi braith in him for the sake o his *investigations*!

He'll no be the first.

I grant, says Pitcairne, that we anatomists can appear ower eager tae inspect a cadaver. But niver, as God is my witness, wid I contemplate such an abomination as whit ye imply. A physick's haunds are healing haunds.

So ye plan tae bring the deid back tae life?

That, as ye ken fou weel, is beyond me or onybody else in my profession and only a necromancer wid hae ye believe itherwise. But the deid are the deid and needs must. A man can nae mair choose the moment o his demise than when he slithers frae his mither's womb. *Mors Patet, Hora Latet*, my freends. Death is sure, the hour obscure and nane but a blockheid wid deny it. And as for travail on the Sabbath, wid ye, if ye were at daith's door on the Lord's Day, bide until the morn's morn afore ye sent for a doctor?

Aye! says one.

Aye, says another, with less conviction.

We'll see if ye're as guid as yir word, says Pitcairne, in yir hour o need.

The real issue, on the Sabbath, with most of the townsfolk on the way to their respective places of worship, is a little different. Pitcairne makes no bones about his unorthodox views on religion. In his cups or out of them, he has a loose tongue and is wont to play the devil's advocate, in part for sport, in part to test the reasoning powers of whatever company he finds himself in, and the man spreads himself around. When folk see him escorting a corpse to his chambers they already know he intends to get out his saws, drills and scalpels and the other grim tools of his trade, and rend the body asunder. And this, many believe, is a violation of the will of God. Except in the case of criminals, whose decomposing heads are on display, most days of the year, at the gibbet in the Grassmarket and also at the Mercat Cross.

Answer me this, he says. Wid ye raither perish frae the tardiness or ignorance o physicks or hae them, helter-skelter, advance their knowledge that ye might be spared a twelvemonth mair? Dae ye believe, if yir threescore and ten years were naewhere near expired, that the Lord wid object tae medical intervention? Answer me this: wha, in fou possession o thir faculties, wid choose tae suffer needless pain?

If we're meant tae suffer, it is the Lord's will and no the whim o some atheistical physick.

My guid sir, says Pitcairne, a physick sweers tae *dae nae hairm*. Does this maxim gang agin yir credo?

Physicks should spend mair time readin the Scriptures than aw yon textbooks.

Ye'd hae me practise my profession on the strength o medical instruction gleaned frae the Scriptures?

Dinna pay *him* ony mind! shouts a burly woman, jabbing an accusing finger in Pitcairne's direction. That ane's the *antichrist*, come tae dupe us, tae deceive us intae believin he brings salvation. He'll send us aw tae perdition!

Pitcairne bows deeply in the woman's direction. I'm flattered, he declares to all and sundry, that this good woman considers me tae possess such fiendish power but truth be telt, I'm but a humble servant o medical science. And the mair I learn, the mair I find there is tae learn! In an aside to Thomas he adds: Atween you and me, I've a mind tae cast some o yon sactimonious gadflies in my next drama.

Thomas thrills at Pitcairne's insouciance, his jocosity, his ability to stand firm against condemnation, neither rising to anger, nor submitting to being brow-beaten. Though he knows that pride is a sin, being chosen by Pitcairne as an assistant makes him glow with pleasure. How can sinning feel so good? These people, with their petty objections are incapable of comprehending the significance of new ideas. They want to be told what to do and what to think at every turn. They do not wish, do not dare, to make decisions for themselves. They prefer to remain ignorant and helpless, to leave their bodies and souls in the hands of a preacher who, after all, is only a man. And if rumour is to be believed, there are men of the cloth who sin as much as the meanest kind of man. He will not let himself become a sheep which blindly follows the herd no matter where the shepherd might lead; he will find his own path, wherever it takes him.

His mind races on, charting out a splendid future for himself: he will laureate with honours; he will study medicine under Pitcairne; he will become a healer; he will discover treatments no-one this side of the equator has even considered, let alone tried and tested and put into practice; he will travel far and wide, study the customs and beliefs of distant lands and make some crucial discovery about the nature of the cosmos. Indeed he will. He will, perhaps, become one of the great minds of his day.

As an idealised future hurtles on in his imagination, one splendid achievement superseding its predecessor, Thomas becomes aware that, from across the street, an incongruous group is observing him, closely: two fellow students, Patrick Middleton and John Neilson, who is further on in his studies; Robert Henderson, Keeper of the Library; and Robert Hutchison, bookseller and printer. Proud to be seen in Pitcairne's company, Thomas raises a hand in greeting. To a man, all turn their backs on him and, deep in conversation, proceed in the direction of St Giles Kirk.

A Frenzy

One inclement afternoon, after concluding his teaching duties – fulfilled with as little enthusiasm as he might have instructed a school of codfish – Alexander Cunningham has been assigned to assist Robert Henderson, Keeper of the Library, with stock-taking. Now that there is a complete catalogue of holdings, stock must be fully accounted for. Henderson is pear-shaped, pernickety and peevish: an ink blot on the register, the manner in which a book is conveyed from his desk to the reading tables, the creaks caused by a body shifting on a chair – any little thing can irk the man, despite the fact that the library is not, customarily, a haven of peace and quiet. The college printer operates on the floor below and generates a great amount of racket, not to mention dizzy-making fumes from printers' ink. Nevertheless, as the college endeavours to preserve its books by keeping a fire burning, the library is popular with students who cannot afford the recent increase in the price of coal. Beneath portraits of Luther, Melanchthon, Zwingli, Calvin, and the newly-installed likeness of the still-controversial René Descartes, they can pursue their studies in relative comfort.

To blunt the tedium and compensate for the burdensome prospect of working with Henderson, whose cussedness oozes from every pasty pore, Cunningham fortifies himself from a flask of brandy. Henderson scrutinises the borrowings, pointing out, with stubby-fingered insistence, the names of those who have signed for Descartes, Hobbes, Blount and Spinoza. Especially Spinoza.

If the books are in the library, says Cunningham, are they no intended for readin?

We'll mak a start when I've dealt wi the returns, Henderson replies. For a heavy man his voice is incongruously reedy. If a job's worth daein, it's worth daein weel.

D'ye think I dinna ken that, man?

There's them that kens and does whit's richt, says Henderson, and them that kens whit's richt but pleases thirsels.

Sniffing, Henderson pads off to the stocks with books stacked like bricks from palm to oxter.

Why, Cunningham wonders, is a man who has such suspicion of books in charge of a library? If Henderson had his way, he'd chain up the books, or lock them away so only the elite might have access, the few so etiolated and intransigent that nothing they read could have any effect on them, unless it be to strengthen the illusion that they already know all that is right and good, sinful and seditious.

The thought of inching round the stocks with Henderson – once the man has finished reshelving the returns – checking titles against the catalogue and the ledger of borrowers, of having to spend several hours in such proximity that he could ascertain the individual constituents of the man's dinner, makes Cunningham reach again for his flask. That and the faintly troubling awareness that Henderson has written proof of who has borrowed what. Does the Keeper of the Library read anything other than titles and authors and names of borrowers? Does he, like all too many others, decide *a priori* that if a book has met with notoriety then it must undoubtedly be pernicious?

Cunningham has no interest in regulating the reading habits of his students but glances at the list of borrowers nevertheless. Halyburton is a prominent borrower, and his choice of reading predictably pious. Aikenhead, who might in time prove to be one of his best students, has borrowed books on everything under the sun and he is heartened to note that some of his own more challenging recommendations are listed. As for Craig, his choice suggests rather more unorthodox tastes than Cunningham might have expected.

Laughter erupts from a table near the fire. Ever alert to irregularity, Henderson pads down the aisle to reprehend the culprits, who are, Cunningham realises with a twist of irritation, his own students: Craig, Mitchell, Middleton and Potter. In recent months Craig has extended his social circle somewhat, and Aikenhead, to whom in their bajan year he attached himself like a very leech, now appears to be only intermittently included in the company. If he were of a mind to intervene he'd advise Aikenhead to steer clear of Craig, yet any student worth his salt would spurn a teacher's advice on such matters. Besides, if he has any sense he'll get the measure of the sly anatomy soon enough. Aikenhead is of no immediate concern. What concerns him at the moment is the party of oafs, directing their attention towards him and only him, and making great sport of their sniggering scrutiny.

A pulse drums at his temple. His chest tightens. He is about to resort to the flask once more but stays his hand. Since the night when Craig caught him with his breeks about his knees, he has been waiting, with a bitter broth of dread and ire, for something to happen: an accusatory finger picking him out on the street; a chap at the door, and the delivery of an advocate's decree or summons to attend the college court slipped beneath it.

Nothing of the sort has transpired. Nothing at all has transpired. As yet. Craig has come to classes as usual, smirking and snivelling as usual, attempting to disrupt lessons and undermine his authority. What Craig lacks in reasoning he makes up for in cunning. Since the night in question, Cunningham has desisted from laying a stave across Craig's ugly back. So far. And so far, Craig has kept his mouth shut: the dog can only be biding his time.

The red-headed lemon seller, who goes by the name Estrella St Clair, was still plying her trade a few weeks back, when she was apprehended during the ceremonial Riding of the Borders, a piece of pomp and nonsense in which magistrates assemble at the foot of the West Bow, leave the city by Society Port and ride around the liberties. The affair is little more than an excuse for the idle to gawp, the beggars to beg, for even more shilpit, destitute folk to worm their way into the city, and for tradesfolk of all descriptions to turn a profit.

Just as the recommendations of the Assembly were beginning to be put into practice and the Kirk Session was pursuing loose young women with savage appetite, while trumpets blared and magistrates trotted by on brushed and tasselled mounts, one of the baillies, presumably not blind to the charms of Estrella St Clair, instructed the Guard to apprehend her before continuing on his ceremonial duties.

She was charged for a whore, branded on the shoulder and warned that, should she come before the courts for a similar offence, the branding iron would be set upon her face. He has since passed her on the street a time or two. Though she covers herself rather more fastidiously than previously and no longer proffers oranges and lemons – such practice having been banned by some expedient trumpery – her sinuous gait and bold gaze suggest that she has not entirely abandoned her whoring. He does not blame her: needs must and how else might a woman sustain herself once she has fallen?

Confined to the library, with daylight drained from the sky by four in the afternoon, amid further eruptions of hilarity from the table by the fire – Henderson's rebuke has had no effect whatsoever – Cunningham becomes convinced that Craig has been relating details of what he spied through the shutters. Why else would his audience vacillate between inane gawping and throaty sniggers?

He sees no sin in what transpired. It was a mutually beneficial transaction. He has read the Greeks, the Romans, knows that intercourse between men and women does not depend exclusively on the holy sacrament of matrimony. He would willingly know the jade again this minute; he would set his teeth to the soft lobe of her ear, listen to the slap of skin on skin, the cries of pleasure mixed with pain; it's what the beasts do when they have the urge, with no aftertaste of shame or guilt. God gave man the apparatus to take pleasure thus, and, by God, it is a pleasure – and what, in God's name, is wrong with pleasure?

He would have her now, in front of the fire, for all to see;

he'd show those sniggering gawpers what it is to be a man. And if she's a whore, so be it: what other kind of woman could he have, without submitting to a lifetime of toil and the inevitable procreation induced by matrimony? He'd rather sell his soul to the devil than bring another brat into a world in which even the mind is bound and gagged, in which all vitality is sapped by vain attempts to please a wrathful, implacable deity, who sends famine and pestilence to test the faith and fortitude of believers, who sends spies and pickthanks to torment a man because he dares to think for himself! And what of these hobbledehoys, with a stirring in their breeches and a fear of the Almighty clamping their very thoughts in thumbikins?

The odours in the library are suffocating: rank male sweat, unwashed clothes, leather, vellum, paper, ink, smoke, dust, ash—

Regent Cunningham, Henderson pipes up, shall we mak a start?

The students exchange gleeful glances as the Keeper of the Library admonishes their regent. The wind gowls round the courtyard and dashes loose grit against the windows.

Tell us aboot the jade's breasts, Craig.

Her legs.

Her arse.

Gie us the haill accoont frae the start.

Sae we can better judge the extent and nature o the sinnin.

Revelling in the attention – not to mention the renewed stirring in his groin – Mungo Craig continues to feed tidbits to Middleton, Mitchell and Potter: the lemon seller opening up her bodice and revealing her breasts, their regent setting his teeth to her nipple, the smooth flesh of her haunches, the dark cleft of her buttocks. Having a tale to tell which simultaneously titillates and scandalises is a far better way to make folk take note of him than making a pest of himself in class.

The excitement around the table rises as steadily as sap from the root of each well-read but practically ignorant young man. They are once more visualising the moment of penetration when Cunningham, acutely aware of how the other students hang on Craig's every word, upends his flask and finds it empty.

Weel, says Henderson, clicking a fingernail down the ribs of the ledger, shall we mak a start?

A start? Cunningham rounds on him. On whit should we mak a start?

The task ye're chairged wi.

Anither task! Anither and then anither! Ye'd hae me at yir tasks till I'm deid. Ye'd hae me labour at taen stock until there's nae braith left in me. And whit then? Pit me in my grave and say *Amen*? A life o toil and penance and denial. Where's the pleasure, man, where's the joy? I'll tell ye where: the only pleasure tae be had in this world is in wine, in song, in the freedom o the mind tae roam where it wishes. And in women. Aye, in women. *Be not forgetful to entertain strangers, for thereby some have entertained angels unawares. Hebrews 13:2* Then again, as onybody kens, the deil has the best tunes.

Cunningham hurls his empty flask across the room. It hits the fireplace then clatters into the grate.

The books! Henderson squeals in alarm. We must attend tae the books!

Attend tae the books? And how wid ye hae me attend tae them? Cunningham sways towards the stacks and plucks out books at random. Here, he says. Here's a pretty pile. Whit wid ye hae me dae wi them, set them tae the flames? They'd gie us heat aplenty. And is it no the best recourse for whit we fear, tae tear it doon, set a flame tae it? Which authors should we burn first? Herbert of Cherbury – now there's a chiel for ye – or Charles Blount? Wid ye say the Deists are best consigned tae the flames forthwith? Deists wid hae us believe that God wid let us proceed wi oor lives, mak oor ain decisions about whit's richt or wrang and stand by oor ain beliefs. Or is it mair pressing tae first dispose o the Talmud, the Qu'ran, tae immolate yon far-flung floo'ers sae they might no contaminate oor Covenanted gairden? Far-flung floo'ers, far-flung floo'ers – damn them aw!

Cunningham bangs against the shelves and lurches towards the window table.

Whit say ye, gentlemen? How wid ye deliberate on this: should we incinerate the prented word or set alight the petticoats o jades and witches? Wid ye agree wi Reverend Knox's deliberations on the female o the species? How did he pit it? Let me see, now, let me see. How wis the great man's critique set doon? Let me see. Ah, here it is, here it is. Pay close attention.

The First Blast of the Trumpet against the Monstruous Regimen of Women

To promote a woman to bear rule, superiority, dominion or empire above any realm, nation, or city, is repugnant to nature, contumely to God, a thing most contrarious to his revealed will and approved ordinance, and finally it is the subversion of good order, of all equity and injustice. In the probation of this proposition, I will not be so curious, as to gather what soever may amplify, set forth, or decore the same, but I am purposed, even as I have spoken my conscience in most plain and few words, so to stand content with a simple proof of every member, bringing in for my witness God's ordinance in nature, his plain will revealed in his word, and the minds of such as be most ancient amongst goodly writers…

How then should we cleanse oorsels, gaird agin contamination? How should we protect oorsels agin the monstruous regimen o women? Weel, Craig, whit say ye?

I dinna ken, sir.

Ye dinna ken? Ye dinna ken? The verra same wha cairries up his sleeve a barb, a jibe, for ilka class o mine he's attended – ye dinna ken? Weel, weel. The wages o ignorance are – the wages o sin are – the wages o idiocy!

Retreating from the window table, Cunningham makes a haphazard tour of the library, pulling out books as he goes. Outside, the wind continues to gowl. Underfoot, the printing press clacks and rattles. Arms stacked with books, he careens towards the fire.

Tae the flames! he shrieks. Tae the flames!

Like a hog that can shift more quickly than his bulk might suggest, Henderson streaks across the library, lunges at Cunningham and brings him down hard, then straddles him and wrenches his arms behind his back with such alacrity it might have been part of his daily regimen. Books clatter across the floor and come to rest like fallen rocks. Cunningham, pinned face down by Henderson, roars and writhes.

This is madness sir! Henderson squeals. Desist, I pray ye!

Pray aw ye like, I'll no desist! Cunningham spits. I'll hae ye chairged wi assailze! I'll hae ye horsewhipped! I'll hae ye—

Fetch a doctor! Henderson orders the students who have risen from their seats to observe, at close quarters, the curious sight of their regent quoshed beneath Henderson's considerable arse. Which doctor should we fetch? says Craig.

Naw *we*. *Ane* o ye fetch a doctor. The rest bide where ye be. I may be needful o reinforcements.

Pitcairne kens the man, says Craig.

Fetch Pitcairne, then. If he's no in his chambers ye ken where tae look.

Awbody kens where tae find Pitcairne, says Middleton. And kens the atheistical chiels he imbibes wi.

And perhaps, says Mitchell, oor Tam will be sat at thir feet.

If Tam's at thir feet, says Craig, he'll no be sittin quiet. He'll be airin that wayward tongue o his, contributin his tuppenceworth tae the proceedins.

Surely mair than tuppenceworth! says Middleton.

This isna the time or place for aw this jabber! squeals Henderson. Fetch the flaming doctor!

I'll gang, says Craig. But whit shall I say is the maitter wi Maister Cunningham?

A frenzy! says Henderson, bearing down with determination on the regent's flailing body. The poor distracted saul has been afflicted wi a frenzy!

A Tincture of Sedative Herbs

While Thomas and his classmates come to the end of the academic year, while they are totting up what remains of a bursary, allowance or loan in the hope it will see them through to the end of their studies, Parliament sits. There are four committees, each with a specific remit: the address to the King, national security, trade, and contested elections. As Catholics have been prevented from voting since William's accession, legislation that favours a covenanted Presbyterianism is far from being a surprise and as voters are required to demonstrate ownership of property, other refinements and exclusions are none too hard to deduce.

The security committee is the largest, comprising peers, barons and burgh representatives in equal measure. The clergy ferrets away in the background, compiling an exhaustive list of caveats relating to the spiritual health of the nation. The Justice of the Court rolls his eyes and sends them away to confine themselves to essentials, and to excise all reference to existing laws. Not content with presenting their grievances to Parliament, the Presbyterian clergy launches simultaneous diatribes from the pulpit. The end is nigh, or at least inevitable; there is no hiding from Judgement day, and so the Episcopal clergy's wish to practise religion *its way* – which in the eyes of the Presbyterians is irreligious and atheistic – could only bring down doom on every head.

In order that Parliament might appease the most belligerent men of the cloth and so proceed to its main business – the establishment of the Company of Scotland Trading to Africa and the Indies, and, more than three years after the event, who must bear the blame for the massacre at Glencoe – it passes, with scant deliberation on the finer points, several acts related to religious matters. 'Irregular' baptisms and marriages, that is those performed by outed clergy, are outlawed. Penalties for profaneness, or public scandal, are increased. Permission is granted to magistrates to reschedule Saturday or Monday markets so that those with a distance to travel might avoid breaking the Sabbath. New legislation on blasphemy, containing specific penalties for mocking and railing against God, is introduced. Punishment for a first offence is imprisonment and the wearing of sackcloth; for a second, a heavy fine, with a portion of the fine going to any informer; for a third offence, death.

***

Things do not improve for Regent Cunningham. In the wake of his frenzy, which culminates in snarling and flailing and foaming at the mouth, Archibald Pitcairne binds his arms and applies a kerchief soaked in dwale to the patient's mouth and nose, until the distracted man succumbs to its stupefying effects. Magnus and Callum Fairweather remove him from the library to Pitcairne's medical rooms where he is subjected to a range of treatments. These include bleeding and the ingestion – violently protested – of several of the doctor's more unorthodox concoctions, the ingredients of which include spider webs, ground human skull, hens' gizzards. All to no avail. Repeated inhalation of dwale affords Cunningham pockets of stupor but a man cannot doze forever and when he surfaces from his dwam he is even more agitated than before. He howls and roars and would bite the hand that treated him were he not firmly restrained. He utters such filthy curses that even Pitcairne, himself no stranger to full-blooded oaths, is at a loss as to how to proceed.

After the best part of a week under close observation, Callum and Magnus transport the patient to his lodgings within the college grounds.

Not one to give up lightly, Pitcairne consults John Sutherland, who has recently been appointed professor of Botanical Medicine. Though Sutherland's expertise is in high demand, the fact that he looks to Rome for his religious guidance has become, for some, cause for controversy. Promotion affords him an amount of protection from bigots but does not stop tongues wagging; nor does it ensure the safety of Zeno who follows his lead on all matters and accepts the notion of transubstantiation as readily as the fact that grass is green. More than once, while planting out seedlings, Zeno has been set upon; he was more distressed by the damage done to the plants than by being forced to eat handfuls of earth. Sutherland has petitioned for the perpetrators to be brought to justice but knows full well that snoops and censors, eager to apprehend drunks, Sabbath breakers and fornicators, can be all too lax in rooting out the lawless and violent within the ranks of the faithful.

With Thomas in tow, Pitcairne pays the beleaguered regent a home visit. It is no great inconvenience to cross the college courtyard, follow the dank corridor's labyrinthine route then climb several flights of stairs at its end.

Mercy, says Pitcairne, reaching for his chypre, the stink in here wid fell an ox!

Thomas picks his way round the study, wrinkling his nose at the smell and looking askance at the squalor: all available surfaces are littered with the mouldering remains of meals; empty bottles stand around the floor, drinking glasses are clarted with dregs of dessicated claret; candle-stubs are clumped together like toadstools; papers are piled in extravagant disarray.

Unkempt and unshaven, Cunningham is in bed, flat on his back, directing a stream of invective at the ceiling.

Guid day tae ye, sir, says Pitcairne.

The wages o sin are the wages o idiocy! bawls Cunningham.

That's as may be, says Pitcairne, but I've a tincture o herbs frae Professor Sutherland.

How d'ye fare, Maister Cunningham? says Thomas.

Cunningham scowls at his visitors then resumes cursing the ceiling.

Weel, says Pitcairne, I canna see ony bogles up there sae will ye try this tincture or will ye no? I'm under strict instructions tae administer the dose *personally* – ower much can be fatal – and I canna tarry here aw day.

The wages o sin are the wages o idiocy! Cunningham bawls, then resumes his filthy cursing.

Has Cunningham simply gone mad, Thomas wonders, or is there some sense in his foul-mouthed rant? Was some trouble, hitherto unacknowledged, now finding its way free through the flood of expletives? To lose one's wits – demonic possession or no – to be at the mercy of a mental aberration which makes a man speak and act in ways contrary to his will, must be intolerable; surely a man thus afflicted deserves a little pity? Pitcairne does not approve of treatments applied to lunatics which purport to drive out the devil. But Pitcairne, according to some, does not believe in God; and if he does not believe in God, how then could he believe in the devil?

Rumour has it, says Pitcairne, that the sin o fornication cost ye yir sanity. I've nae truck wi that kind o superstition. I'm a healer. A healer disna concern hissel wi a man's morals but wi his malady.

If ye please, Maister Cunningham, says Thomas, try the tincture. It grieves me tae see ye in such a condition.

Cunningham pauses in his cursing but continues to glower at the ceiling.

I'll be blunt, says Pitcairne. Whether or no ye're possessed wi deils, ye're a freethinker, a heterodox, wi interests far beyond the tight-knit web o the Kirk. And oor new Principal, wha adheres tae the Convenant like a wasp tae syrup, needs scant encouragement tae suspend ye, in perpetuity, frae yir duties.

At this, Cunningham roars and pulls a blanket over his head.

We came tae yir pigsty o oor ain free will, says Pitcairne, waving the phial of chypre under his nose. We'll try again the morn's morn. And the day efter. Beyond that, ye're in the hands o the Almighty.

Hircus Cervus

A miserable summer, so lacking in warmth that even the flies and clegs fail to hatch, is followed by a wailing witch of an autumn and an interminable winter freeze. Food becomes scarce. In parts of the country the crop yield is too poor and harvested too late in the year to have any value; livelihoods rot on stalks. Fuel is running low and some unfortunates who have been sleeping rough are found dead in doorways, closes and wynds but the new Incorporation of Chirurgeon Apothecaries – replacing the Guildbrether of Barbers and Chirurgeons – already has sufficient corpses at its disposal on which to practice dissection. In exchange for the incorporation's commitment to build a medical school within two years or lose its privileges, the council has granted it permission to take possession of the bodies of foundlings, weaned but not yet of an age to attend school or enter a trade, as well as the remains of those troubled souls proven to have committed *felo de se*.

During the same period, outed episcopal clergy are compelled to swear an Oath of Allegiance to the King if they wish to retain any benefices. Despite whatever moral quagmire they sense themselves descending into, over a hundred sign the oath, to the disgruntlement of extreme Presbyterians. The General Assembly, due to take place in October, is postponed and when it eventually meets in December the streets are awash with hollow-cheeked beggars. A holding centre is commissioned to house them until such time as they can be sent back to their own parishes. The work is undertaken less from charity than from an attempt to contain the problems that vagrant beggars bring – disease, brawling, thievery, an eagerness to eat anything they can find. Rumours of anthropophagy abound. Elsewhere in the country, plague has broken out and the movement of beggars is causing concern. As is the movement of soldiers.

To have a harvest fail one year suggests, to the faithful, that God is angry. To have it fail two years in succession indicates that those made in His own image need to take drastic action, forthwith, to stay calamity. Surely, if the wrath of God is plain as day, outlawing Catholic Priests and Quakers might be a direct route to appeasement?

The Kirk steps up its campaign against any perceived to stray from the path of orthodoxy and many attend the rousing fire and brimstone sermons delivered by James Webster, minister of the Tolbooth Kirk. Beggars continue to freeze to death on the city streets and cottars, attempting to harvest worthless crops, lose feet and hands to frostbite. The number of desperately hungry continues to rise and, in response, the Kirk once again feels the need to address itself to the dissemination of dangerous ideas: it passes an act against the atheistical opinions of the Deists.

South of the Border, the Licensing Law has lapsed and books which hitherto might have run up against opposition from the censors can now be printed; this includes John Toland's *Christianity not Mysterious*, which challenges the tenets of revealed religion and denies the divine hand of Providence at work in the universe. Its author does not deny the existence of a supreme being but still, provocatively, envisions the universe as a self-regulating mechanism. Toland's name is on many lips and his reputation as a firebrand travels far and wide. Some admire his forthrightness, his daring, his gift of the gab; others, including the scrupulous John Locke, find his barn-storming attack on the fabric of belief distasteful, and disconcerting.

The physical, spiritual and moral collapse of Regent Cunningham has prompted his former students to chew over the situation. Now that Cunningham has, according to the faithful, been struck down by the Almighty for his evil ways and dangerous ideas – and had his teaching contract revoked – it is vital that his former students investigate the literature he recommended and consider all the influences which might have contributed to his downfall. So, at least, says Mungo

Craig, and few demur.

While Thomas's attention has been taken up with more practical matters, Craig has become something of a guiding light amongst his peers. Without Cunningham to call him to account, he is free to challenge the regent's teachings, and does so with relish, revealing the extent of his own study to be greater than he had hitherto been given credit for. Even Thomas Halyburton, darling of devout Presbyterians, though he won't set foot in Hutchison's bookshop, dips into works by Deists, Jansenists, Socinians and Epicureans, if only to ascertain where, precisely, the road to damnation lies. Halyburton's flirtation with danger is brief: he sees the error of his ways before the errors of others might corrupt him, and turns his back on those who might seduce him from the true path of Presbyterian goodness. But that is Halyburton, already marked out for the ministry, who knows full well the side on which his bread is buttered.

Cunningham, it is generally agreed, has been justly punished by God by being reduced to a broken, raving madman though Thomas does not share his classmates' relish in Cunningham's downfall. True, he rarely felt the crack of the stave across his back while others, Craig in particular, were punished repeatedly and at times brutally; but the tables have turned and Cunningham has become a wretch. How can his fellow students, who study as much theology and philosophy as he, remain so hard-hearted?

The college has become taxed by the students' preference for taverns, billiard halls and skittle alleys over lecture halls, and has forbidden them to enter such establishments during class time. Spies receive financial reward for every offender's name supplied and pursue their task with zeal. So far no such restrictions have been imposed on visiting a bookstore. Who could be sure that a reputable regent – which, now, would be one appointed by Principal Gilbert Rule and his Board of Governors – had not sent a party of students to seek recommended reading materials as yet unavailable in the college library? By some inexplicable means, the languishing lamentable Cunningham had hitherto hung on to an appointment granted when James Stewart was on the throne, a time when a staunch Protestant like Rule was about as welcome in the corridors of learning as a Papist is now.

It is a bitter winter morning, still dark, icy underfoot. Dozens of students tramp briskly down the College Wynd, as much to keep warm as to hasten to their classes.

Welcome back tae *mens sanitas*, says Craig, as he catches up with Thomas. Nae tellin whit hairm a man might come tae frae bein owerlang in the company o a dement.

Pink-cheeked from the cold but snug in his warm coat, Thomas strides along eagerly. Craig struggles to keep up with him.

Maister Cunningham's a tormented saul, says Thomas.

He'll get nae sympathy frae me, says Craig. He's a vicious bully. No tae mention a filthy libertine.

A vile sinner, says Middleton, falling in with the pair of them, and blowing on thin, chilblained fingers as he lopes along. A pernicious sinner tae. Think o the hairm he could have done tae aw yon pliant minds entrusted tae his care.

Wid ye say *ye've* a pliant mind, Middleton? says Thomas. Wid ye say Cunningham has done ye a personal mischief?

I sincerely hope he hasna.

The point is, says Craig, there's nae tellin ane way or anither until it's ower late. And it's aye better tae be safe and sure.

Is it no better, says Thomas, tae mind ye dinna bend whitiver way the wind blaws?

We'll see, says Craig.

While a replacement for Cunningham was sought and sporadic lessons delivered by Principal Rule and others of his religious persuasion, regular classes are about to resume and Thomas and his fellow students are curious to meet their new regent.

Cunningham's replacement is one John Row who, from the outset, is a disappointment. Dogged, dull as mud, Row makes no attempt to introduce himself, nor to gain favour through jest or pleasantry, despite the fact that the classroom is so cold that the breath condenses in foggy plumes. He looks them over, counts heads then launches into lecturing. Row is dark, sallow-skinned, hollow-eyed, sepulchral-voiced. The bones of his narrow face are set off by a short, pointed beard. He does not appear to know how to smile. He follows the curriculum to the letter, insisting doggedly that ethics is the supreme tenet of philosophy, that no matter how much knowledge a student may acquire, his greatest aim, and achievement, must be to love God. The class is set to study geometry for the entire morning. Thomas has no objection to geometry but, like so many others, he is hungry, and hunger makes him restive. Row drones on about how the principles of geometry were given by God so that his people might labour more efficiently. Stomachs rumble, pens scratch, numb arses shift.

Regent Row, says Thomas, in the Latin as ever, may I speak, sir?

If you must.

Thank you, Sir. I was thinking that if God is responsible for the rules of geometry, which can be mathematically proven like the rules of logic, why is it not possible to apply a similar computation to the Creator Himself? When I consider, for example, Theantropos, it appears to me a conundrum, in the manner of *quadratum rotundum,* or *hircus cervus.* A circle cannot be made from a square, nor can a goat and a hart combine to create a single creature.

The acoustics are such that his words hang in the air like the breath of his classmates, before they evaporate. Row's expression remains unreadable. Perhaps he should stop now, but no, he continues: As Aristotle posited, we can *imagine* a creature which is half goat and half hart, but know that it does not exist. We may be able to *imagine* a man incarnating God while knowing he does not exist. Man's imagination, with art and industry, can create anything.

Some of his classmates respond with a ripple of mirth; others are more circumspect.

Chou D'Or

Netherstane, November 1695

Dearest Brother,

You cannot imagine what joy it was for both of us to visit you earlier in the year, even if my gladness was undone by the dreadful news about Jeremiah. I beg your pardon for how unforthcoming I was: I had no words then for what I was feeling. Six months on and I cannot but hope that the great wave that rent his ship also carried him to a place of safety where he remains alive and well. But the Lord giveth and the Lord taketh away and if He deems that I become an old maid, so be it; it is not for me to question His will, nor to squander my days in pining.

We miss you terribly. Anna would tell you this herself but will not write to a student at the College of Edinburgh – even if this is her own brother – in case she errs. She is as adamant in her refusal as she is shamed by her difficulty with letters. Nevertheless, she fares well. I regret not meeting any of your college friends but Anna admits some distaste for those she met. It may be that we fail to appreciate the nature of friendship between educated folk but why, we wonder, does our brother befriend folk who do not treat him with respect?

On our return to Netherstane we shared the coach with a foppish art master, a Frenchman who goes by the name of Hippolyte Fer-de-Lance, who looked askance at my tears but offered little comfort. His efforts would have been in vain; that day, and for many days thereafter, I was inconsolable. Monsieur Hippolyte was engaged in the main for Alasdair who, as ever, cannot settle on what to do with his life. He insisted on a studio with tall windows and a north-facing aspect which, he claimed, has the most constant light, and the upstairs guest room was given over to him. It was no surprise to anybody – bar Lady Hester – that limning was little more for

Alasdair than a passing fancy. He can barely hold a brush in the proper manner, never mind produce a fair likeness of anybody or anything on God's earth. When the art master became impatient with his lack of application and tardy progress, he invited Anna and me to take lessons as well. Euphemie, as you can imagine, had too much else on her mind.

It turns out that I have little talent for art but Anna shines at the limning and the Frenchman was fair taken with her early essays and, of course, her yellow hair. Mon petit chou d'or, he called her. Anna was not fond of being called a cabbage, even a golden one, but Sir Patrick was so pleased to discover her aptitude that he charged her to make likenesses of every member of the household, including the servants. She worked at this with fervour. From first light she was at the easel with rags and brushes, bemoaning how few hours of daylight the winter months offer.

One by one her subjects took up an agreed position, sitting or standing, and this process uncovered some particular vanities: Alasdair wanted to know whether his nose looked finer one way or t'other; Euphemie changed her mind a dozen times about how she should wear her hair; Madge swithered between her blue blouse and her white; John Barr sought the opinion of all as to whether he should sit, coachwhip in hand, or stand and pretend to clap the mare's head; Lady Hester had to be convinced that without a doubt she could be mistaken for a lady of the French courts. This provided us with some amusement but could not, of course, compensate for your absence.

For my part, I was content to serve as Anna's assistant: grinding pigments; mixing in egg yolk, casein and wax; cleaning brushes. There is a great deal to be done before and after making marks on a panel than you might imagine. Sir Patrick promised that when all the likenesses were complete, we would receive recompense for our industry. It pleased us to feel that we were less of a burden on his bounty but things have taken an unexpected turn.

The art master is no longer with us and before he left he caused quite a stir. Lady Hester, who was, at first, tickled by his attentions and his French ways – a siller tongue and an avid eye – caught him and Aleen together in the brewhouse. Modesty prevents me from saying more. The next day the mistress sent him packing, with his tail between his legs and his bag of brushes over his shoulder.

Some say he went to the city and inveigled himself into another household; others that he set sail back to France. Whether it is more dangerous for a Papist to take his chances in the city or to cross the water, I know not, but Aleen has extra duties now, and hard slaps and pinches from Lady Hester. As further punishment, Anna has been forbidden to paint her likeness and Aleen weeps about this more than the slaps. She did not encourage the Frenchman's attention in the least – she seeks a husband, not a paramour – and it makes my blood boil to see her so ill-used.

The upshot of the art master's dalliance is that Sir Patrick and Lady Hester now squabble constantly. Madge mutters about business ventures of Sir Patrick's going awry, about dowry payments being hard to raise, about Lady Hester's indiscretions and extravagances being at the root of the disharmony. Whatever the cause, Sir Patrick has never again mentioned remuneration for the likenesses and we do not like to mention it for fear he will snap at us as he snaps at his wife.

The crops on the estate have not been hit as hard as elsewhere but stores are woefully low. You might think the grave situation with the harvest would have shamed Lady Hester into more frugal preparations for Yule but if anything her extravagance has increased. As goods cannot be brought by road, she has them brought by sea, irrespective of the cost or risk others take to satisfy her whims.

It has been a dreadful season, wet and cold. The roads have been impassable for months. Worse, the crops have been so slow in ripening that farmers could not bring in the harvest until this month and there was little value in what they harvested. There is much hunger in the villages, also in Queensferry and Borrowstounness. The churches take collections every week and all repentance money goes to those whose crops have failed. Some say that the more folk sin, the more the poor will benefit; either way it is a sorry state of affairs. Each day, courtesy of Madge, Anna and I take parcels of food to the most needy families on the estate.

There is also much social unrest. In recent weeks we have seen men-o-war in the firth and, for able-bodied men, the threat of being pressed grows daily. When an English battleship docked in Queensferry the other week, the townsmen avoided the taverns and bolted their doors.

Might you visit for Yule? By hook or by crook there will be sufficient to eat. Fires will be piled high, if the mistress has her way, though as soon as she orders Aleen to build up the fires, the Maister tells her to damp them down. The lass doesn't know which way to turn.

We hope that you are thriving and studying hard, and count the days until we see you again.

Your loving sisters, Katharine and Anna

Postscript: Maister Naysmith assisted me with the drafting of this letter but be assured he did not read every word of it. He sends his best regards and says: keep yir een wide and yir mooth shut!

Poetical Fictions and Extravagant Chimaeras

Thomas and Mungo Craig are on Leith links, for the horse racing. The crowd is large, cheerful, diverse, hailing from town houses and tenement lands, from country seats and rural hovels. Folk meet and greet, and make leisurely perambulations of the track, noting the conditions of the ground and the favourable weather: it is clear and warm. A fresh breeze blowing off the water sets the petals of dog roses aflutter.

When horses and riders are gathered together and paraded around the makeshift paddock, the merchants and burghers cease talk about trade, and guidwives suspend their assessment of each other's hats and gowns in order to appraise the horses: they note a good pair of shoulders, a glossy coat, alert eyes, a spirited gait. The jockeys too, are inspected – for lightness, leanness, compactness, for ardour and ambition. Even those who know little about racing pay close attention to horses and riders, and consider their assessment to be sound.

In honour of his father's fondness for a wager, and of his own childhood fascination with the entrancing properties of quicksilver, Thomas puts a small sum on a horse by the name of Mercury, a long-legged grey colt with lively eyes. Mungo Craig considers backing the favourite, a black filly called Salvation, but changes his mind at the last moment. The horn sounds and they're off, thundering down the track to the crack of whips and lusty exhortation from the spectators. It's a rough race, with horses down and riders toppled from their mounts. By the final stretch the only two serious contenders are Mercury and Salvation, which, with mounting excitement from the crowd, remain neck and neck almost to the finish when Salvation, whipped on furiously by his rider, edges in front and wins by a short head.

Shame, says Thomas. Yir instinct wis true!

My instinct tae forego a wager wis true. Whereas ye pit siller on a horse wi the name o the deil's metal.

Ach, the deil's name is ascribed tae aw and sundry. But we're baith losers. You lost the chance tae fill yir pocket and I a portion o whit remains o my allowance.

Them that struggle tae mak ends meet canna be sae free wi thir coin.

That's no how it is wi gamin, says Thomas. Ye can learn frae loss as weel as gain. Look aboot ye. There's poor folk playin fast and loose wi whit little they hae and ithers wi plenty tae spare, feart tae risk a merk.

I widna ken aboot the rich.

Slick with sweat and breathing hard, the horses which have just finished racing are being walked round the paddock, to cool them down and slow their galloping hearts. Mercury tosses his head and lifts his hooves high. The groom claps his shoulders and talks in his ear. Salvation stumbles, nostrils flaring, breath rasping. Her flanks are streaming with sweat and blood.

It's as weel ye didna put a wager on Salvation, says Thomas. Look at the pitiful state o her now!

The horse wis pit on this earth tae serve man.

Is it God's will that we should mistreat it? Mercury ran weel enough withoot a thrashin.

It's God's will an animal does man's biddin.

Where's the need tae cut a beast tae shreds for the sake o a race?

Ilka cratur on God's earth should ken its place.

Ach, man, it's a day for plain pleasures. Oor heids will bow again soon enough frae the weight o the doctrine o theology.

It's oor duty tae bow beneath it.

The sun is shinin, the lasses are smilin, says Thomas, throwing his arms wide as if to welcome any lasses who might step forward. None do, though one or two cast fleeting glances in his direction.

He delighteth not in the strength of the horse; he taketh not pleasure in the legs of man – Psalm a hunder and fourtie sevin.

Ye're weel-versit on yir bible, I'll gie ye that.

We were born tae serve the Lord, says Craig. Nae mair, nae less.

But were we born tae be cowed and constrained at ilka turn, or tae glory in the joys o life?

The Lord delights in those who fear him, who put their hope in his unfailing love. Verse elevin.

Ach, says Thomas. If ye ask me, the doctrine o theology is a rhapsody o feigned and ill-invented nonsense. It's patched up pairtly o the moral doctrine o philosophers, and pairtly o poetical fictions and extravagant chimaeras.

Craig blinks. His thin lips stretch into a mirthless smile.

Ye were aye ane for sailin close tae the wind, Aikenhead.

If ye say so!

Thomas sups his ale and scans the racecourse. What's the point in going to the races at all if you can't take any pleasure in it, if all you can do is seek – and so surely find – fault?

A dozen more horses are being led off to the starting point for the next race. He is tempted to put on another bet in the hope of recouping his earlier loss but contents himself to be a spectator without a stake. The horses which ran earlier are being rubbed down by grooms. Mercury appears calm and composed, though the glint in his eye suggests he'd be willing to run again if the opportunity were to present itself.

Salvation has not recovered from her exertions. Her head droops, her breath comes in loud, ragged pants and she trembles all over. The groom attempts to lead her out of the paddock but she shies, wild-eyed, nostrils flaring, and flails around. After a prolonged spasm of violent shuddering, with a long, forlorn whinny, she collapses. She has been run too hard and her heart has given out.

Wis that the Lord's will? says Thomas.

Now now, Tam. I'm nae the hertless chiel ye'd cry me. Yon's a dule sicht tae be sure. But come awa, he says, clapping Thomas on the back. Shall we tak a walk roon the perimeter, in the hope that the sea breezes and the sicht of merry folk will raise oor spirits?

As ye wish, says Thomas, mollified.

While the second race is run, to rather more subdued exhortation from the jockeys and onlookers, the dead horse is piled on a cart and dragged to the far side of the links, then to the butchers.

It is a fine evening and folk remain out of doors, enjoying the mild air and the remaining hours of daylight. Thomas and Craig are with Mitchell, Middleton and Potter, whom they met at the racecourse at the end of the day. Despite Craig's persistent carping, Mitchell and Potter continue to crow about their success in backing winners.

So, Craig, ye'd decline the drap o ale oor profit wid buy ye? says Potter.

Why no turn the vice o gamin intae the virtue o generosity? says Mitchell, prompting lengthy debate on whether good can come from ill, whether a good deed can negate a bad deed and so on.

As the light begins to fade and a cool breeze skitters up the High Street, they are joined by John Neilson. A former student now in the employ of the Court of Session, Neilson persuades them to repair to Lucky McCloud's where he stands a round of drinks.

So ye'll accept Neilson's generosity, Craig, but no oors? says Mitchell.

We didna say that, says Craig.

Indeed we didna, says Middleton.

Tempus volat, hora fugit, says Neilson. Dinna be wastin yir braith on quibbles. Yir health, ane and aw!

Then, as he is wont to do, he regales his drinking companions with tales from the courts. He is enjoying the elevated status afforded a graduate in gainful employment. He has taken to smoking and puffs meditatively on a pipeful of Dutch tobacco. The aromatic smoke provokes in Thomas a twinge of nostalgia.

One drink leads to another and one topic of conversation

leads to another: from court business to moral frailty, from horse racing to human cruelty, from politics to philosophy, from serious debate to banter and bawdy talk, from quiddity to dreams and ideals. Just after the ten o'clock bell tolls and the tavernkeeper prepares to close up for the night, in that moment of limbo when drinkers pause and consider where and how the hours have gone, the talk once more spools back to the racecourse, and Craig presses Thomas to repeat to the assembled company 'his curious phrase about rhapsody and chimaeras'. At first he can't recall what Craig refers to but after some prompting – *efter sayin ye were in nae rush tae bow beneath the weight o theology* – and more than a little loose-tongued from the ale, Thomas obliges. Willingly. Eager to impress with his fine phrase.

Printer's Deil

It is a chill, late October day. The air has a smoky, autumnal reek to it and the sky is streaked with threads of cirrus. The trees on College Wynd are shedding what few leaves remain on their branches.

Are ye comin in, or d'ye intend tae press yir neb agin the gless for eternity?

Ye caught me switherin, says Thomas, stepping inside and closing the door behind him.

In my line o work, replies Robert Hutchison, returning to his press, he that swithers neglects an opportunity. Ye're chitterin forby. Chitterin and switherin isna a guid combination.

Indeed it isna! says Thomas.

Blowing on his hands and rubbing some warmth into his arms, Thomas, as ever, casts a greedy eye around the shop, relishing the rich waft of leather, printers' ink and paper. The press and binding table dominate the room. The walls are lined with bookshelves from floor to ceiling and every inch of available floor space is taken up with teetering stacks of pamphlets and broadsheets. Display tables feature Hutchison's own publications and a range of titles from London, Paris and Amsterdam.

It must be gratifyin tae see the fruits o yir labour pass frae ane haund tae anither.

If siller shifts in my direction, it can hae its compensations.

Hutchison lowers the ratcheted candleholder to inspect a printed plate. He is a barrel-chested man in middle years, with deft, inky fingers.

Whit an admirable invention is the prentin press! says Thomas. Tae consider that, afore its existence, few folk had the privilege tae read the great works o their times, and o antiquity forby. We must aye mind whit the Greeks and Romans teach us, and the Egyptians, the Babylonians, the Chinese—

I've work tae dae, lad. Yir man is through the back.

May I ask whit's on the press?

If ye bide a while, ye'll find oot. But awa and get a heat.

Hutchison's door is always open. He keeps his opinions to himself – mostly – and his ears pricked for any breath of scandal: there's money in scandal, if it's set in print smartly enough. Students are not the most lucrative customers but the browsers of today may become the doctors, lawyers or preachers of tomorrow, for whom building a library is essential. Thomas hopes to become a regular customer once he has laureated, though the likelihood of completing his studies, never mind entering into a profession has, in recent months, become fraught with uncertainty.

At short notice and for reasons unspecified, Sir Patrick has withdrawn his financial support. Thomas would have appreciated knowing how this irksome situation has arisen. Katharine's letter of the previous winter hinted at financial troubles. Perhaps the man is too proud to admit as much but Thomas has been too busy to dwell on his guardian's lack of communication. On top of having to move to insalubrious lodgings with a glum, hunched tailor and his mousy wife, he now lacks the means to pay the final year of his college fees. He remains optimistic nevertheless; finding themselves in straitened circumstances, others have come through unscathed. If he has to delay laureation, so be it. The knowledge he has already acquired will not go to waste and friends will surely keep him abreast of new ideas.

He edges down a narrow corridor between more crammed bookshelves and on through to a small but well-proportioned room where Hutchison holds more protracted business meetings, often accompanied by wine and cheese and even, if occasion demands, some musical entertainment. The back shop is devoid of bookshelves; instead, its painted walls are hung with framed frontispieces from Hutchison's own publications. A smoky fire hisses in the grate. Mungo Craig, his cheeks pink from the fire, is feeding the flames with spoiled sheets from the press. Coffee brews on the hob.

Ah Tam, he says. It's been a while.

Twa month or mair. Beggin yir pardon but I've had maitters tae attend tae.

So it wid appear, says Craig. Pu' up a chair.

Thomas shivers and draws close to the fire.

Nae coat on such a snell day? says Craig.

Naw, says Thomas. But this is a fine parlour! Ye're weel-appointed, says Thomas, And wi such a deal o literature tae haund!

I'm content wi a guid price for bed and board, says Craig. Hutchison can aye dae wi an extra pair o haunds and it does nae hairm tae learn the methods o prent-makkin. But whit o yir ain situation? I hear ye've had tae flit?

The least said aboot that, Thomas groans, the better.

Ach weel. *Tae ilka time there is a season, and a time tae ilka purpose* – but ye dinna need me quotin Ecclesiastes. Whit brings ye here?

Ye invited me!

So I did, says Craig. It slipped my mind.

Besides, says Thomas, I wanted tae congratulate ye on yir laureation.

It wis the Guid Lord's wish. There's nae cause for congratulations.

Efter aw yon time burnin the midnicht oil? I canna see how the wishes o the Lord come intae play. And why strive at aw if yir fate's been decided?

Weel, weel. The gospel accordin tae Tam Aikenhead.

If I'd laureated, says Thomas, I'd trumpet the fact frae the West Port tae the Canongate.

Aye, Aikenhead. Ye're vainglorious and nae mistake.

But might it no be mair gratifyin tae the Almighty that a man mak his way by his ain effort than by predestination?

Are ye sayin ye got where ye are by dint o yir ain effort? That a wealthy patron, niver mind the ear o a professor or twa, has nae bearin on yir situation?

My *present* situation isna guid at aw! says Thomas. I've had tae hawk my coat tae pay a deposit on my new lodgins. But we dinna choose oor circumstances, he says cheerfully, basking in the fire's warmth, and I thank God for my guardian's generosity. Had it continued a twelvemonth mair, I'd have been even mair grateful.

Weel, says Craig, I widna choose tae be a cobbler's son.

Once a cobbler's son, aye a cobbler's son! says Hutchison, appearing in the doorway, a page of print nipped between thumb and index finger. Am I richt in thinkin my tenant's a dunderheid? He grins widely, as if being a dunderhead were laudable.

No in the least! says Thomas.

I'm only gaen by whit the regents say. And regents ken best, dae they no?

Wi respect, Maister Hutchison, says Craig, some regents ken *warst*.

Bold words! says Hutchison. He spreads the printed sheet on the table. The text is smudged in places and the page has been printed askew but the text is black and solid and clearly legible. So, he says. Whit d'ye mak o my first impression?

It's no yir fairest assemblage, says Craig.

But such a rough and ready broadside is affordable tae sae mony, says Thomas. Is that not ane o the wonders o prent?

Hark at him! says Craig.

He's richt, says Hutchison. A broadsheet's value is in the content, no in the design or the quality. And this ane should fly off the press as fast as Lucky Lorimer's pasties leave the chafin dish.

Or jades raise thir skirts, says Craig.

True, says Hutchison. But once this case comes tae trial, yon lasses will mind thir step and no mistake. He picks up the broadsheet again, angles it towards the firelight, takes a deep breath and declaims:

On the WANTONNESS of a WHORE: the True Tale of One Such and her Path to DAMNATION by James Morrison, burgher of Edinburgh and elder of the Tron Kirk, in which he Examines the FALL from GRACE of one EXECRABLE WOMAN of this Toun, who has continued to PRACTISE her FILTHY TRADE after being BRANDED as a WHORE, first on ye SHOULDER, and second on ye CHEEK, thus making her SIN VISIBLE for all the WORLD to see and who now Awaits TRANSPORTATION to the AMERICAS or DEATH.

Ye've a way wi words, Maister Hutchison, says Thomas.

I've yir man Craig tae thank for the text.

Indeed? Aw the same, says Thomas, might pity raither than punishment no lead a lass back tae the path o righteousness mair swiftly? Perhaps those that try her will agree.

If they dae, says Craig, they'll be dolts.

Whitiver the case, says Hutchison, I need copies aboot the toun posthaste. Efter sentence is passed, folk are loath tae pairt wi thir penny. Sae I'm thinkin, Maister Aikenhead, wid ye be willin tae mind the shop while Craig and I dae the roonds o the taverns and coffee houses?

It wid be my pleasure, says Thomas, as I couldna, in aw conscience, pit aboot a text which appears tae accuse the woman afore she's been tried.

Dear, dear, says Craig. Tam and his high principles.

That's settled then, says Hutchison. It shouldna tak us mair than an oor or twa. I'll treat baith o ye tae a bite when we're done. I hear Lucky Lorimer has a fine side o pork on her hob. Frae Haddington, which didna suffer the cruel harvest suffered by the rest o the Lothians.

Lucky Lorimer disna serve students, says Thomas.

Ah, but Craig's my tenant forby. And sometime printer's deil.

I'd sooner gang by anither name, sir.

I dinna ken anither name, says Hutchison, cheerily. And ye're a braw wee deil, are ye no?

Delighted to have the shop to himself, Thomas paces around, inspecting this and that, imagining himself as the shop's proprietor. He would enlarge the windows to let in more daylight, add more ceiling lamps. He would reorganise the stock, removing stacks from the floor where they are prone to damage from damp and dirty shoes, enabling browsers to move around more freely and thus encourage sales. As for the back shop, there is surely no need for a room solely given over to entertaining: a good-sized table and chairs is all that might be required for close inspection of a book, or for serving refreshments. Would he move the press into the back shop or add shelves? What kind of titles would be best held in the back – imports or costly, illustrated works?

He realises that Hutchison made no mention of what he should do should anyone wish to make a purchase but is confident that he can come to some satisfactory arrangement; he would enjoy having the opportunity to persuade a customer to choose one book over another. Nevertheless, being free to browse is a grand treat in itself.

A wide range of publications are on display: medical treatises; travelogues; sermons so numerous they have a table to themselves; bawdy ballads; fantastical narratives involving faeries or other supernatural creatures; philosophical and mathematical treatises; instruction manuals; and, perhaps in response to the recent establishment of the Bank of Scotland, endless meditations on money. But the title which most draws him is *Christianity not mysterious, or, A treatise shewing that there is nothing in the Gospel contrary to reason, nor above it and that no Christian doctrine can be properly call'd a mystery,* by John Toland.

How favourably Mungo Craig has spoken of this man in the past and now he has the opportunity to peruse his ideas with no-one looking over his shoulder. He is turning the pages, nodding in agreement with some parts of Toland's argument, shaking his head at others, when the door opens and five members of the Town Guard troop inside. They have left their long pikes outside, resting against the wall but, even so, once the door has been pushed to, the shop feels very crowded.

Can I assist ye, gentlemen? says Thomas, pleased to have the opportunity to welcome visitors to the bookshop, even though the Guard is not noted for its literary appetite. I'm afraid the proprietor is outwith the premises and may not return for some time. Ye're welcome tae wait but might prefer instead tae return later in the efternoon.

Are ye Thomas Aikenhead? growls the tallest and broadest of them.

I am. How did ye ken?

O St Mary's Wynd, by Gassman the Goldsmith's?

That wis my former lodgins. I've since relocated tae—

And ye're a student at the College o Edinburgh?

I am.

Then ye must come wi us.

Beggin yir pardon, gentlemen, but I gave my word I'd mind the shop until the proprietor returned.

Ane o us will mind the shop. Thomas Aikenhead, a chairge of blasphemy has been laid agin ye, and by the power that is invested in the Toun Gaird ye must accompany us tae the Tolbooth forthwith.

Blasphemy? Thomas splutters. There must be some mistake. And a mistake I hope will cleared up in the verra near future. Blasphemy? It's inconceivable that I should be chairged wi such. The mistake may not have been made by yirsels and I widna haud the Gaird tae accoont but a mistake, maist certainly, has been made—

Come alang, sir.

By aw means. The sooner this is cleared up, the better.

A
SATYR
AGAINST
𝕬𝖙𝖍𝖊𝖎𝖘𝖙𝖎𝖈𝖆𝖑 𝕯𝖊𝖎𝖘𝖒
With the Genuine Character of a
DEIST
To Which is Prefixt,

An Account of **Mr. AIKINHEAD's** *NOTIONS,*

Who is now in Prifon for the fame Damnable

APOSTACY

By *MUNGO CRAIG* S.Ph & Sac.Th.

When the heavy door shuts behind them, Mungo Craig and Patrick Middleton stand side by side and peer through the gloom. The air is mephitic and they take shallow, reluctant breaths, inclining their nostrils in the direction of the small, barred window. Middleton lowers his head to prevent it from scraping against the ceiling, and scans the bare walls, the floor. Craig, who barely reaches Middleton's shoulder, coolly observes the prisoner huddled on a filthy pallet.

Thomas glowers at his visitors. He has lost weight, is covered in flea bites, and scratches relentlessly. Beside him is a bible, writing materials and a crumpled, heavily annotated copy of Craig's pamphlet.

Ye're taciturn the day, says Craig. For a man sae pairtial tae the soond o his ain blab I'd have thocht yir salutation wid've been a veritable cataract o verbiage.

Ye'd have thocht it, wid ye? And whit else, Judas, wid ye have thocht?

That ye'd appreciate ony company at aw, says Craig.

At a time like this, says Middleton.

Warden! I dinna wish tae entertain fause-faces. I dinna wish it! Bein locked up is punishment enough. Haein tae thole such loathsome company is saut in the wound. Warden!

He'll no hear ye, says Middleton, inclining his head towards the grille in the door. He's awa doon the corridor.

I believe, says Craig, some liege has sent a consignment o Lindsay's pies tae ease the confinement o John Fraser. You'll forgive us for no bringin ye a bite.

We considered ye'd be mair in need o spiritual sustenance, says Middleton. And bein o a charitable, Christian disposition—

I wish nane o yir Christian charity. Nane! D'ye hear?

My, my, says Craig. Is it wise tae cast aspersions on Christian charity at a time like this?

I'm no castin aspersions on *Christian charity*, Craig, I'm castin aspersions on *you*. And on Middleton. And the ithers that pit me here.

If I had ony nigglin doots aboot settin doon my concerns, says Craig, ye've swept them awa at ane fell swoop.

Did ye come tae gloat? Tae verify the result o yir tattle?

It wisna me that bent the ear o the Privy Cooncil, says Craig.

Wid ye sweer on the bible that ye didna turn me in? Wid ye?

Thomas lunges forward, fists out. The shackle at his ankle prevents him from punching anything but air but Craig and Middleton step back a pace. Middleton tries but fails to find a comfortable angle for his head. Out of harm's way, Craig smirks, blinks, tugs at an ear.

I'm no on trial for my life. I needna defend mysel tae a pernicious blasphemer like yirsel.

Wid ye sweer it?

I willna sweer, says Craig. I'm no obliged tae sweer.

And whit o Maister Middleton? says Thomas.

As Maister Craig says, I'm no on trial for my life. I willna sweer tae ocht.

D'ye chime wi ilka word yon snake utters? says Thomas.

Indeed I dinna, says Middleton. But I concur wi my companion.

If ye canna sweer, ye're guilty.

We dinna say we *canna* sweer, says Craig. We say we *willna*. And let that be an end tae it.

An end tae whit – my life? Thomas shrieks. And how can it be that I'm tae be tried for my life – *my life!* – for a first offence, if in truth I've committed ony offence at aw, when John Fraser's sentence wis sackcloth? Is the law no intended tae be fair and just? How is it fair and just tae deny ane the same lenience as anither?

Wha kens? says Craig. Perhaps Fraser has mair freends in high places.

It may be, says Middleton, that Aikenhead is considered a worse offender.

But it's still a *first offence*! says Thomas. And sackcloth is the stated punishment for a first offence!

I dinna ken the ins and oots o the law. Ye'd hae tae ask John Neilson aboot that.

Neilson's no here, says Thomas. And for aw he professes tae ken the workins o the courts, I expect he'd hae tae ask anither. And that wid aw tak time. He's no here, though lik yirsels, he's ane o my accusers. As is Potter and Mitchell. So, Craig, if ye canna sweer that ye didna turn me in, ye're guilty.

Aw this talk o guilt in advance o yir trial is reckless. Mind that we may be summoned as witnesses.

Ye didna turn me in but yet ye'd be witnesses? *Mendacem memorem esse portet,* or if the Latin as weel as the truth has deserted ye: Liars should have guid memories. Guid memories!

The thick walls absorb Thomas's protest, sap its energy.

No content wi my incarceration, Thomas continues, holding Craig's pamphlet aloft, ye further set opinion agin me wi yir damnable *Satyr.* In whit unforgiveable manner have I offended ye?

I acted solely in accordance wi my conscience and my earnest wish tae please God.

Yir conscience wid send a sometime freend tae kick the wind, and on the 'evidence' o works *you* urged me tae read?

It's no the publications that concerned me but the blasphemous conclusions ye came tae.

And for that ye'd turn the world agin me? Are ye sae witless ye canna tell atween a hairmless jest tae brichten a drear nicht and the 'Genuine Character of a Deist', as ye cry me in this execrable pamphlet?

Certainly my *Satyr* contains some execrable notions, Aikenhead. Yir ain.

The light is poor but Thomas can see Middleton's long sallow face, his knitted brows and pursed lips, his nostrils twitching at the stink in the cell. Of Craig he can see the fish eyes darting around the close confines of the cell, the thin, lopsided smile, the small, pointed teeth. These were once the faces of friends.

Whit ye accuse me o is nonsense. Ye say I believe I could fly tae the moon: ony bairn kens that flyin tae the moon is pure fancy. Ye say I claim it possible tae reconstruct a livin creature frae a corpse *rent in twain like a speldered haddock*. Ye ken that wis a jamph, Craig, ye ken *fou weel*! Is there no place in this world for fancy, for sport, for wit?

Where lies wit, says Craig, lies mockery, and the Lord mustna be mockit.

I didna *mock* the Lord. Perhaps I chafed my fellow man. Perhaps my fellow man chafed me. Where's the hairm? Must righteousness aye equate wi unsullied solemnity? In this weary life, can a man no rejoice in a moment's levity?

The Lord mustna be mockit.

Tae think I considered ye a freend! When naebody else wid tak yir side, I stood by ye.

Yon days are past, says Craig. I've a mind tae enter the ministry and must pit behind me aw allegiances that might compromise my virtue—

Yir virtue wis compromised lang syne. If iver ye possessed it.

As I wis sayin afore ye interrupted me – which has aye been yir habit, Aikenhead – whit a man pens may present an aggrandised version o the facts, for the purpose o composin a work o literature.

Yir *Satyr* isna literature.

My readers might disagree. And a deal o folk have already paid thir penny.

It's nocht but an odious twistin o the truth, a tawdry fabrication!

My loyalties lie wi the True Church o the Covenant and those that live by its laws. Ye must understand, Aikenhead, though ye havna yet a publication tae yir name – and scant likelihood o ane now, barring a gallows speech—

I will hear nae mair. Leave! This minute! And Craig, for the benefit o mankind, I hope and pray ye're afflicted wi scrivener's palsy. Warden! Warden!

As ye ken, says Craig, the warden canna hear ye. He'll be back in his ain time tae liberate me and Middleton. In the meantime, ye'll hae tae thole oor company. And surely ony company is a boon at this pairticular time.

A Rhapsody of Feigned and Ill-Invented Nonsense

The courtroom is packed to capacity and the abundance of heavy winter clothing makes for a rich animal reek. His sisters, eyes downcast as if they were in church, sit between Sir Patrick and Lady Hester. Attired in a velvet gown and fur cape, as if she might be attending a theatrical production, Lady Hester fans herself with a copy of Craig's *Satyr*, which was on sale outside the courts, and surveys the crowd, to ascertain who is and is not in attendance. Sir Patrick exchanges the briefest of nods with Campbell of Aberuchil. Thomas recalls the ruddy, wall-eyed judge visiting Netherstane one morning and staying for the midday dinner. He was genial at table but coarse with the housemaids and harsh with his horse. Will it avail him any that Campbell and Sir Patrick are acquainted? Of the others who will try his case, David Hume of Crossrig, John Lauder of Fountainhall and Archibald Hope of Rankeillor are some of the most renowned judges in the country. Does it bode well that his fate will rest on those well-versed in the intricacies and fine distinctions of the law?

Before the witnesses are called, the list of jurors and their occupations is read out. How many folk are required to consider his case! The jury comprises burgesses and guildmen, former baillies, merchants and three printer-booksellers. That one of these is George Mosman, printer to the Kirk, will not go in Thomas's favour; Mosman will have no option but to side with the Kirk. Five of those summoned, however, have refused to stand jury and in their absence are issued with a fine. What would make these men stay away and be prepared to pay the price for doing so? Did they wish to distance themselves from such unconscionable proceedings or simply to avoid stepping over the door on a bitter morning, two days before Yule?

Thomas has no defence counsel. He is young. His words have been wilfully misconstrued. The notions he is said to have expounded are no more than an interpretation of works he read, rather than any statement of own beliefs. He has insisted, over and over, on his unshakeable and orthodox belief in God, on his fervent adherence to the Christian faith. He has affirmed that should the charges be dropped his own remorse and sorrow, combined with prayer and study of the bible, would prevent him from straying from the path of righteousness forever more. And so on.

It is not a question of what he really believes but of what the Privy Council wants, needs to hear. He is no longer sure what he believes or whether what he believes matters. Would it change anything at all if he did not believe that the earth revolves around the sun? He has made two petitions in advance of the trial but the charges were not dropped and no-one has offered to act as his defence counsel so here he is, defending himself. Perhaps it's for the best. Though he had not thought there would be so many he would have to convince of his innocence.

It will not aid his case that the Lord Justice Clerk, Adam Cockburn, has an insatiable appetite for the pursuit of irreligion, nor that James Stewart of Goodtrees, the Lord Advocate, is held to give over the entirety of every Sabbath to his devotions. Nevertheless, the rule of law may yet triumph. Thomas is a first-time offender who has barely achieved majority. The correct punishment for a first offence is sackcloth and a term of imprisonment. That is all! That is the punishment John Fraser received for maintaining that there was no God to whom men owed reverence, worship and obedience, and that established religion was made to keep folk under the thumb of the Kirk.

Did he say worse than Fraser? Indeed he did not. Surely between so many carefully chosen, upstanding members of the community they can come to a just decision? What could possibly make his case any different from Fraser's? Nothing. Nothing. But he is being tried for his life! There must be some mistake. It should never have come to this but common sense will prevail. It must.

Thomas Aikenhead, son to the deceased James Aikenhead, chirurgeon apothecary in Edinburgh, prisoner in the Tolbooth thereof. You are indicted and accused, at the insistence of Sir James Stewart, His Majesty's advocate for His Highness's interest, and by special order of the lords of His Majesty's Privy Council, that whereby the laws of God, and by the laws of this and all other well-governed Christian realms, the crime of blasphemy against God, or any of the persons of the blessed Trinity, or against the holy Scriptures, or our holy religion, is a crime of the highest nature, and ought to be severely punished: Likeas by the act of parliament, first parliament of Charles Second, Act 21, entitled 'Act against the crime of blasphemy', it is stated and ordained, that whosoever not being distracted in his wits shall rail upon or curse God, or any of the persons of the blessed Trinity, shall be processed before the chief justice, and being found guilty, shall be punished with death: and by the 11th act of the 5th session of the present parliament, the aforesaid act is not only ratified but it is further stated, that whosoever shall in their writing or discourse deny, impune or quarrel, or argue, or reason against the being of God, or any of the persons of the blessed Trinity, or the authority of the holy Scriptures, or the Old and New Testaments, or the Providence of God in the government of the world...

And so the Lord Advocate for the King continues in flat, drear tones to state the lengthy account of the charges against him, itemising each and every punishable utterance he is said to have made over a period of more than a twelvemonth. A twelvemonth! That Craig and others have conspired against him for so long, garnering words that tripped off his tongue in unguarded moments of levity; that the mesh of their duplicity has caused him to be tried for his life – it is beyond belief.

How could it be that the same lads who enthused about gaming halls and suggested – needless to say when none of the college spies was in earshot – that sins of the flesh might be the greatest pleasures of all, saw fit to commit him to this dire situation, while he has tried to interest them in Spinoza's concept of goodness or Locke's thoughts on free will and human understanding? What cardinal grievance against him prompted them to take such a step? Of course intellectual disagreements flared up from time to time but surely, for scholars, a day without debate is like oatmeal without salt? He cannot recall exhibiting – or feeling – animosity towards any of them, not even towards Craig himself, the snake! Until now.

The assize lawfully sworn, no objection of the law in the contraire, it is reported that on several occasions and without any encouragement, the pannall, Thomas Aikenhead... affirmed that the doctrine of theology was a rhapsody of feigned and ill-invented nonsense, patched up partly of the moral doctrine of philosophers, and partly of poetical fictions and extravagant chimaeras, or words to this effect or purpose...

Aye. That day at the races. Mercury and Salvation. A lost wager. A poor, ill-treated filly. Craig and his cant. Later, his sly, sly tricks: *Say whit ye said again, Thomas.* And, eager to impress the assembled company with his fine phrase, he had obliged. Vain bladderskate. Cocksure dupe.

...you scoffed at and ridiculed the holy scriptures, calling the Old Testament Ezra's fables, and Ezra the inventor thereof... of the New Testament, you did not only scoff but did most blasphemously rail upon our Lord and Saviour, calling the said new Testament the History of the Impostor Christ, and affirming him to have learned magick in Egypt, and that coming into Judea he picked up a few blockish fisher fellows, whom he knew by his skill in physiognomy had strong imaginations... and on them played his pranks as you blasphemously term his miracles.

Scoff – ridicule – rail – fables – imposter – magick – pranks – miracles – now when and where was he doing and saying such? He should have been studying hard for his final examinations if he hoped to laureate the following summer, but the more he read, the more he was drawn to study outwith the curriculum. Through his continued contact with Archibald Pitcairne, he was learning much more than the naming of the bones. In the late autumn, when the churchmen arrived in town to find the General Assembly had been postponed yet again – and notice of postponement came too late for many to alter their travel arrangements so the city was full of impotent, irate clergy – the doctor completed the penning of his satirical drama: *Assembly*.

As he had been unsparing in his lampooning of the Presbytery, Pitcairne thought the better of publishing; instead he circulated the manuscript privately and Thomas felt privileged to be a reader. Inspired by the pithiness of the drama, emboldened by association with such an illustrious character, it slipped his mind that wealth and position afforded the doctor a degree of latitude denied to a mere student. Seduced by the sound of his own voice, the desire to entertain and the pleasing flow of one phrase into another, he found himself expounding an irreverent interpretation of the prophesies of Ezra. What also slipped his mind was the possibility that anyone might take him seriously.

How could he have been so remiss? Which days or nights did he utter these words and who, in addition to the sometime friends now champing at the bit to give evidence against him, heard them said? Hutchison the bookseller and Henderson, Keeper of the Library, both stand in the long line of witnesses, as does his landlord, the tailor George Dickson and his wife Jonet Elder who, from their hunched shoulders and relentless foot shuffling, seem abashed by the situation they find themselves in. He can't imagine why they've been called. They might have something to say about him owing them rent but he's never done more than offer a polite greeting or comment on the weather. In all there are seventeen witnesses, seventeen souls who claim to have heard him commit the horrid crime of blasphemy!

Your tongue, Thomas, your loose, foolish tongue…

…you scoff at the Trinity, affirming blasphemously that Theantropos is as great a contradiction as Hircus Cervus or a quadratum rotundum…

That one he does remember. Regent Row. Dull as mud. Goat-beard. God-given Geometry.

…you say redemption is a proud and presumptuous device, deny

the existence of spirits and maintain that God, the world and nature are one and the same, and from eternity. You claim that man's imagination, with art and industry can achieve anything...

Think, Thomas. Think! All the thinking you've already done amounts to nothing if you can't find a way out of this. Denying the existence of spirits is tantamount to denying the existence of witches or devils – which is atheistical – but when did this punishable statement pass your lips – when? And to whom did you say it?

He must remember when he spoke these words – and how precisely he phrased the statement. This is no time for imprecision. The wording, the exact wording, might tip the scales in his favour. Or otherwise. If he could put happiness itself on the scales, it would be light and frothy as a spray of camomile. And sadness would be dark and heavy as a lump of pitch.

He denied the existence of spirits and claimed man's imagination could achieve anything... so in effect claimed that man's imagination could have invented God! In denying spirits, he has also, in effect, claimed that God the spirit is merely a figment of man's imagination. Did he really say this? Did he mean it? He must try the words out in his head. Again. Again! Can he recapture the scene? Who was there? Middleton with his lugubrious humming and hawing, his paraphrasing of other's sentiments? Or Mitchell, he of the roving eye, who prefers mechanical inventions to philosophy and theology? Or sleekit, mealy-mouthed Potter? Not that he would have described Potter in such terms before he discovered his falsity – no, first he was smart Potter, shy Potter! Or Neilson, who is already earning a good wage – while he himself is penniless, unlaureated and on trial for his life? Or Craig? He has no words vile enough for Craig.

Were they indoors or out? Was it morning or evening, summer or winter? But more to the point, what prompted such reckless outpouring? Such statements don't spring forth apropos of nothing. Unless he is truly distracted in his wits, there has to be a chain of connection which leads, by some form of logic, to a conclusion.

To deny the existence of spirits, would this not presuppose someone else insisting, in the first place, on the *existence* of spirits? And then he, delighting in debate as ever, feeling obliged to counter the other's statement? That's what it must have been, his simple, innocent delight in debate; mental sport, no more or less. But add to this his alleged statement that *man's imagination can achieve anything* – no, he is in deep water and the only hope he has of hauling himself to safety is to put his statements in context, consider them clearly and logically and find a way out of this abominable predicament. But he can't. He simply cannot remember when, how or why he uttered such words. Perhaps he did not utter them at all.

…you prefer Mahomet to the blessed Jesus and hope to see Christianity greatly weakened…

Now why would he have said that when it it not something he has ever knowingly considered?

…you have been so bold in the aforesaid blasphemies, that when you had found yourself cold, you have wished to be in the place that Ezra calls Hell, to warm yourself there…

Has no-one ever been cold to the bone but still wishes to make a jest of it? Does no-one appreciate the value of laughter?

Sometimes the day drags; sometimes it hurtles forward. The only witnesses to be called are fellow students, former friends. Mitchell is followed by Neilson, Middleton by Potter. One after another they confirm that the accused was heard to declare one or other blasphemous statement, sometimes on one occasion, sometimes on several occasions. It seems to Thomas – and so it must also seem to the jury – that he spent a great deal of his time blaspheming. Potter has nothing new to add to Mitchell's statement. Though he is in no doubt that everybody in the courtroom is scrutising him closely, no-one will meet his eye, except Anna, with whom he exchanges fleeting glances as each new witness takes the stand. When the last witness is called, Anna gasps and draws back in her seat. Thomas thinks too that when Mungo Craig takes the stand, she shakes her head, but he may be mistaken; it may be his own head that is shaking.

Craig has given some thought to his appearance. He is wearing a crisp new shirt and a sober waistcoat, and his hair has been trimmed. His solemn demeanour is studied. As the Lord Advocate reads out his statement, he nods in agreement with his own damnable words. Until now, had judge and jury been of a mind to take into account the youth of the accused, they might have construed his statements as hare-brained blather but Craig's testimony dispels any inclination towards lenience. Rather than presenting the accused as little more than a braggart, albeit a vexatious one, Craig's testimony emphasises more dangerous and damning aspects: his railing against God and his alleged hope to see *Christianity greatly weakened, and shortly to be extirpated.* If that weren't enough to create a clatter of perturbation in the courtroom, Craig's statement also alleges that, should Thomas be banished, he would wreak revenge and through his writings *make all Christianity tremble.*

Banished? When did he ever speak of being banished? When did he ever think of it? Why on earth would such a notion have occurred to him? Certainly he argued *against* banishment when Hutchison presented his impression on the punishment for whores. But he argued for lenience as being a better path to righteousness! That was all he'd spoken of, all there had been time to speak of: Craig and Hutchison couldn't be off fast enough to hawk their pamphlets and thereby clear the way for the arrival of the Guard! A dirty trick, if ever there was one.

Though Craig confirms his testimony, with ingratiating deference towards the Lord Advocate and a suitably grave countenance, Thomas is convinced that a smirk plays about his thin lips. He protests the allegations vehemently, argues against Craig's reliability as a witness due to the extent of his own deceit.

How much did they pay ye, Craig? he shouts. Awbody kens there are rewards for bringin chairges against folk. Did they pay ye weel for yir trouble?

The Lord Justice Clerk orders Thomas to be silent and requests that Craig step down from the stand. After the Lord Advocate has given his summary of the charges, putting particular emphasis on the mocking, scoffing and railing against God, and the dangerous threats to Christianity's wellbeing, as testified by a single witness – Mungo Craig – the jury is sent off and requested to come to a decision by noon the following day. Thomas wishes dearly that the present day, indeed the last twelvemonth of days, could start all over again.

Nightshade

Through the long hours of darkness – and it has been dark since three in the afternoon – Thomas does not sleep a wink. He works relentlessly on his speech and also, in case the speech does not say what he wants it to, on a subsequent letter to his friends. Whoever they might now be. Now that he is a criminal, convicted of a capital crime, he is in deep doubt as to whom he might count as a friend.

Beyond the scrabbling of the rats, the creaking of the joists and the night terrors of other prisoners, voices call out his name, deploring the severity of the sentence and urging him to stand firm on his beliefs. For the past week folk have been gathering outside the jail, protesting his sentence. Ye're nae alane! they cry, but he is: so alone now, so terribly alone. Their support gives him some comfort but cannot bring him the reprieve he has hoped and prayed for since the sentence was passed. At first he worried that the protests on his behalf might attract unfavourable attention and make things go worse for him; this is no longer of the slightest concern.

What has happened is unthinkable and yet it consumes his every waking moment. The unanimous verdict of guilty was delivered. The judges, in their dark caps and gowns, rose to their feet and the frightful words of the sentence clanged through the courtroom. He gripped the dock so hard his fingernails made indentations in the wood. He looked down at his feet, half-expecting his innards to have spilled out of him. Anna sobbed and tore at her hair. Katharine prayed to the heavens. Sir Patrick and Lady Hester shifted in their seats, anxious to leave. Cockburn, the Lord Justice Clerk, called upon those present to curb their clamour. As soon as the noise had died down, Thomas begged the judges to grant him a stay of execution.

Dae ye wish respite in the hope ye might save yir life, asked Cockburn, or tae better prepare yirsel for daith?

Tae mak fou repentance and better prepare tae meet my Makar. Fifteen days isna lang enough tae mak my peace.

Then ye must be a terrible sinner! came a voice from the benches.

Once more Cockburn called for order and leaned over to confer, *sotto voce*, with the judges. A few rumbles of dissatisfaction persisted but only a few. Meanwhile, the chancellor and clerk of the jury, a former baillie and a merchant, who had been charged with delivering its verdict, surveyed the courtroom, which was rather less crowded than the day before. If the jurors were surprised by the sentence, there was no evidence of this in their obdurate expressions. As on the day of the trial, no-one but Anna would meet Thomas's eye. It was as if he had become so loathsome that catching his glance might infect a beholder with loathsomeness.

After a moment, Cockburn declared that the decision of his learned fellows was that no respite should be granted. After repeating the sentence, that the accused *would be taken to the Gallowlee betwixt Leith and Edinburgh, upon Friday the eighth day of January next to come, betwixt two and four o clock in the afternoon, and there to be hanged on a gibbet until dead,* Thomas was led back to the Tolbooth.

Since then, he has left his cell three times: on New Year's Eve, to hear his first petition decisively outvoted; four days later, to attend the Tolbooth Kirk and endure a hellfire sermon from James Webster, in which every blistering word seemed directed at himself; and yesterday morning, to hear the vote on his final petition. The vote was many hours ago. The fifteenth day has been and gone. He must put it out of his mind. He must do what he can: revise his speech and a letter to his friends. All his past words are like chaff before the wind. But how can it be that chaff carries so much weight?

Who are his friends? Perhaps these strangers who decry his predicament are now his only friends. So many of those he had considered friends, indeed his *firmest* friends, have shown themselves to be the willing and deliberate agents of his doom. There was no accident and no coercion; these false friends were put under no pressure. They have all betrayed him of their own free will. And for their own gain. What does the bible say about self-seeking? He has noted it down, along with many other biblical promises and threats: *For those who are self-seeking and do not obey the truth, but obey unrighteousness, there will be wrath and fury. Romans 2:8*

And what of his sisters – where are his sisters when he needs them most – pacing the shoreline, wringing their hands, while the cold sea lashes the sand and seabirds wheel and cry, while a chill draught blows through the corridors of Netherstane and the mistress orders Aleen to bank up the fires? Why have his sisters not come to visit him? Katharine would have been consumed by shame and humiliation to find herself related to a convicted blasphemer but does she understand his own very real and urgent need? And what of Anna, who cried the loudest in the courtroom and reached out her arms to him as he was taken back to his cell? Perhaps Katharine has written and the letter has not been delivered. It is winter and the roads are impassable. Perhaps they have been forbidden to communicate with him. Of course they may be afraid of association, of possible repercussions. These are anxious times. Authority must be demonstrated. And exerted.

This morning he still had some hope. A few days back he had a visit from one of the judges to try his case, Lauder of Fountainhall, and Sir William Anstruther, a Privy Councillor. Fountainhall had brought some dried fruit; Sir William, writing paper and ink. The two men expressed approval of his study of the Scriptures, and though chary of commenting on any aspects of the trial, evinced some sympathy for his plight. Encouraged by their visit, Thomas submitted a second petition: if one judge had changed his mind, others might do likewise.

He could not simply ask to be pardoned; he could only beat his repentant breast and ask, once again, for more time to make amends, in the hope that the Privy Council would, of its own accord, decide to reduce the sentence. Such an outcome was not unheard of. Indeed, only the other day, a thief had his death sentence reduced to banishment. How that man must have rejoiced at his good fortune – he would live! And who knows, a banished man – or woman – might in some foreign land find a better life than what they left behind, a life in which there was no need for sin. Or find a place on this earth where sin did not exist and folk did not live in fear of God or their fellow man! Thomas would welcome finding himself in such a place. But then, how could the courts have contemplated banishment for such a dangerous blasphemer as Craig, master of the poison tongue and poison pen, suggests he is?

He must no longer speak extempore. Each word must be weighed like a granule of precious matter; each must contribute to a true representation of his beliefs. How hard it is to bend words to one's intention when so much is at stake! He must pay scrupulous attention to the wording of his speech and the letter to his friends. Distinctions need to be made, clear distinctions: whether or not he accepts this or that, whether or not he believes this or that happens, has happened, might happen. But what does he believe? He must be steady, unswerving, but what if he discovers through this process of putting down his words that his conclusions are false? What if there is an angry, vengeful God who will punish him for eternity because he has dared to say that he cannot, in all truthfulness, make sense of every word of the Scriptures?

No sooner has he put down a line or two than he feels the need to qualify the statement he has just made with some caveat or modification and when he reads over what he has written, he sees a jumble of contradictions – the work of a madman! Isn't it the law that one who is distracted in his wits should be exonerated? If the Privy Council could not be sure, could not *prove* that he did not lose his wits some time *before* the trial, can the sentence stand? It is too late to make a case for this: he should have ranted at the trial, ranted like poor demented

Cunningham. But then, only those who are *truly* distracted in their wits can rant; if you dissemble in your ranting you are not distracted, you are deceitful, and therefore guilty and deserving of punishment. Thomas does not feel guilt, only regret. He is brimful of regret.

When he was led into the court to hear the outcome of his second petition, he recognised most by face, if not by name. A sizeable number of senior clergy were in attendance. Was it possible that one or two, aware of the spiritual counsel he had received from men of the cloth, might be convinced that he had turned over a new leaf? Would they vote to treat him with lenience?

Sir William Anstruther was present, and on this occasion, the man met his eye. What fervid hope the briefest of glances can ignite! What vain hope. His pleas were rejected by a single vote. One single *nay* was all that stood between clemency and doom. Might Lauder of Fountainhall, had he been present, have made a difference to the outcome? What if an adamant minister or two had been laid low by the ague? Could it truly be justice that whoever happened to turn up on a given day could decide a man's fate by the raising of a gloved hand?

Snow

As always in the depths of winter, daylight is long a-coming.
Thomas has always loved the light but because time has fallen
utterly out of kilter and the day to come has a finality about it
like no other, he does not pray for dawn. He does not pray for
anything. He has done all the praying and soul-searching a
condemned man might undertake and it has brought no solace.
And no reprieve.

It begins to snow, lightly at first but soon the flakes are falling
thick and fast, like goose down shaken from a mattress, a pale
flurry swirling gently in the globe of illumination cast by the
street lamp. He has spent so many hours of the longest nights
of his life, staring out at the flickering lamp and whatever is
caught in its beam. For once he does not long for daylight. If he
could, he would stop time altogether: dawn would never arrive;
the snowflakes would hang in the frigid air and the world
remain suspended between darkness and light for eternity –
but surely even God cannot hold back time?

The city still sleeps. His head seethes – your tongue, your
tongue – look what it has brought you to! So keen to speak your
mind, to cavil. So quick to mock, to belittle what others hold
dear, to ignore what was staring you in the face. So caught up
in foolish, vain ambition, as foolish and vain as a lass tying
bows in her hair in the hope that the lad she loves will glance in
her direction – the lad she loves! And who loves you, Thomas?
Do you even know what it is to love? Who, now, would admit
to a jot of affection?

And your friends, those you believed were friends – how
could you have been so green, so remiss? You didn't pay

proper attention to how your words were received: a cocked eye, a smirk, a nudge, a whisper. You were too taken up with spouting ideas, opinions, half-digested theories, expounded for the benefit of whoever cared to listen and in this town the walls most certainly have ears. As you were romancing yourself into the company of the great minds of Europe, the wynds were carrying rumours of your flagrant irreverence from Castlehill to Holyrood. What a fool you've been. What a fool.

As the lamplighter douses the flame, and in doing so announces the irrevocable arrival of the day, everything takes on an excruciating clarity: an early bird – a robin – pauses on the lamp, its red breast bright as blood; it hops; it chirrs. Snowflakes glister. The dark bars gleam with a patina of sweat where his hands have gripped them, as he watched the snow fall and waited for the coming of the light.

At the night soil bucket, his bladder pulses but all he can release is a thin dribble of piss. Nothing escapes the vice of his sphincter. From his work with Pitcairne, he knows what happens when a man kicks the wind, and would discharge every drop of his body's waste in advance of the noose but it would seem that, even for dignity's sake, he has no power over his bodily functions.

The prison wakes. Bolts are scraped back. Keys grind in locks. Every sound is spiked with doom. Irked to wake and find themselves still constrained, other inmates demonstrate their disgruntlement. They moan, roar, rattle the bars of their cells. They curse the cold, the filth, the insufficiency of the food and the plump judges who put them in this place of pain and misery, deprivation and dread.

Thomas expects the guards to lead him out of the Tolbooth straight away but instead they bring bread and water – and it is fresh bread, still warm – and say he must wait a while longer. Rather than eat the bread, he presses it to his cheek and imagines it is not fired dough but a warm hand – his mother's hand, Katharine's, Anna's hand, the hand of the bookseller's lass at the Ferry Fair whose name he never discovered –

stroking his cheek, his neck, shoulder, breastbone. He will not eat the bread. He has no need of food at this moment, no need of it ever again.

Was it really only a day ago that his final appeal was turned down, really only a single day he has been wrestling with his final words to the world? He has revised and rephrased his speech until his words shriek back at him, like the wailing of some accursed soul. Which is what he is.

Footsteps. The rattle of chains. For him and none other. This is his day. His last.

The snow continues to fall. The sun is spectral. He would have wished for a deserted street but it is as full of folk as the day the elephant was led through town, its great head nodding and swaying as it dragged itself onto the platform and drank itself into a stupor. No elephant today, no pantalooned showman, no lovely tumbling girls with flashing eyes and supple, burnished limbs. Today, in sackcloth and chains, he is the spectacle.

The air is charged and the crowd fractious. Volleys of cheers from one side of the street are matched by jeers from the other. Some throw hard-packed snowballs at him, stones, some curse him to hell. Others, less clamorously, urge him to be steadfast, to die bravely for his beliefs. They have had enough of indignity and humiliation, of pillories, of jougs and branks; of being told who and what to believe; of living in fear. It has got out that the Kirk declined to intervene on his behalf, that it wished, needed, to see him hang. *As Ane Example and Terror* was the reason given. An example! A terror! Has blindfold justice, with sword and scales, carried out her duties to the best of her ability? The Kirk had the authority to save him but chose not to. What then should God-fearing citizens surmise? What indeed.

This is no a murderer nor a fornicator.

They say he's niver lain wi a woman.

He mockit the scriptures. Railed agin the Almighty.

It wis a first offence!

This is no a traitor nor a thief.

He hasna laid a finger on a saul.

Nor made off wi a mite or a maidenheid.

He practised magick and ony that practise magick are in league wi the deil.

This is a lad wi a loose tongue and precious little else to his name.

It wis a first offence!

He should've kent better.

He must be punished.

This is a lad.

How the snow changes things. All detail is concealed, all boundaries blurred. The street he has walked up and down so often, picking out landmarks and admiring architectural details, is now little more than a soft white arm reaching from the Palace below to the Castle above. As the High Street joins Castlehill, the road bends. He cannot see the house where he lived and yet, in his mind's eye, he can see it so clearly: the shop sign swinging above the door; the shelves lined with gleaming bottles and jars; his father resting his elbows on the counter and poring over Culpeper or greeting a customer; his mother preparing dinner; Katharine combing Anna's fluffy hair; the cat ensconced in the window seat. In his mind's eye the house is in soft summer light, not this sharp winter sun which after weeks of prison gloom assaults his eyes.

Flanked on either side by fusiliers, he is ordered to set forth. He passes the Tron Kirk, the scene of one of his alleged offences. He cannot remember what he is meant to have said there but such detail is now of no account. He passes through the Netherbow. The snow has obscured the devastation from the fire in the Canongate though the bitter stink of burnt matter still hangs in the air. He passes between the Trinity Kirk and the House of Correction.

He is a small boy and the frozen Nor' Loch is a cloudy plate. It is night-time and his father is skating by the light of the Great Comet's glorious tail. Anna, rosy-cheeked, slides on the ice and squeals with laughter. His mother berates him for moaning about the cold, urges him to enjoy himself while he can.

The shackles chafe and drag him down when more than ever he needs to hold his head high, to walk strong and straight, to feel his blood surge, to truly feel alive, to think, while he can, of what it means to be alive. Must they chain him? Do they expect him to break through a line of fusiliers, who jab the heels of their pikes into the snow at every step? Where on God's earth would he, could he run to?

It is downhill all the way, a long slow slope from the top of Leith Wynd, in the direction of the Firth of Forth which, today, is a broad grey collar. He will never skim a stone across the surface of the firth, never dip his toes in its waters, never walk hand in hand with a lass on the shore, never hold her close. He will never again hold anyone close and no-one will hold him. No-one will wash his body in preparation for the grave. No-one will wrap his body carefully in a mort cloth of clean or soiled linen. His remains will be tossed in the ground at the foot of the gibbet, to rot alongside those of every other soul for whom the Gallowlee is the end of the road.

The light is crisp and clear and he can see all the way to the Bass. He counts three ships on the water. Anna, with her extraordinary eyes, might well have seen more. Katharine might have reminded him of the fanatics imprisoned on the island. His sisters – where are his sisters? Who are all these people and why are they not taken up with gainful employment? Why do they trudge through snow which is turning to slush beneath their boots? They do not need to make this journey. They are free to turn around, return to the city and go about their business. Why do they choose to accompany the grim spectacle that he has become? What do they hope to gain, to learn?

He cannot feel his feet, his hands. By the side of the road, someone has built a snowman. It has lumps of coal for eyes and a noose around its neck. It reminds him of a rumour about orphanage bairns who hanged a cat because it could not say the catechism. Were these children terrified of guilt by association or simply curious and cruel? He will never know. The crowd grows, renews its taunts and jibes, its conflicting exhortations. Repent. Stand fast. If only it were quiet. If only there were not so many people. He does not recognise a soul: not true friends, false friends, not neighbours, dominies, regents and professors, not doctors and gardeners, librarians and booksellers, lairds and ministers, lawyers and tavern keepers, mothers and daughters, fathers and sons, not the women who weep, who scream in his face, who turn away in disgust, not lissom lasses who whisper of sinful pleasures, not hawkers and beggars, drunkards and scolds, thieves and cheats, not judges, jury, witnesses or spies. He must have seen many of these people before. Why does he not recognise a single one?

There are those who betrayed him to the authorities and those who would have betrayed him, had the opportunity arisen. There are those who could not say what they might have done and those who would not open their mouths, no matter that they might be put to the boots, because they believe in something he is not at all sure that he still believes in. He does not know what he believes in now, is not sure he believes in anything at all. What does it mean, what does it matter, to believe? If you believe the world is flat, do you betray a friend because he believes it is round?

The bible he carries has become damp, the pages creased. He slips it inside the rough sackcloth and presses it tightly to his breast. His heart hammers like a lost traveller beating on a door, begging to be let in from the cold. At the boundary between the jurisdictions of Edinburgh and Leith, the dreary procession turns off Leith Wynd towards the Gallowlee. There is no going back.

Afterword

Copy of his LETTER to his friends from Edinburgh Tolbooth, the day of his death:

January 8th 1697

Being now wearing near the last moment of my time of living in this vain world, I have by the enclosed under my own hand, now when I am steping into eternity, breifly as my time could only allow, given a true relation to the world in generall, for whose use I am to give some copies of the enclosed at my last end to the ministers and magistrats who shall be by me, and to my dear and worthy freinds (whom I from good ground may term parents) in particular, for whose use I will order this enclosed principall to be delivered by the bearer, to be present, of the original rise, matter, and manner of my doubtings and inquisitions, for which as I am now to die, so I desired not to live further than might have contribute to the glory of God, and good of his people by my after short time (for which I was demanding a repreive) and my own soul's eternal welfare, by my more serious and incessant application to the throne of mercy for my great sins, which I hope shall be all forgiven by the mercy of God, through the merits of my Redeemer Jesus Christ, tho alace my time hath been short since my sentence, so I have trifled away and mispent too much thereof, however, as my time hath allowed me, the enclosed will give satisfaction to you in particular, and to the world in generall, and after I am gone produce more charity than hath been my fortune to be trysted hitherto with, and remove the apprehensions, which I hear are various with many about my case, being the last words of a dying person, and proceeding from the sincerity of my heart.

Ther is one thing I hear I am aspersed with, which is not in the enclosed, which is, that I am suspected to have practised magick and conversed with devils, which I here declare in the presence of

Almighty God, to be altogether false and without any solid ground. I desire you may call for extracts of my petitions to the councell and justiciary, which I related to in my last speech, which I recommend to your care, that I may be vindicated from any false aspersions.
  Sic Subscribitur

THOMAS AIKENHEAD

Notes on the text

Some aspects of the narrative are based on historical fact; I hope that any departures from recorded fact – or liberties taken with it – make for plausible fiction.

I have incorporated a small amount of period material into the text, as follows:

The titles of two chapters were transcribed, in part, from facsimiles of 17th century publications accessed via Early English Books Online, http://eebo.chadwyck.com.

These are:

Increase Mather, *Heaven's Alarm to the World* (1682), Library of Congress.

Mungo Craig, *A Satyr Against Atheistical Deism* (1696), Harvard University Library.

In the chapter entitled 'Venice Treacle', parts of 'Matthiolus's great antidote against Poison and Pestilence' were adapted from:

Nicholas Culpeper, *The Complete Herbal and English Physician Enlarged*, London: Thomas Kelly, 1843: 337-338.

As the extract from John Knox's infamous polemic, 'The First Blast of the Trumpet against the Monstruous Regimen of Women' (1558), is spoken aloud, I have updated the spelling to aid comprehension.

In 'A Rhapsody of Feigned and Ill-Invented Nonsense', extracts from the records of the trial and Thomas's Letter to his Friends were transcribed and as, with Knox's text, updated from:

William Cobbett and Thomas Howell (eds). *A Complete Collection of State Trials*, 34 vols. London: Hansard (1809-28): 920-930.

Acknowledgements

An earlier version of the opening chapter appeared in *Edinburgh Review* 131.

I'd like to thank a number of people who, in various ways, have helped bring this book to completion, in particular: Dorothy McMillan, Douglas Dunn, Alan Riach, Alan Gillis, Greg Walker, Tom Webster, Elspeth Wills, Frances Dow, Richard Smith, Brian McCabe, Anne Ferguson, Joan Parr, Lesley Glaister, Sally Whitton and, it goes without saying, Geraldine Cooke. A special thanks must also go to Rodge Glass for thorough yet sensitive editorial input, and to all of the team at Freight Books. I would also like to add my gratitude for a Leverhulme Research Fellowship and a residency at Ledig House Writers' Centre, both of which were invaluable in the early stages of the work.